The Bloomsbury Phantastics

EX LIBRIS

ALSO AVAILABLE IN THE SERIES

CORALINE
&
OTHER STORIES

Neil Gaiman

with illustrations by Dave McKean

BLOOMSBURY

LONDON · NEW DELHI · NEW YORK · SYDNEY

Bloomsbury Publishing, London, New Delhi, New York and Sydney

Coraline first published in Great Britain in 2002 by Bloomsbury Publishing Plc
All other stories in this edition originally published as *M is for Magic,* first published in
Great Britain in 2008 by Bloomsbury Publishing Plc
This paperback edition first published 2009
Bloomsbury Publishing Plc, 50 Bedford Square, London, WC1B 3DP

A CIP catalogue record for this book is available from the British Library

ISBN 978 1 4088 0345 5

MIX
Paper from
responsible sources
FSC® C020471

Typeset by Dorchester Typesetting Group Ltd
Printed and bound in Great Britain by CPI Group (UK) Ltd, Croydon CR0 4YY

13

www.bloomsbury.com/thebloomsburyphantastics

Contents

Introduction

I LOVE CHILDREN'S FICTION. I think I love it mostly because when I was a child I read a lot, and each of the stories I read changed me and affected me. Each of them affected me in different ways. They made me happy or they made me sad or they made me wonder. Sometimes they scared me.

When *Coraline* was filmed, the *New York Times* wrote a review that began by explaining that this was a scary film for children, and that *that was a good thing*.

I found myself shaking my head at the idea of a world in which people thought there was something wrong with scaring children. I had loved to be scared as a child, as long as the fear was on the page. There were good books of ghost stories when I was a boy and I read all of them, graduating quickly to the *Pan Book of Horror Stories*. When I was eleven, my favourite comics were horror comics, with quirky twist-endings. Sometimes the monsters were the heroes and sometimes they were not.

It is hard to describe the joy of literary fear, or an appreciation of the uncanny, to those who do not enjoy it, but I feel obligated here at the least to make the attempt:

Funny fiction should make us laugh. Sad fiction should make us cry. And scary fiction . . .

. . . that should be the tapping of the twig on the window, late at night, when you're alone in the house. The way that shadows slide, amended by imagination, and the whisper of something that may only be the wind.

For me, it all goes back to something that Ogden Nash, the American poet, said. 'Where there's a monster', he wrote, 'there's a miracle'. A world in which there are monsters, and ghosts, and things that want to steal your heart is a world in which there are angels and dreams and, above all, a world in which there is hope.

Coraline began when my daughter Holly came home from kindergarten to the house we lived in in Nutley, Sussex, and climbed on my lap and began to dictate stories. She was four. In her stories a small girl came home to find her mother was being impersonated by a witch. Soon she was imprisoned in the cellar, and, with a girl called Lucy Jane (who may or may not have been a ghost, Holly was never entirely sure), had to escape to find her real mother (who had gone to America).

It was scary, wonderful stuff. I sent her stories to my friends – one of them drew part of Holly's story as a comic and another published it, because they found them so strange and troubling. And I began looking around for good Gothic horror for little girls. I asked at local bookshops and got strange looks. The books of ghost stories for children I had enjoyed had dried up and blown away with the years. Such things did not exist, not any longer. Not then.

So I started to write a story for Holly. I took things from my life. Coraline's flat and the house in which it was found was the house and flat we lived in when I wrote it; I borrowed the door from a house, long-since demolished, in which I had lived when I was a boy, a door that opened onto a brick wall. I remembered a story by a Victorian writer named Lucy Clifford, who wrote odd, disturbing stories for children, in which children were threatened with a New Mother, and I remember deciding that an Other Mother sounded better. I do not remember where I found the buttons. I did not think that anyone would ever want to know.

I would write it in my own time, grabbing an hour here, an hour there. I wrote it until August 1992, when we moved to America. I wrote

'Hullo,' said Coraline. 'How did you get in?' The cat didn't
say anything.

Coraline got out of bed

and stopped for six years without even finishing the sentence. I
was writing it in my own time, I told people, and I had run out of my
own time, and that was sort of true. And while I knew exactly how the
book would end, I was not entirely certain what would happen when
Coraline and the Cat went back to the place the Beldam waited. And
besides, nobody was even waiting for it.

Holly was thirteen when I restarted *Coraline*. She now had a little
sister, Maddy, who was the age Holly had been when I started thinking about the book. I sent the book to an editor who liked it, who
gave me a contract to finish it. And, over the next two years, writing a
few words every night before I slept, I did.

Coraline was published in 2002, illustrated by Dave McKean, and
she went out into the world, accompanied by Miss Spink and Miss
Forcible, not to mention her Other Mother, and scared many adults
and fewer children. I was proud of her, proud of them all. And then I
was able to gaze on, still proud but less immediately as I watched her
transmute into an animated character in Henry Selick's marvellous
film, into an actress on stage in Stephin Merritt's haunting musical,
into beautiful lines on paper in P. Craig Russell's graphic novel.

I do not know why it has worked so well, nor why it has changed
its shape while never changing its essence. I think it's because, at the
end of the day (which is twilit and is about the time when the bats
come out), it is not a story about fear, but one about bravery. After
all, if a dragon is going to be defeated, it should be worth the fight,
and the thing that calls herself the Other Mother is that.

Beyond *Coraline* and, more recently, *The Graveyard Book*, I have
written very few short stories intended for the young. The stories that
accompany *Coraline* here were written, on the whole, for adults,
although they have proved popular with readers of all ages.

'The Witch's Headstone' was the first story I wrote about Bod, and
the first story that would become a part of my novel *The Graveyard
Book* (it's chapter four). There are tiny differences between this, the

original version, and the one in the finished book (Silas is described ever-so-slightly differently, for a start).

Some of these stories have fear as an ingredient (although it does not make a meal). There are cats and graveyards, Jack-in-a-boxes, strange meals and late nights.

Here then, *Coraline*, and a handful of stories to accompany her. Read her in peace. And do not worry. It was only a twig, tapping on the window, and not your own Other Mother's fingernails. Not her fingernails at all.

Neil Gaiman, June 2009

CORALINE

Fairy tales are more than true: not because they tell us that dragons exist, but because they tell us that dragons can be beaten.

G. K. Chesterton

I started this for Holly
I finished it for Maddy

1

CORALINE DISCOVERED THE door a little while after they moved into the house.

It was a very old house – it had an attic under the roof and a cellar under the ground and an overgrown garden with huge old trees in it.

Coraline's family didn't own all of the house, it was too big for that. Instead they owned part of it.

There were other people who lived in the old house.

Miss Spink and Miss Forcible lived in the flat below Coraline's, on the ground floor. They were both old and round, and they lived in their flat with a number of ageing Highland terriers who had names like Hamish and Andrew and Jock. Once upon a time Miss Spink and Miss Forcible had been actresses, as Miss Spink told Coraline the first time she met her.

'You see, Caroline,' Miss Spink said, getting Coraline's name wrong, 'both myself and Miss Forcible were famous actresses, in our time. We trod the boards, lovey. Oh, don't let Hamish eat the fruit-cake, or he'll be up all night with his tummy.'

'It's Coraline. Not Caroline. Coraline,' said Coraline.

In the flat above Coraline's, under the roof, was a crazy old man with a big moustache. He told Coraline that he was training a mouse circus. He wouldn't let anyone see it.

'One day, little Caroline, when they are all ready, everyone in the whole world will see the wonders of my mouse circus. You ask me why you cannot see it now. Is that what you asked me?'

'No,' said Coraline quietly, 'I asked you not to call me Caroline. It's Coraline.'

'The reason you cannot see the mouse circus,' said the man upstairs, 'is that the mice are not yet ready and rehearsed. Also, they refuse to play the songs I have written for them. All the songs I have written for the mice to play go *oompah oompah*. But the white mice will only play *toodle oodle*, like that. I am thinking of trying them on different types of cheese.'

Coraline didn't think there really was a mouse circus. She thought the old man was probably making it up.

The day after they moved in, Coraline went exploring.

She explored the garden. It was a big garden: at the very back was an old tennis court, but no one in the house played tennis and the fence around the court had holes in it and the net had mostly rotted away; there was an old rose garden, filled with stunted, flyblown rose bushes; there was a rockery that was all rocks; there was a fairy ring, made of squidgy brown toadstools which smelled dreadful if you accidentally trod on them.

There was also a well. On the first day Coraline's family moved in, Miss Spink and Miss Forcible made a point of telling Coraline how dangerous the well was, and they warned her to be sure she kept away from it. So Coraline set off to explore for it, so that she knew where it was, to keep away from it properly.

She found it on the third day, in an overgrown meadow beside the tennis court, behind a clump of trees – a low brick circle almost hidden in the high grass. The well had been covered over by wooden boards, to stop anyone falling in. There was a small knothole in one of the boards, and Coraline spent an afternoon dropping pebbles and acorns through the hole, and waiting, and counting, until she heard the *plop* as they hit the water, far below.

Coraline also explored for animals. She found a hedgehog, and a snakeskin (but no snake), and a rock that looked just like a frog, and a toad that looked just like a rock.

There was also a haughty black cat, who would sit on walls and tree stumps and watch her, but would slip away if ever she went over to try to play with it.

That was how she spent her first two weeks at the house – exploring the garden and the grounds.

Her mother made her come back inside for dinner and for lunch; and Coraline had to make sure she dressed up warmly before she went out, for it was a very cold summer that year; but go out she did, exploring, every day until the day it rained, when Coraline had to stay inside.

'What should I do?' asked Coraline.

'Read a book,' said her mother. 'Watch a video. Play with your toys. Go and pester Miss Spink or Miss Forcible, or the crazy old man upstairs.'

'No,' said Coraline. 'I don't want to do those things. I want to explore.'

'I don't really mind what you do,' said Coraline's mother, 'as long as you don't make a mess.'

Coraline went over to the window and watched the rain come down. It wasn't the kind of rain you could go out in, it was the other kind, the kind that threw itself down from the sky and splashed where it landed. It was rain that meant business, and currently its business was turning the garden into a muddy, wet soup.

Coraline had watched all the videos. She was bored with her toys, and she'd read all her books.

She turned on the television. She went from channel to channel to channel, but there was nothing on but men in suits talking about the stock market, and sports programmes. Eventually, she found something to watch: it was the last half of a natural-history programme about something called protective coloration. She watched animals, birds and insects which disguised themselves as leaves or twigs or other animals to escape from things that could hurt them. She enjoyed it, but it ended too soon, and was followed by a programme about a cake factory.

It was time to talk to her father.

Coraline's father was home. Both of her parents worked, doing things on computers, which meant that they were home a lot of the time. Each of them had their own study.

'Hello, Coraline,' he said when she came in, without turning round.

'Mmph,' said Coraline. 'It's raining.'

'Yup,' said her father. 'It's bucketing down.'

'No,' said Coraline, 'it's just raining. Can I go outside?'

'What does your mother say?'

'She says, "You're not going out in weather like that, Coraline Jones".'

'Then, no.'

'But I want to carry on exploring.'

'Then explore the flat,' suggested her father. 'Look – here's a piece of paper and a pen. Count all the doors and windows. List everything blue. Mount an expedition to discover the hot-water tank. And leave me alone to work.'

'Can I go into the drawing room?' The drawing room was where the Joneses kept the expensive (and uncomfortable) furniture Coraline's grandmother had left them when she died. Coraline wasn't allowed in there. Nobody went in there. It was only for best.

'If you don't make a mess. And you don't touch anything.'

Coraline considered this carefully, then she took the paper and pen and went off to explore the inside of the flat.

She discovered the hot-water tank (it was in a cupboard in the kitchen).

She counted everything blue (153).

She counted the windows (21).

She counted the doors (14).

Of the doors that she found, thirteen opened and closed. The other, the big, carved, brown wooden door at the far corner of the drawing room, was locked.

She said to her mother, 'Where does that door go?'

'Nowhere, dear.'

'It has to go somewhere.'

Her mother shook her head. 'Look,' she told Coraline.

She reached up, and took a string of keys from the top of the kitchen doorframe. She sorted through them carefully and selected the oldest, biggest, blackest, rustiest key. They went into the drawing room. She unlocked the door with the key.

The door swung open.

Her mother was right. The door didn't go anywhere. It opened on to a brick wall.

'When this place was just one house,' said Coraline's mother, 'that door went somewhere. When they turned the house into flats, they simply bricked it up. The other side is the empty flat on the other side of the house, the one that's still for sale.'

She shut the door and put the string of keys back on top of the kitchen doorframe.

'You didn't lock it,' said Coraline.

Her mother shrugged. 'Why should I lock it?' she asked. 'It doesn't go anywhere.'

Coraline didn't say anything.

It was nearly dark now, and the rain was still coming down, pattering against the windows and blurring the lights of the cars in the street outside.

Coraline's father stopped working and made them all dinner.

Coraline was disgusted. 'Daddy,' she said, 'you've made a *recipe* again.'

'It's leek and potato stew, with a tarragon garnish and melted Gruyère cheese,' he admitted.

Coraline sighed. Then she went to the freezer and got out some microwave chips and a microwave mini-pizza.

'You know I don't like recipes,' she told her father, while her dinner went round and round and the little red numbers on the microwave oven counted down to zero.

'If you tried it, maybe you'd like it,' said Coraline's father, but she shook her head.

That night, Coraline lay awake in her bed. The rain had stopped, and she was almost asleep when something went *t-t-t-t-t*. She sat up in bed.

Something went *kreeee* . . .

. . . *aaaak*.

Coraline got out of bed and looked down the hall, but saw

nothing strange. She walked down the hallway. From her parents'
bedroom came a low snoring – that was her father – and an occasional sleeping mutter – that was her mother.

Coraline wondered if she'd dreamed it, whatever it was.

Something moved.

It was little more than a shadow, and it scuttled down the darkened
hall fast, like a little patch of night.

She hoped it wasn't a spider. Spiders made Coraline intensely
uncomfortable.

The black shape went into the drawing room and Coraline
followed it in, a little nervously.

The room was dark. The only light came from the hall, and
Coraline, who was standing in the doorway, cast a huge and distorted
shadow on to the drawing- room carpet: she looked like a thin giant
woman.

Coraline was just wondering whether or not she ought to turn on
the light when she saw the black shape edge slowly out from beneath
the sofa. It paused, and then dashed silently across the carpet
towards the farthest corner of the room.

There was no furniture in that corner of the room.

Coraline turned on the light.

There was nothing in the corner. Nothing but the old door that
opened on to the brick wall.

She was sure that her mother had shut the door, but now it
was ever so slightly open. Just a crack. Coraline went over to it
and looked in. There was nothing there – just a wall, built of red
bricks.

Coraline closed the old wooden door, turned out the light, and
went back to bed.

She dreamed of black shapes that slid from place to place, avoiding the light, until they were all gathered together under the moon.
Little black shapes with little red eyes and sharp yellow teeth.

They started to sing:

We are small but we are many
We are many, we are small

We were here before you rose
We will be here when you fall.

Their voices were high and whispery and slightly whiny. They made Coraline feel uncomfortable.

Then Coraline dreamed a few commercials, and after that she dreamed of nothing at all.

2

THE NEXT DAY it had stopped raining, but a thick white fog had lowered over the house.

'I'm going for a walk,' said Coraline.

'Don't go too far,' said her mother. 'And dress up warmly.'

Coraline put on her blue coat with a hood, her red scarf and her yellow wellington boots.

She went out.

Miss Spink was walking her dogs. 'Hello, Caroline,' said Miss Spink. 'Rotten weather.'

'Yes,' said Coraline.

'I played Portia once,' said Miss Spink. 'Miss Forcible talks about her Ophelia, but it was my Portia they came to see. When we trod the boards.'

Miss Spink was bundled up in pullovers and cardigans, so she seemed more small and circular than ever. She looked like a large, fluffy egg. She wore thick glasses that made her eyes seem huge.

'They used to send flowers to my dressing room. They *did*,' she said.

'Who did?' asked Coraline.

Miss Spink looked around cautiously, looking first over one shoulder and then over the other, peering into the mist as though someone might be listening.

'*Men*,' she whispered. Then she tugged the dogs to heel and waddled off back towards the house.

Coraline continued her walk.

She was three quarters of the way around the house when she saw Miss Forcible, standing at the door to the flat she shared with Miss Spink.

'Have you seen Miss Spink, Caroline?'

Coraline told her that she had, and that Miss Spink was out walking the dogs.

'I do hope she doesn't get lost; it'll bring on her shingles if she does, you'll see,' said Miss Forcible. 'You'd have to be an explorer to find your way around in this fog.'

'I'm an explorer,' said Coraline.

'Of course you are, lovey,' said Miss Forcible. 'Don't get lost, now.'

Coraline continued walking through the garden in the grey mist. She always kept in sight of the house. After about ten minutes of walking she found herself back where she had started.

The hair over her eyes was limp and wet, and her face felt damp.

'Ahoy! Caroline!' called the crazy old man upstairs.

'Oh, hello,' said Coraline.

She could hardly see the old man through the mist.

He walked down the steps on the outside of the house that led up past Coraline's front door to the door of his flat. He walked down very slowly. Coraline waited at the bottom of the steps.

'The mice do not like the mist,' he told her. 'It makes their whiskers droop.'

'I don't like the mist much, either,' admitted Coraline.

The old man leaned down, so close that the bottom of his moustache tickled Coraline's ear. 'The mice have a message for you,' he whispered.

Coraline didn't know what to say.

'The message is this. *Don't go through the door.*' He paused. 'Does that mean anything to you?'

'No,' said Coraline.

The old man shrugged. 'They are funny, the mice. They get things wrong. They got your name wrong, you know. They kept saying Coraline. Not Caroline. Not Caroline at all.'

12

He picked up a milk bottle from the bottom step, and started back up to his attic flat.

Coraline went indoors. Her mother was working in her study. Her mother's study smelt of flowers.

'What shall I do?' asked Coraline.

'When do you go back to school?' asked her mother.

'Next week,' said Coraline.

'Hmph,' said her mother. 'I suppose I shall have to get you new school clothes. Remind me, dear, or else I'll forget,' and she went back to typing things on the computer screen.

'What shall I *do?*' repeated Coraline.

'Draw something.' Her mother passed her a sheet of paper and a ballpoint pen.

Coraline tried drawing the mist. After ten minutes of drawing she still had a white sheet of paper with

M ST
I

written on it in one corner, in slightly wiggly letters. She grunted and passed it to her mother.

'Mm. Very modern, dear,' said Coraline's mother.

Coraline crept into the drawing room and tried to open the old door in the corner. It was locked once more. She supposed her mother must have locked it again. She shrugged.

Coraline went to see her father.

He had his back to the door as he typed. 'Go away,' he said cheerfully as she walked in.

'I'm bored,' she said.

'Learn how to tap-dance,' he suggested, without turning round.

Coraline shook her head. 'Why don't you play with me?' she asked.

'Busy,' he said. 'Working,' he added. He still hadn't turned around to look at her. 'Why don't you go and bother Miss Spink and Miss Forcible?'

Coraline put on her coat and pulled up her hood and went out of the house. She went down the steps. She rang the door of Miss Spink and Miss Forcible's flat. Coraline could hear a frenzied woofing as the Scottie dogs ran out into the hall. After a while Miss Spink opened the door.

'Oh, it's you, Caroline,' she said. 'Angus, Hamish, Bruce, down now, lovies. It's only Caroline. Come in, dear. Would you like a cup of tea?'

The flat smelt of furniture polish and dogs.

'Yes, please,' said Coraline. Miss Spink led her into a dusty little room, which she called the parlour. On the walls were black and white photographs of pretty women, and theatre programmes in frames. Miss Forcible was sitting in one of the armchairs, knitting hard.

Miss Spink poured Coraline a cup of tea in a little pink bone-china cup with a saucer, and gave her a dry Garibaldi biscuit to go with it.

Miss Forcible looked at Miss Spink, picked up her knitting, and took a deep breath. 'Anyway, April. As I was saying: you still have to admit, there's life in the old dog yet,' she said.

'Miriam, dear, neither of us is as young as we were.'

'Madame Arcati,' replied Miss Forcible. 'The nurse in *Romeo*. Lady Bracknell. Character parts. They can't retire you from the stage.'

'Now, Miriam, we ag*reed*,' said Miss Spink.

Coraline wondered if they'd forgotten she was there. They weren't making much sense; she decided they were having an argument as old and comfortable as an armchair, the kind of argument that no one ever really wins or loses, but which can go on for ever, if both parties are willing.

She sipped her tea.

'I'll read the leaves, if you want,' said Miss Spink to Coraline.

'Sorry?' said Coraline.

'The tea leaves, dear. I'll read your future.'

Coraline passed Miss Spink her cup. Miss Spink peered short-sightedly at the black tea leaves in the bottom. She pursed her lips.

'You know, Caroline,' she said after a while, 'you are in terrible danger.'

Miss Forcible snorted and put down her knitting. 'Don't be silly, April. Stop scaring the girl. Your eyes are going. Pass me that cup, child.'

Coraline carried the cup over to Miss Forcible. Miss Forcible looked into it carefully, and shook her head, and looked into it again.

'Oh dear,' she said. 'You were right, April. She *is* in danger.'

'See, Miriam,' said Miss Spink triumphantly. 'My eyes are as good as they ever were . . . '

'What am I in danger from?' asked Coraline.

Misses Spink and Forcible stared at her blankly. 'It didn't say,' said Miss Spink. 'Tea leaves aren't reliable for that kind of thing. Not really. They're good for generalities, but not for specifics.'

'What should I do then?' asked Coraline, who was slightly alarmed by this.

'Don't wear green in your dressing room,' suggested Miss Spink.

'Or mention the Scottish play,' added Miss Forcible.

Coraline wondered why so few of the adults she had met made any sense. She sometimes wondered who they thought they were talking to.

'And be very, very careful,' said Miss Spink. She got up from her armchair and went over to the fireplace. On the mantelpiece was a small jar, and Miss Spink took off the top of the jar and began to pull things out of it. There was a tiny china duck, a thimble, a strange little brass coin, two paperclips, and a stone with a hole in it.

She passed Coraline the stone with a hole in it.

'What's it for?' asked Coraline. The hole went all the way through the middle of the stone. She held it up to the window and looked through it.

'It might help,' said Miss Spink. 'They're good for bad things, sometimes.'

Coraline put on her coat, said goodbye to Misses Spink and Forcible, and to the dogs, and went outside.

The mist hung like blindness around the house. She walked slowly to the steps up to her family's flat, and then stopped and looked around.

In the mist, it was a ghost-world. *In danger?* thought Coraline to herself. It sounded exciting. It didn't sound like a bad thing. Not really.

Coraline went back up the steps, her fist closed tightly around her new stone.

3

THE NEXT DAY the sun shone, and Coraline's mother took her into the nearest large town to buy clothes for school. They dropped her father off at the railway station. He was going into London for the day to see some people.

Coraline waved him goodbye.

They went to the department store to buy the school clothes.

Coraline saw some Day-glo green gloves she liked a lot. Her mother refused to get them for her, preferring instead to buy white socks, navy-blue school underpants, four grey blouses, and a dark grey skirt.

'But Mum, *everybody* at school's got grey blouses and everything. *Nobody's* got green gloves. I could be the only one.'

Her mother ignored her; she was talking to the shop assistant. They were talking about which kind of pullover to get for Coraline, and were agreeing that the best thing to do would be to get one that was embarrassingly large and baggy, in the hope that one day she might grow into it.

Coraline wandered off, and looked at a display of wellington boots shaped like frogs and ducks and rabbits.

Then she wandered back.

'Coraline? Oh, there you are. Where on earth were you?'

'I was kidnapped by aliens,' said Coraline. 'They came down from outer space with ray guns, but I fooled them by wearing a wig and laughing in a foreign accent, and I escaped.'

'Yes, dear. Now, I think you could do with some more hairclips, don't you?'

'No.'

'Well, let's say half a dozen, to be on the safe side,' said her mother.

Coraline didn't say anything.

In the car on the way back home, Coraline said, 'What's in the empty flat?'

'I don't know. Nothing, I expect. It probably looks like our flat before we moved in. Empty rooms.'

'Do you think you could get into it from our flat?'

'Not unless you can walk through bricks, dear.'

'Oh.'

They got home around lunchtime. The sun was shining, although the day was cold. Coraline's mother looked in the fridge, and found a sad little tomato and a piece of cheese with green stuff growing on it. There was only a crust in the bread bin.

'I'd better dash down to the shops and get some fishfingers or something,' said her mother. 'Do you want to come?'

'No,' said Coraline.

'Suit yourself,' said her mother, and left. Then she came back and got her purse and car keys and went out again.

Coraline was bored.

She flipped through a book her mother was reading about native people in a distant country; how every day they would take pieces of white silk and draw on them in wax, then dip the silks in dye, then draw on them more in wax and dye them some more, then boil the wax out in hot water, and then, finally, throw the now-beautiful cloths on a fire and burn them to ashes.

It seemed particularly pointless to Coraline, but she hoped that the people enjoyed it.

She was still bored, and her mother wasn't yet home.

Coraline got a chair and pushed it over to the kitchen door. She climbed on to the chair, and reached up. She clambered down, and got a broom from the broom cupboard. She climbed back on the chair again, and reached up with the broom.

Chink.

She climbed down from the chair and picked up the keys. She smiled triumphantly. Then she leaned the broom against the wall and went into the drawing room.

The family did not use the drawing room. They had inherited the furniture from Coraline's grandmother, along with a wooden coffee table, a side table, a heavy glass ashtray and the oil painting of a bowl of fruit. Coraline could never work out why anyone would want to paint a bowl of fruit. Other than that, the room was empty: there were no knick-knacks on the mantelpiece, no statues or clocks; nothing that made it feel comfortable or lived-in.

The old black key felt colder than any of the others. She pushed it into the keyhole. It turned smoothly, with a satisfying clunk.

Coraline stopped and listened. She knew she was doing something wrong, and she was trying to listen for her mother coming back, but she heard nothing. Then Coraline put her hand on the doorknob and turned it; and, finally, she opened the door.

It opened on to a dark hallway. The bricks had gone, as if they'd never been there. There was a cold, musty smell coming through the open doorway: it smelled like something very old and very slow.

Coraline went through the door.

She wondered what the empty flat would be like – if that was where the corridor led.

Coraline walked down the corridor uneasily. There was something very familiar about it.

The carpet beneath her feet was the same carpet they had in their flat. The wallpaper was the same wallpaper they had. The picture hanging in the hall was the same that they had hanging in their hallway at home.

She knew where she was: she was in her own home. She hadn't left.

She shook her head, confused.

She stared at the picture hanging on the wall: no, it wasn't exactly the same. The picture they had in their own hallway showed a boy in old-fashioned clothes staring at some bubbles. But now the expression on his face was different – he was looking at the bubbles as if he was planning to do something very nasty indeed to them. And there was something peculiar about his eyes.

Coraline stared at his eyes, trying to work out what exactly was different.

She almost had it when somebody said, 'Coraline?'

It sounded like her mother. Coraline went into the kitchen, where the voice had come from. A woman stood in the kitchen with her back to Coraline. She looked a little like Coraline's mother. Only . . .

Only her skin was white as paper.

Only she was taller and thinner.

Only her fingers were too long, and they never stopped moving, and her dark-red fingernails were curved and sharp.

'Coraline?' the woman said. 'Is that you?'

And then she turned round. Her eyes were big black buttons.

'Lunchtime, Coraline,' said the woman.

'Who are you?' asked Coraline.

'I'm your other mother,' said the woman. 'Go and tell your other father that lunch is ready.' She opened the door of the oven. Suddenly Coraline realised how hungry she was. It smelled wonderful. 'Well, go on.'

Coraline went down the hall, to where her father's study was. She opened the door. There was a man in there, sitting at the keyboard, with his back to her. 'Hello,' said Coraline. 'I – I mean, she said to say that lunch is ready.'

The man turned round.

His eyes were buttons – big and black and shiny.

'Hello, Coraline,' he said. 'I'm starving.'

He got up and went with her into the kitchen. They sat at the kitchen table and Coraline's other mother brought them lunch. A huge, golden-brown roasted chicken, fried potatoes, tiny green peas. Coraline shovelled the food into her mouth. It tasted wonderful.

'We've been waiting for you for a long time,' said Coraline's other father.

'For me?'

'Yes,' said the other mother. 'It wasn't the same here without you. But we knew you'd arrive one day, and then we could be a proper

21

family. Would you like some more chicken?'

It was the best chicken that Coraline had ever eaten. Her mother sometimes made chicken, but it was always out of packets, or frozen, and was very dry, and it never tasted of anything. When Coraline's father cooked chicken he bought real chicken, but he did strange things to it, like stewing it in wine, or stuffing it with prunes, or baking it in pastry, and Coraline would always refuse to touch it on principle.

She took some more chicken.

'I didn't know I had another mother,' said Coraline cautiously.

'Of course you do. Everyone does,' said the other mother, her black-button eyes gleaming. 'After lunch I thought you might like to play in your room with the rats.'

'The rats?'

'From upstairs.'

Coraline had never seen a rat, except on television. She was quite looking forward to it. This was turning out to be a very interesting day after all.

After lunch her other parents did the washing- up, and Coraline went down the hall to her other bedroom.

It was different from her bedroom at home. For a start it was painted in an off-putting shade of green and a peculiar shade of pink.

Coraline decided that she wouldn't want to have to sleep in there; but that the colour scheme was an awful lot more interesting than the one in her own bedroom.

There were all sorts of remarkable things in there she'd never seen before: wind-up angels that fluttered around the bedroom like startled sparrows; books with pictures that writhed and crawled and shimmered; little dinosaur skulls that chattered their teeth as she passed. A whole toybox filled with wonderful toys.

This is more like it, thought Coraline. She looked out of the window. Outside, the view was the same one she saw from her own bedroom: trees, fields and, beyond them, on the horizon, distant purple hills.

Something black scurried across the floor and vanished under the bed. Coraline got down on her knees and looked under the bed.

Fifty little red eyes stared back at her.

'Hello,' said Coraline. 'Are you the rats?'

They came out from under the bed, blinking their eyes in the light. They had short, soot-black fur, little red eyes, pink paws like tiny hands, and pink, hairless tails like long, smooth worms.

'Can you talk?' she asked.

The largest, blackest of the rats shook its head. It had an unpleasant sort of smile, Coraline thought.

'Well,' asked Coraline, 'what *do* you do?'

The rats formed a circle.

Then they began to climb on top of each other, carefully but swiftly, until they had formed a pyramid with the largest rat at the top.

The rats began to sing, in high, whispery voices,

We have teeth and we have tails
We have tails, we have eyes
We were here before you fell
You will be here when we rise.

It wasn't a pretty song. Coraline was sure she'd heard it before, or something like it, although she was unable to remember exactly where.

Then the pyramid fell apart, and the rats scampered, fast and black, towards the door.

The other crazy old man upstairs was standing in the doorway, holding a tall black hat in his hands. The rats scampered up him, burrowing into his pockets, into his shirt, up his trouser-legs, down his neck.

The largest rat climbed on to the old man's shoulders, swung up on the long grey moustache, past the big black-button eyes, and on to the top of the man's head.

In seconds the only evidence that the rats were there at all were the restless lumps under the man's clothes, forever sliding from place to place across him; and there was still the largest rat, who stared down, with glittering red eyes, at Coraline from the man's head.

The old man put his hat on, and the last rat was gone.

'Hello, Coraline,' said the other old man upstairs. 'I heard you were here. It is time for the rats to have their dinner. But you can come up with me, if you like, and watch them feed.'

There was something hungry in the old man's button eyes that made Coraline feel uncomfortable. 'No, thank you,' she said. 'I'm going outside to explore.'

The old man nodded, very slowly. Coraline could hear the rats whispering to each other, although she couldn't tell what they were saying.

She was not certain that she wanted to know what they were saying.

Her other parents stood in the kitchen doorway as she walked down the corridor, smiling identical smiles, and waving slowly. 'Have a nice time outside,' said her other mother.

'We'll just wait here for you to come back,' said her other father.

When Coraline got to the front door, she turned back and looked at them. They were still watching her, and waving, and smiling.

Coraline walked outside, and down the steps.

4

THE HOUSE LOOKED exactly the same from the outside. Or almost exactly the same; around Miss Spink and Miss Forcible's door were blue and red lightbulbs that flashed on and off spelling out words, the lights chasing each other around the door. On and off, around and around. ASTOUNDING! was followed by A THEATRICAL and then TRIUMPH!!!

It was a sunny, cold day, exactly like the one she'd left.

There was a polite noise from behind her.

She turned round. Standing on the wall next to her was a large black cat, identical to the large black cat she'd seen in the grounds at home.

'Good afternoon,' said the cat.

Its voice sounded like the voice at the back of Coraline's head, the voice she thought words in, but a man's voice, not a girl's.

'Hello,' said Coraline. 'I saw a cat like you in the garden at home. You must be the other cat.'

The cat shook its head. 'No,' it said. 'I'm not the other anything. I'm me.' It tipped its head on one side; green eyes glinted. 'You people are spread all over the place. Cats, on the other hand, keep ourselves together. If you see what I mean.'

'I suppose. But if you're the same cat I saw at home, how can you talk?'

Cats don't have shoulders, not like people do. But the cat

shrugged, in one smooth movement that started at the tip of its tail and ended in a raised movement of its whiskers. 'I can talk.'

'Cats don't talk at home.'

'No?' said the cat.

'No,' said Coraline.

The cat leapt smoothly from the wall to the grass, near Coraline's feet. It stared up at her.

'Well, you're the expert on these things,' said the cat drily. 'After all, what would I know? I'm only a cat.'

It began to walk away, head and tail held high and proud.

'Come back,' said Coraline. 'Please. I'm sorry. I really am.'

The cat stopped walking, and sat down, and began to wash itself, thoughtfully, apparently unaware of Coraline's existence.

'We . . . we could be friends, you know,' said Coraline.

'We *could* be rare specimens of an exotic breed of African dancing elephants,' said the cat. 'But we're not. At least,' it added cattily, after darting a brief look at Coraline, '*I'm* not.'

Coraline sighed.

'Please. What's your name?' Coraline asked the cat. 'Look, I'm Coraline. Okay?'

The cat yawned slowly, carefully, revealing a mouth and tongue of astounding pinkness. 'Cats don't have names,' it said.

'No?' said Coraline.

'No,' said the cat. 'Now, *you* people have names. That's because you don't know who you are. We know who we are, so we don't need names.'

There was something irritatingly self-centred about the cat, Coraline decided. As if it were, in its opinion, the only thing in any world or place that could possibly be of any importance.

Half of her wanted to be very rude to it; the other half of her wanted to be polite and deferential. The polite half won.

'Please, what is this place?'

The cat glanced around briefly. 'It's here,' said the cat.

'I can see that. Well, how did you get here?'

'Like you did. I walked,' said the cat. 'Like this.'

Coraline watched as the cat walked slowly across the lawn. It walked behind a tree, but didn't come out the other side. Coraline went over to the tree and looked behind it. The cat was gone.

She walked back towards the house. There was another polite noise from behind her. It was the cat.

'By the by,' it said. 'It was sensible of you to bring protection. I'd hang on to it, if I were you.'

'Protection?'

'That's what I said,' said the cat. 'And anyway – '

It paused, and stared intently at something that wasn't there.

Then it went down into a low crouch and moved slowly forward, two or three steps. It seemed to be stalking an invisible mouse. Abruptly, it turned tail and dashed for the woods.

It vanished among the trees.

Coraline wondered what the cat had meant.

She also wondered whether cats could all talk where she came from and just chose not to, or whether they could only talk when they were here – wherever *here* was.

She walked down the brick steps to the Misses Spink and Forcible's front door. The blue and red lights flashed on and off.

The door was open, just slightly. She knocked on it, but her first knock made the door swing open, and Coraline went in.

She was in a dark room that smelled of dust and velvet. The door swung shut behind her, and the room was black. Coraline edged forward into a small anteroom. Her face brushed against something soft. It was cloth. She reached up her hand and pushed at the cloth. It parted.

She stood blinking on the other side of the velvet curtains, in a poorly lit theatre. Far away, at the edge of the room, was a high wooden stage, empty and bare, a dim spotlight shining on to it from above.

There were seats between Coraline and the stage. Rows and rows of seats. She heard a shuffling noise, and a light came towards her, swinging from side to side. When it was closer she saw the light was coming from a torch being carried in the mouth of a large black Scottie dog, its muzzle grey with age.

'Hello,' said Coraline.

The dog put the torch down on the floor and looked up at her. 'Right. Let's see your ticket,' it said gruffly.

'Ticket?'

'That's what I said. Ticket. I haven't got all day, you know. You can't watch the show without a ticket.'

Coraline sighed. 'I don't have a ticket,' she admitted.

'Another one,' said the dog gloomily. 'Come in here, bold as anything, "Where's your ticket?" "Haven't got one." I don't know . . .' It shook its head, then shrugged. 'Come on, then.'

The dog picked up the torch in its mouth and trotted off into the dark. Coraline followed. When it got near to the front of the stage it stopped and shone the torch on to an empty seat. Coraline sat down and the dog wandered off.

As her eyes got used to the darkness she realised that the other inhabitants of the seats were also dogs.

There was a sudden hissing noise from behind the stage. Coraline decided it was the sound of a scratchy old record being put on to a record player. The hissing became the noise of trumpets, and Miss Spink and Forcible came on to the stage.

Miss Spink was riding a one-wheeled bicycle, and juggling balls. Miss Forcible skipped on behind her, holding a basket of flowers. She scattered the flower petals across the stage as she went. They reached the front of the stage, and Miss Spink leapt nimbly off the unicycle, and the two old women bowed low.

All the dogs thumped their tails and barked enthusiastically. Coraline clapped politely.

Then they unbuttoned their fluffy round coats and opened them. But their coats weren't all that opened: their faces opened, too, like empty shells, and out of the old empty fluffy round bodies stepped two young women. They were thin, and pale, and quite pretty, and had black-button eyes.

The new Miss Spink was wearing green tights and high brown boots that went most of the way up her legs. The new Miss Forcible wore a white dress and had flowers in her long yellow hair.

Coraline pressed back against her seat.

Miss Spink left the stage, and the noise of trumpets squealed as the gramophone needle dug its way across the record and was pulled off.

'This is my favourite bit,' whispered the little dog in the seat next to her.

The other Miss Forcible picked a knife out of a box on the corner of the stage. 'Is this a dagger that I see before me?' she asked.

'Yes!' shouted all the little dogs. 'It is!' Miss Forcible curtseyed, and all the dogs applauded again. Coraline didn't bother clapping this time.

Miss Spink came back on. She slapped her thigh, and all the little dogs woofed.

'And now,' Miss Spink said, 'Miriam and I proudly present a new and exciting addendum to our theatrical exposition. Do I see a volunteer?'

The little dog next to Coraline nudged her with its front paw. 'That's you,' it hissed.

Coraline stood up, and walked up the wooden steps to the stage.

'Can I have a big round of applause for the young volunteer?' asked Miss Spink. The dogs woofed and squealed and thumped their tails on the velvet seats.

'Now, Coraline,' said Miss Spink. 'What's your name?'

'Coraline,' said Coraline.

'And we don't know each other, do we?'

Coraline looked at the thin young woman with black-button eyes and shook her head, slowly.

'Now,' said the other Miss Spink, 'stand over here.' She led Coraline over to a board by the side of the stage, and put a balloon on top of Coraline's head.

Miss Spink walked over to Miss Forcible. She blindfolded Miss Forcible's button eyes with a black scarf and put the knife into her hands. Then she turned her round three or four times and pointed her at Coraline. Coraline held her breath and squeezed her fingers into two tight fists.

Miss Forcible threw the knife at the balloon. It popped loudly, and the knife stuck into the board just above Coraline's head and twanged there. Coraline breathed out.

The dogs went wild.

Miss Spink gave Coraline a very small box of chocolates and thanked her for being such a good sport. Coraline went back to her seat.

'You were very good,' said the little dog.

'Thank you,' said Coraline.

Misses Forcible and Spink began juggling with huge wooden clubs. Coraline opened the box of chocolates. The little dog looked at them longingly.

'Would you like one?' she asked it.

'Yes, please,' whispered the dog. 'Only not toffee ones. They make me drool.'

'I thought chocolates weren't very good for dogs,' she said, remembering something Miss Forcible had once told her.

'Maybe where you come from,' whispered the little dog. 'Here, it's all we eat.'

Coraline couldn't see what the chocolates were, in the dark. She took an experimental bite of one which turned out to be coconut. Coraline didn't like coconut. She gave it to the dog.

'Thank you,' said the dog.

'You're welcome,' said Coraline.

Miss Forcible and Miss Spink were doing some acting. Miss Forcible was sitting on a stepladder, and Miss Spink was standing at the bottom.

'What's in a name?' asked Miss Forcible. 'That which we call a rose by any other name would smell as sweet.'

'Have you got any more chocolates?' said the dog.

Coraline gave the dog another chocolate.

'I know not how to tell thee who I am,' said Miss Spink to Miss Forcible.

'This bit finishes soon,' whispered the dog. 'Then they start folk dancing.'

'How long does this go on for?' asked Coraline. 'The theatre?'

'All the time,' said the dog. 'For ever and always.'

'Here,' said Coraline. 'Keep the chocolates.'

'Thank you,' said the dog. Coraline stood up.

'See you soon,' said the dog.

'Bye,' said Coraline. She walked out of the theatre and back into the garden. She had to blink her eyes at the daylight.

Her other parents were waiting for her in the garden, standing side by side. They were smiling.

'Did you have a nice time?' asked her other mother.

'It was interesting,' said Coraline.

The three of them walked back up to Coraline's other house together. Coraline's other mother stroked Coraline's hair with her long white fingers. Coraline shook her head.

'Don't do that,' said Coraline.

Her other mother took her hand away.

'So,' said her other father. 'Do you like it here?'

'I suppose,' said Coraline. 'It's much more interesting than at home.'

They went inside.

'I'm glad you like it,' said Coraline's other mother. 'Because we'd like to think that this is your home. You can stay here for ever and always. If you want to.'

'Hmm,' said Coraline. She put her hands in her pockets and thought about it. Her fingertips touched the stone that the real Misses Spink and Forcible had given her the day before, the stone with the hole in it.

'If you want to stay,' said her other father. 'There's only one little thing we'll have to do, so you can stay here for ever and always.'

They went into the kitchen. On a china plate on the kitchen table were a spool of black cotton and a long silver needle and, beside them, two large black buttons.

'I don't think so,' said Coraline.

'Oh, but we want you to,' said her other mother. 'We want you to stay. And it's just a little thing.'

'It won't hurt,' said her other father.

Coraline knew that when grown-ups told you something wouldn't hurt it almost always did. She shook her head.

Her other mother smiled brightly and the hair on her head drifted like plants under the sea. 'We only want what's best for you,' she said.

She put her hand on Coraline's shoulder. Coraline backed away.

'I'm going now,' said Coraline. She put her hands back in her pockets. Her fingers closed around the stone with the hole in.

Her other mother's hand scuttled off Coraline's shoulder like a frightened spider.

'If that's what you want,' she said.

'Yes,' said Coraline.

'We'll see you soon, though,' said her other father. 'When you come back.'

'Um,' said Coraline.

'And then we'll all be together as one big happy family,' said her other mother. 'For ever and always.'

Coraline backed away. She turned and hurried into the drawing room and pulled open the door in the corner. There was no brick wall there now – just darkness; a night-black underground darkness that seemed as if things in it might be moving.

Coraline hesitated. She turned back. Her other mother and her other father were walking towards her, holding hands. They were looking at her with their black-button eyes. Or at least she *thought* they were looking at her. She couldn't be sure.

Her other mother reached out her free hand and beckoned gently with one white finger. Her pale lips mouthed, 'Come back soon,' although she said nothing aloud.

Coraline took a deep breath and stepped into the darkness, where strange voices whispered and distant winds howled. She became certain that there was something in the dark behind her: something very old and very slow. Her heart beat so hard and so loudly she was scared it would burst out of her chest. She closed her eyes against the dark.

Eventually she bumped into something, and opened her eyes, startled. She had bumped into an armchair, in her drawing room.

The open doorway behind her was blocked by rough red bricks.

She was home.

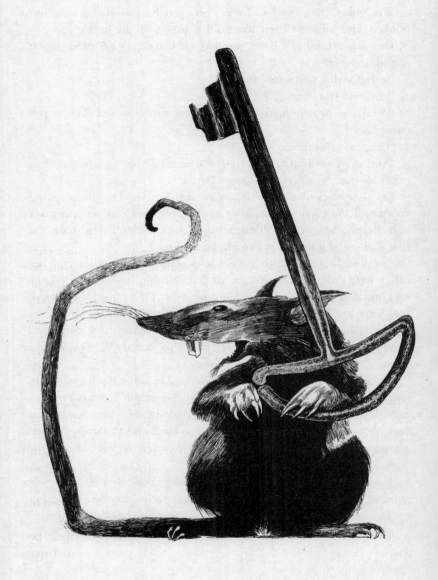

5

CORALINE LOCKED THE door of the drawing room with the cold black key.

She went back into the kitchen, and climbed on to a chair. She tried to put the bunch of keys back on top of the door again. She tried four or five times before she was forced to accept that she just wasn't big enough, and she put them down on the counter next to the door.

Her mother still hadn't returned from her shopping expedition.

Coraline went to the freezer and took out the spare loaf of frozen bread in the bottom compartment. She made herself some toast, with jam and peanut butter. She drank a glass of water.

She waited for her parents to come back.

When it began to get dark, Coraline microwaved herself a frozen pizza.

Then Coraline watched television. She wondered why grown-ups gave themselves all the good programmes, with all the shouting and running around in.

After a while she started yawning. Then she undressed, brushed her teeth and put herself to bed.

In the morning she went into her parents' room, but their bed hadn't been slept in, and they weren't around. She ate tinned spaghetti for breakfast.

For lunch she had a block of cooking chocolate and an apple. The apple was yellow and slightly shrivelled, but it tasted sweet and good.

For tea she went down to see Misses Spink and Forcible. She had three digestive biscuits, a glass of limeade, and a cup of weak tea. The limeade was very interesting. It didn't taste anything like limes. It tasted bright green and vaguely chemical. Coraline liked it enormously. She wished they had it at home.

'How are your dear mother and father?' asked Miss Spink.

'Missing,' said Coraline. 'I haven't seen either of them since yesterday. I'm on my own. I think I've probably become a single child family.'

'Tell your mother that we found the Glasgow Empire press clippings we were telling her about. She seemed very interested when Miriam mentioned them to her.'

'She's vanished under mysterious circumstances,' said Coraline, 'and I believe my father has as well.'

'I'm afraid we'll be out all day tomorrow, Caroline lovey,' said Miss Forcible. 'We'll be staying with April's niece in Royal Tunbridge Wells.'

They showed Coraline a photographic album, with photographs of Miss Spink's niece in it, and then Coraline went home.

She opened her money box and walked down to the supermarket. She bought two large bottles of limeade, a chocolate cake, and a new bag of apples, and went back home and ate them for dinner.

She cleaned her teeth, and went into her father's office. She woke up his computer and wrote a story.

CORALINE'S STORY

THERE WAS A GIRL HER NAME WAS APPLE. SHE USED TO
DANCE A LOT. SHE DANCED AND DANCED UNTIL HER FEET
TURND INTO SOSSAJES. THE END.

She printed out the story and turned off the computer. Then she drew a picture of the little girl dancing underneath the words on the paper.

She ran herself a bath with too much bubble bath in it, and the bubbles ran over the side and went all over the floor. She dried herself, and the floor as best she could, and went to bed.

Coraline woke up in the night. She went into her parents' bedroom, but the bed was made and empty. The glowing green numbers on the digital clock glowed 3:12 a.m.

All alone, in the middle of the night, Coraline began to cry. There was no other sound in the empty flat.

She climbed into her parents' bed, and, after a while, she went back to sleep.

Coraline was woken by cold paws batting her face. She opened her eyes. Big green eyes stared back at her. It was the cat.

'Hello,' said Coraline. 'How did you get in?'

The cat didn't say anything. Coraline got out of bed. She was wearing a long T-shirt and pyjama bottoms. 'Have you come to tell me something?'

The cat yawned, which made its eyes flash green.

'Do you know where Mummy and Daddy are?'

The cat blinked at her slowly.

'Is that a yes?'

The cat blinked again. Coraline decided that that was indeed a yes. 'Will you take me to them?'

The cat stared at her. Then it walked out into the hall. She followed. It walked the length of the corridor and stopped down at the very end, where a full-length mirror hung. The mirror had been, a long time before, the inside of a wardrobe door. It had been hanging there on the wall when they moved in, and, although Coraline's mother had spoken occasionally of replacing it with something newer, she never had.

Coraline turned on the light in the hall.

The mirror showed the corridor behind her; that was only to be expected. But also reflected in the mirror were her parents. They stood awkwardly in the reflection of the hall. They seemed sad and alone. As Coraline watched, they waved to her, slowly, with limp hands. Coraline's father had his arm around her mother.

In the mirror Coraline's mother and father stared at her. Her father opened his mouth and said something, but she could hear nothing at all. Her mother breathed on the inside of the mirror-glass, and quickly, before the fog faded, she wrote:

with the tip of her forefinger. The fog on the inside of the mirror faded, and so did her parents, and now the mirror reflected only the corridor, and Coraline, and the cat.

'Where are they?' Coraline asked the cat. The cat made no reply, but Coraline could imagine its voice, dry as a dead fly on a windowsill in winter, saying, *Well, where do you think they are?*

'They aren't going to come back, are they?' said Coraline. 'Not under their own steam.'

The cat blinked at her. Coraline took it as a yes.

'Right,' said Coraline. 'Then I suppose there is only one thing left to do.'

She walked into her father's study. She sat down at his desk. Then she picked up the telephone, and opened the phone book and called the local police station.

'Police,' said a gruff male voice.

'Hello,' she said. 'My name is Coraline Jones.'

'You're up a bit after your bedtime, aren't you, young lady?' said the policeman.

'Possibly,' said Coraline, who was not going to be diverted, 'but I am ringing to report a crime.'

'And what sort of crime would that be?'

'Kidnapping. Grown-up-napping, really. My parents have been stolen away into a world on the other side of the mirror in our hall.'

'And do you know who stole them?' asked the police officer. Coraline could hear the smile in his voice, and she tried extra hard to sound like an adult might sound, to make him take her seriously.

'I think my other mother has them both in her clutches. She may want to keep them and sew their eyes with black buttons, or she may simply have them in order to lure me back into reach of her fingers. I'm not sure.'

'Ah. The nefarious clutches of her fiendish fingers, is it?' he said. 'Mm. You know what I suggest, Miss Jones?'

'No,' said Coraline. 'What?'

'You ask your mother to make you a big old mug of hot chocolate,

and then give you a great big old hug. There's nothing like hot chocolate and a hug for making the nightmares go away. And if she starts to
tell you off for waking her up at this time of night, why you tell her
that that's what the policeman said.' He had a deep, reassuring voice.

Coraline was not reassured.

'When I see her,' said Coraline, 'I shall tell her that.' And she put
down the telephone.

The black cat, who had sat on the floor grooming its fur through
this entire conversation, now stood up and led the way into the hall.

Coraline went back into her bedroom and put on her blue dressing
gown and her slippers. She looked under the sink for a torch, and
found one, but the batteries had long since run down and it barely
glowed with the faintest straw-coloured light. She put it down again
and found a box of in-case-of-emergency white wax candles, and thrust
one into a candlestick. She put an apple into each pocket. She picked
up the ring of keys and took the old black key off the ring.

She walked into the drawing room and looked at the door. She had
the feeling that the door was looking back at her, which she knew was
silly, and knew on a deeper level was somehow true.

She went back into her bedroom, and rummaged in the pocket of
her jeans. She found the stone with the hole in it, and put it into her
dressing-gown pocket.

She lit the candle wick with a match and watched it sputter and
light, then she picked up the black key. It was cold in her hand. She
put the key into the keyhole in the door, but did not turn it.

'When I was a little girl,' said Coraline to the cat, 'when we lived in
our old house, a long, long time ago, my dad took me for a walk on
the wasteland between our house and the shops.

'It wasn't the best place to go for a walk, really. There were all these
things that people had thrown away back there – old cookers and broken dishes and dolls with no arms and no legs, and empty cans and
broken bottles. Mum and Dad made me promise not to go exploring
back there, because there were too many sharp things, and tetanus
and such.

'But I kept telling them I wanted to explore it. So one day my dad
put on his big brown boots and his gloves and put my boots on me and

my jeans and sweater, and we went for a walk.

'We must have walked for about twenty minutes. We went down this hill, to the bottom of a gully, where a stream was, when my Dad suddenly said to me, "Coraline – run away. Up the hill. Now!" He said it in a tight sort of way, urgently, so I did. I ran away up the hill. Something hurt me on the back of my arm as I ran, but I kept running.

'As I got to the top of the hill I heard somebody thundering up the hill behind me. It was my dad, charging like a rhino. When he reached me he picked me up in his arms and swept me over the edge of the hill.

'And then we stopped and we puffed and we panted, and we looked back down the gully.

'The air was alive with yellow wasps. We must have stepped on a wasps' nest in a rotten branch as we walked. And while I was running up the hill, my dad stayed and got stung, to give me time to run away. His glasses had fallen off when he ran.

'I only had the one sting on the back of my arm. He had thirty-nine stings, all over him. We counted later, in the bath.'

The black cat began to wash its face and whiskers in a manner that indicated increasing impatience. Coraline reached down and stroked the back of its head and neck. The cat stood up, walked several paces until it was out of her reach, then it sat down and looked up at her again.

'So,' said Coraline, 'later that afternoon my dad went back again to the wasteland, to get his glasses back. He said if he left it another day he wouldn't be able to remember where they'd fallen.

'And soon he got home, wearing his glasses. He said that he wasn't scared when he was standing there and the wasps were stinging him and hurting him and he was watching me run away. Because he knew he had to give me enough time to run, or the wasps would have come after both of us.'

Coraline turned the key in the door. It turned with a loud clunk.

The door swung open.

There was no brick wall on the other side of the door: only darkness. A cold wind blew through the passageway.

Coraline made no move to walk through the door.

'And he said that wasn't brave of him, doing that, just standing there and being stung,' said Coraline to the cat. 'It wasn't brave because he wasn't scared: it was the only thing he could do. But going back again to get his glasses, when he knew the wasps were there, when he was really scared. *That* was brave.'

She took her first step down the dark corridor.

She could smell dust and damp and mustiness.

The cat padded along beside her.

'And why was that?' asked the cat, although it sounded barely interested.

'Because,' she said, 'when you're scared but you still do it anyway, *that's* brave.'

The candle cast huge, strange, flickering shadows along the wall. She heard something moving in the darkness, beside her, or to one side of her, she could not tell. It seemed as if it was keeping pace with her, whatever it was.

'And that's why you're going back to *her* world, then?' said the cat. 'Because your father once saved you from wasps?'

'Don't be silly,' said Coraline. 'I'm going back for them because they are my parents. And if they noticed I was gone I'm sure they would do the same for me. You know you're talking again?'

'How fortunate I am,' said the cat, 'in having a travelling companion of such wisdom and intelligence.' Its tone remained sarcastic, but its fur was bristling, and its brush of a tail stuck up in the air.

Coraline was going to say something, like *sorry* or *wasn't it a lot shorter walk last time?* when the candle went out as suddenly as if it had been snuffed by someone's hand.

There was a scrabbling and a pattering, and Coraline could feel her heart pounding against her ribs. She put out one hand . . . and felt something wispy, like a spider's web, brush her hands and her face.

At the end of the corridor the electric light went on, blinding after the darkness. A woman stood, silhouetted by the light, a little ahead of Coraline.

'Coraline? Darling?' she called.

'Mum!' said Coraline, and she ran forward, eager and relieved.

'Darling,' said the woman. 'Why did you ever run away from me?'

Coraline was too close to stop, and she felt the other mother's cold arms enfold her. She stood there, rigid and trembling as the other mother held her tightly.

'Where are my parents?' Coraline asked.

'We're here,' said her other mother, in a voice so close to her real mother's that Coraline could scarcely tell them apart. 'We're here. We're ready to love you and play with you and feed you and make your life interesting.'

Coraline pulled back, and the other mother let her go, with reluctance.

The other father, who had been sitting on a chair in the hallway, stood up and smiled. 'Come on into the kitchen,' he said. 'I'll make us a midnight snack. And you'll want something to drink – hot chocolate, perhaps?'

Coraline walked down the hallway until she reached the mirror at the end. There was nothing reflected in it but a young girl in her dressing gown and slippers, who looked like she had recently been crying but whose eyes were real eyes, not black buttons, and who was holding tightly to a burned-out candle in a candlestick.

She looked at the girl in the mirror and the girl in the mirror looked back at her.

I will be brave, thought Coraline. No, I *am* brave.

She put down the candlestick on the floor, then she turned round. The other mother and the other father were looking at her hungrily.

'I don't need a snack,' she said. 'I have an apple. See?' And she took an apple from her dressing-gown pocket, then bit into it with relish and an enthusiasm that she did not really feel.

The other father looked disappointed. The other mother smiled, showing a full set of teeth, and each of the teeth was a tiny bit too long. The lights in the hallway made her black-button eyes glitter and gleam.

'You don't frighten me,' said Coraline, although they did frighten her, very much. 'I want my parents back.'

The world seemed to shimmer a little at the edges.

'Whatever would I have done with your old parents? If they have left you, Coraline, it must be because they became bored with you, or tired. Now, I will never become bored with you, and I will never aban-don you. You will always be safe here with me.' The other mother's wet-looking black hair drifted around her head, like the tentacles of a creature in the deep ocean.

'They weren't bored of me,' said Coraline. 'You're lying. You stole them.'

'Silly, silly Coraline. They are fine wherever they are.'

Coraline simply glared at the other mother.

'I'll prove it,' said the other mother, and brushed the surface of the mirror with her long white fingers. It clouded over, as if a dragon had breathed on it, and then it cleared.

In the mirror it was daytime already. Coraline was looking at the hallway, all the way down to her front door. The door opened from the outside and Coraline's mother and father walked inside. They carried suitcases.

'That was a fine holiday,' said Coraline's father.

'How nice it is, not to have Coraline any more,' said her mother with a happy smile. 'Now we can do all the things we always wanted to do, like go abroad, but were prevented from doing by having a little daughter.'

'And,' said her father, 'I take great comfort in knowing that her other mother will take better care of her than we ever could.'

The mirror fogged and faded and reflected the night once more.

'See?' said her other mother.

'No,' said Coraline. 'I don't see. And I don't believe it either.'

She hoped that what she had just seen was not real, but she was not as certain as she sounded. There was a tiny doubt inside her, like a maggot in an apple core. Then she looked up and saw the expression on her other mother's face: a flash of real anger, which crossed her face like summer lightning, and Coraline was sure in her heart that what she had seen in the mirror was no more than an illusion.

Coraline sat down on the sofa and ate her apple.

'Please,' said her other mother. 'Don't be difficult.' She walked into the drawing room and clapped her hands twice. There was a rustling noise and a black rat appeared. It stared up at her. 'Bring me the key,' she said.

The rat chittered, then it ran through the open door that led back to Coraline's own flat.

The rat returned, dragging the key behind it.

'Why don't you have your own key on this side?' asked Coraline.

'There is only one key. Only one door,' said the other father.

'Hush,' said the other mother. 'You must not bother our darling Coraline's head with such trivialities.' She put the key in the keyhole and twisted. The lock was stiff, but it clunked closed.

She dropped the key into her apron pocket.

Outside, the sky had begun to lighten to a luminous grey.

'If we aren't going to have a midnight snack,' said the other mother, 'we still need our beauty sleep. I am going back to bed, Coraline. I would strongly suggest that you do the same.'

She placed her long white fingers on the shoulders of the other father, and she walked him out of the room.

Coraline walked over to the door at the far corner of the drawing room. She tugged on it, but it was tightly locked. The door of her other parents' bedroom was now closed.

She was indeed tired, but she did not want to sleep in the bedroom. She did not want to sleep under the same roof as her other mother.

The front door was not locked. Coraline walked out into the dawn and down the stone steps. She sat down on the bottom step. It was cold.

Something furry pushed itself against her side in one smooth, insinuating motion. Coraline jumped, then breathed a sigh of relief when she saw what it was.

'Oh. It's you,' she said to the black cat.

'See?' said the cat. 'It wasn't so hard recognising me, was it? Even without names.'

'Well, what if I wanted to call you?'

The cat wrinkled its nose and managed to look unimpressed. 'Calling cats,' it confided, 'tends to be a rather overrated activity. Might as well call a whirlwind.'

'What if it was dinnertime?' asked Coraline. 'Wouldn't you want to be called then?'

'Of course,' said the cat. 'But a simple cry of 'Dinner!' would do nicely. See? No need for names.'

'Why does she want me?' Coraline asked the cat. 'Why does she want me to stay here with her?'

'She wants something to love, I think,' said the cat. 'Something that isn't her. She might want something to eat as well. It's hard to tell with creatures like that.'

'Do you have any advice?' asked Coraline.

The cat looked as if it were about to say something else sarcastic. Then it flicked its whiskers, and said, 'Challenge her. There's no guarantee she'll play fair, but her kind of thing loves games and challenges.'

'What kind of thing is that?' asked Coraline.

But the cat made no answer, simply stretched, luxuriantly, and walked away. Then it stopped, and turned, and said, 'I'd go inside if I were you. Get some sleep. You have a long day ahead of you.'

And then the cat was gone. Still, Coraline realised, it had a point. She crept back into the silent house, past the closed bedroom door beyond which the other mother and the other father . . . what? she wondered. Slept? Waited? And then it came to her that, should she open the bedroom door, she would find it empty, or, more precisely, that it was an empty room and it would remain empty until the exact moment that she opened the door.

Somehow, that made it easier. Coraline walked into the green and pink parody of her own bedroom. She closed the door and hauled the toybox in front of it – it would not keep anyone out, but the noise somebody would make trying to dislodge it would wake her, she hoped.

The toys in the toybox were still mostly asleep, and they stirred and muttered as she moved their box, and then they went back to sleep. Coraline checked under her bed, looking for rats, but there was nothing there. She took off her dressing gown and slippers and climbed into bed and fell asleep with barely enough time to reflect, as she did so, on what the cat could have meant by *a challenge*.

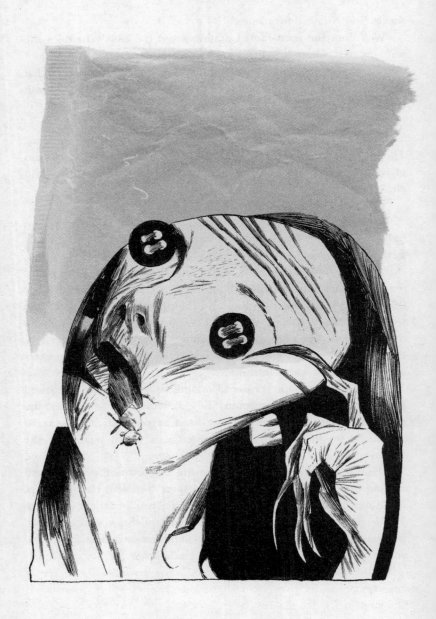

6

CORALINE WAS WOKEN by the mid-morning sun, full on her face. For a moment she felt utterly dislocated. She did not know where she was; she was not entirely sure *who* she was. It is astonishing just how much of what we are can be tied to the beds we wake up in in the morning, and it is astonishing how fragile that can be.

Sometimes Coraline would forget who she was while she was daydreaming that she was exploring the Arctic, or the Amazon rainforest, or darkest Africa, and it was not until someone tapped her on the shoulder or said her name that Coraline would come back from a million miles away with a start, and all in a fraction of a second have to remember who she was, and what her name was, and that she was even there at all.

Now there was sun on her face, and she was Coraline Jones. Yes. And then the green and pinkness of the room she was in, and the rustling of a large painted paper butterfly as it fluttered and beat its way about the ceiling, told her where she had woken up.

She climbed out of the bed. She could not wear her pyjamas, dressing gown and slippers during the day, she decided, even if it meant wearing the other Coraline's clothes. (Was there an other Coraline? No, she decided, there wasn't. There was just her.) There were no proper clothes in the cupboard, though. They were more like dressing-up clothes or (she thought) the kind of clothes she

47

would love to have hanging in her own wardrobe at home: there was a raggedy witch costume; a patched scarecrow costume; a future-warrior costume with little digital lights on it that glittered and blinked; a slinky evening dress all covered in feathers and mirrors. Finally, in a drawer, she found a pair of black jeans that seemed to be made of velvet night, and a grey sweater the colour of thick smoke with faint and tiny stars in the fabric which twinkled.

She pulled on the jeans and the sweater. Then she put on a pair of bright-orange boots she found at the bottom of the cupboard.

She took her last apple out of the pocket of her dressing gown, and then, from the same pocket, the stone with the hole in it.

She put the stone into the pocket of her jeans, and it was as if her head had cleared a little. As if she had come out of some sort of a fog.

She went into the kitchen, but it was deserted.

Still, she was sure that there was someone in the flat. She walked down the hall until she reached her father's study, and discovered that it was occupied.

'Where's the other mother?' she asked the other father. He was sitting in the study, at a desk which looked just like her father's, but he was not doing anything at all, not even reading gardening catalogues as her own father did when he was only pretending to be working.

'Out,' he told her. 'Fixing the doors. There are some vermin problems.' He seemed pleased to have somebody to talk to.

'The rats, you mean?'

'No, the rats are our friends. This is the other kind, big black fellow, with his tail high.'

'The cat, you mean?'

'That's the one,' said her other father.

He looked less like her true father today. There was something slightly vague about his face – like bread dough that had begun to rise, smoothing out the bumps and cracks and depressions.

'Really, I mustn't talk to you when she's not here,' he said. 'But don't you worry. She won't be gone often. I shall demonstrate our tender hospitality to you, such that you will not even think about ever going back.' He closed his mouth and folded his hands in his lap.

'So what am I to do now?' asked Coraline.

The other father pointed to his lips. *Silence.*

'If you won't even talk to me,' said Coraline, 'I am going exploring.'

'No point,' said the other father. 'There isn't anywhere but here. This is all she made: the house, the grounds, and the people in the house. She made it and she waited.' Then he looked embarrassed and he put one finger to his lips again, as if he had just said too much.

Coraline walked out of his study. She went into the drawing room, over to the old door, and she pulled it, rattled and shook it. No, it was locked fast, and the other mother had the key.

She looked around the room. It was so familiar – that was what made it feel so truly strange. Everything was exactly the same as she remembered: there was all her grandmother's strange-smelling furniture, there was the painting of the bowl of fruit (a bunch of grapes, two plums, a peach and an apple) hanging on the wall, there was the low wooden table with the lion's feet, and the empty fireplace which seemed to suck heat from the room.

But there was something else, something she did not remember seeing before. A ball of glass, up on the mantelpiece.

She went over to the fireplace, went up on tiptoes, and lifted it down. It was a snow-globe, with two little people in it. Coraline shook it and set the snow flying, white snow that glittered as it tumbled through the water.

Then she put the snow-globe back on the mantelpiece, and carried on looking for her true parents and for a way out.

She went out of the flat. Past the flashing-lights door, behind which the other Misses Spink and Forcible performed their show for ever, and set off into the woods.

Where Coraline came from, once you were through the patch of trees, you saw nothing but the meadow and the old tennis court. In this place, the woods went on further, the trees becoming cruder and less tree-like the further you went.

Pretty soon they seemed very approximate, like the idea of trees: a greyish-brown trunk below, a greenish splodge of something that might have been leaves above.

Coraline wondered if the other mother wasn't interested in trees, or if she just hadn't bothered with this bit properly because nobody was expected to come out this far.

She kept walking.

And then the mist began.

It was not damp, like a normal fog or mist. It was not cold and it was not warm. It felt to Coraline like she was walking into nothing.

I'm an explorer, thought Coraline to herself. And I need all the ways out of here that I can get. So I shall keep walking.

The world she was walking through was a pale nothingness, like a blank sheet of paper or an enormous, empty white room. It had no temperature, no smell, no texture and no taste.

'It certainly isn't mist,' thought Coraline, although she did not know what it was. For a moment she wondered if she might have gone blind. But no, she could see herself, plain as day. There was no ground beneath her feet, just a misty, milky whiteness.

'And what do you think you're doing?' said a shape to one side of her.

It took a few moments for her eyes to focus on it properly. She thought it might be some kind of lion, at first, some distance away from her; and then she thought it might be a mouse, close beside her. And then she knew what it was.

'I'm exploring,' Coraline told the cat.

Its fur stood straight out from its body and its eyes were wide, while its tail was down and between its legs. It did not look a happy cat.

'Bad place,' said the cat. 'If you want to call it a place, which I don't. What are you doing here?'

'I'm exploring.'

'Nothing to find here,' said the cat. 'This is just the outside, the part of the place *she* hasn't bothered to create.'

'She?'

'The one who says she's your other mother,' said the cat.

'What *is* she?' asked Coraline.

The cat did not answer, just padded through the pale mist beside Coraline.

Something began to appear in front of them, something high and towering and dark.

'You were wrong!' she told the cat. 'There *is* something there!'

And then it took shape in the mist: a dark house, which loomed at them out of the formless whiteness.

'But that's—' said Coraline.

'The house you just left,' agreed the cat. 'Precisely.'

'Maybe I just got turned around in the mist,' said Coraline.

The cat curled the high tip of its tail into a question mark, and tipped its head on to one side. '*You* might have done,' it said. '*I* certainly would not. Wrong, indeed.'

'But how can you walk away from something and still come back to it?'

'Easy,' said the cat. 'Think of somebody walking around the world. You start out walking away from something and end up coming back to it.'

'Small world,' said Coraline.

'It's big enough for her,' said the cat. 'Spiders' webs only have to be large enough to catch flies.'

Coraline shivered.

'He said that she's fixing all the gates and the doors,' she told the cat, 'to keep you out.'

'She may *try*,' said the cat, unimpressed. 'Oh yes. She may try.' They were standing under a clump of trees now, beside the house. These trees looked much more likely. 'There's ways in and ways out of places like this that even *she* doesn't know about.'

'Did she make this place, then?' asked Coraline.

'Made it, found it, what's the difference?' asked the cat. 'Either way, she's had it a very long time. Hang on—' and it gave a shiver and a leap and before Coraline could blink the cat was sitting with its paw holding down a big black rat. 'It's not that I like rats at the best of times,' said the cat conversationally, as if nothing had happened, 'but the rats in this place are all spies for her. She uses them as her eyes and hands . . .' and with that the cat let the rat go.

It ran for almost a metre and then the cat, with one bound, was upon it, batting it hard with one sharp-clawed paw while holding it down with the other. 'I love this bit,' said the cat happily. 'Want to see me do that again?'

'No,' said Coraline. 'Why do you do it? You're torturing it.'

'Mm,' said the cat. It let the rat go.

The rat stumbled, dazed, for a few steps, then it began to run. With a blow of its paw, the cat knocked the rat into the air, and caught it in its mouth.

'Stop it!' said Coraline.

The cat dropped the rat between its two front paws. 'There are those,' it said with a sigh, in tones as smooth as oiled silk, 'who have suggested that the tendency of a cat to play with its prey is a merciful one – after all, it permits the occasional funny little running snack to escape, from time to time. How often does your dinner get to escape?'

And then it picked the rat up in its mouth and carried it off into the woods, behind a tree.

Coraline walked back into the house.

All was quiet and empty and deserted. Even her footsteps on the carpeted floor seemed loud. Dust motes hung in a beam of sunlight.

At the far end of the hall was the mirror. She could see herself walking towards the mirror, looking, reflected, a little braver than she actually felt. There was nothing else there in the mirror. Just her, in the corridor.

A hand touched her shoulder, and she looked up. The other mother stared down at Coraline with big black-button eyes.

'Coraline, my darling,' she said. 'I thought we could play some games together this morning, now you're back from your walk. Hopscotch? Monopoly? Happy Families?'

'You weren't in the mirror,' said Coraline.

The other mother smiled. 'Mirrors,' she said, 'are never to be trusted. Now, what game shall we play?'

Coraline shook her head. 'I don't want to play with you,' she said. 'I want to go home and be with my real parents. I want you to let them go. To let us all go.'

The other mother shook her head, very slowly. 'Sharper than a serpent's tooth,' she said, 'is a daughter's ingratitude. Still, the proudest spirit can be broken, with love.' And her long white fingers waggled and caressed the air.

'I have no plans to love you,' said Coraline. 'No matter what. You can't make me love you.'

'Let's talk about it,' said the other mother, and she turned and walked into the sitting room. Coraline followed her.

The other mother sat down on the big sofa. She picked up a brown handbag from beside the sofa, and took out a white, rustling, paper bag from inside it.

She extended the hand with the paper bag in it to Coraline. 'Would you like one?' she asked politely.

Expecting it to be a toffee or a butterscotch ball, Coraline looked down. The bag was half-filled with large shiny blackbeetles, crawling over each other in their efforts to get out of the bag.

'No,' said Coraline. 'I don't want one.'

'Suit yourself,' said her other mother. She carefully picked out a particularly large and black beetle, pulled off its legs (which she dropped, neatly, into a big glass ashtray on the small table beside the sofa), and popped the beetle into her mouth. She crunched it happily.

'Yum,' she said, and took another.

'You're sick,' said Coraline. 'Sick and evil and weird.'

'Is that any way to talk to your mother?' her other mother asked, with her mouth full of blackbeetles.

'You aren't my mother,' said Coraline.

Her other mother ignored this. 'Now, I think you are a little overexcited, Coraline. Perhaps this afternoon we could do a little embroidery together, or some watercolour painting. Then dinner, and then, if you have been good, you may play with the rats a little before bed. And I shall read you a story and tuck you in, and kiss you goodnight.' Her long white fingers fluttered gently, like a tired butterfly, and Coraline shivered.

'No,' said Coraline.

The other mother sat on the sofa. Her mouth was set in a line; her lips were pursed. She popped another blackbeetle into her mouth, and then another, like someone with a bag of chocolate-covered raisins. Her big black-button eyes looked into Coraline's hazel eyes. Her shiny black hair twined and twisted about her neck and shoulders, as if it were blowing in some wind that Coraline could not touch or feel.

They stared at each other for over a minute. Then the other mother said, 'Manners!' She folded the white paper bag, carefully, so no blackbeetles could escape, and she placed it back in the shopping bag. Then she stood up, and up, and up: she seemed taller than Coraline remembered. She reached into her apron pocket and pulled out first the black door key, which she frowned at and tossed into her handbag, then a tiny silver-coloured key. She held it up triumphantly. 'There we are,' she said. 'This is for you, Coraline. For your own good. Because I love you. To teach you manners. Manners makyth man, after all.'

She pulled Coraline back into the hallway and advanced upon the mirror at the end of the hall. Then she pushed the tiny key into the fabric of the mirror, and she *twisted* it.

The mirror opened like a door, revealing a dark space behind it. 'You may come out when you've learned some manners,' said the other mother. 'And when you're ready to be a loving daughter.'

She picked Coraline up and pushed her into the dim space behind the mirror. A fragment of beetle was sticking to her lower lip, and there was no expression at all in her black-button eyes.

Then she swung the mirror-door closed, and left Coraline in darkness.

7

SOMEWHERE INSIDE HER Coraline could feel a huge sob welling up. And then she stopped it, before it came out. She took a deep breath and let it go. She put out her hands to touch the space in which she was imprisoned. It was the size of a broom cupboard: tall enough to stand in or to sit in, not wide or deep enough to lie down in.

One wall was glass, and it felt cold to the touch.

She went around the tiny room a second time, running her hands over every surface that she could reach, feeling for doorknobs or switches or concealed catches – some kind of way out – and found nothing.

A spider scuttled over the back of her hand and she choked back a shriek. But apart from the spider she was alone in the cupboard, in the pitch dark.

And then her hand touched something that felt for all the world like somebody's cheek and lips, small and cold, and a voice whispered in her ear, 'Hush! And shush! Say nothing, for the beldam might be listening!'

Coraline said nothing.

She felt a cold hand touch her face, fingers running over it like the gentle beat of a moth's wings.

Another voice, hesitant and so faint Coraline wondered if she were imagining it, said, 'Art thou – art thou *alive?*'

'Yes,' whispered Coraline.

'Poor child,' said the first voice.

'Who are you?' whispered Coraline.

'Names, names, names,' said another voice, all faraway and lost. 'The names are the first things to go, after the breath has gone, and the beating of the heart. We keep our memories longer than our names. I still keep pictures in my mind of my governess on some May morning, carrying my hoop and stick, and the morning sun behind her, and all the tulips bobbing in the breeze. But I have forgotten the name of my governess, and of the tulips too.'

'I don't think tulips have names,' said Coraline. 'They're just tulips.'

'Perhaps,' said the voice sadly. 'But I have always thought that these tulips must have had names. They were red, and orange-and-red, and red-and-orange- and-yellow, like the embers in the nursery fire of a winter's evening. I remember them.'

The voice sounded so sad that Coraline put out a hand to the place where it was coming from, and she found a cold hand, and she squeezed it tightly.

Her eyes were beginning to get used to the darkness. Now Coraline saw, or imagined she saw, three shapes, each as faint and pale as a moon in the daytime sky. They were the shapes of children about her own size. The cold hand squeezed her hand back. 'Thank you,' said the voice.

'Are you a girl?' asked Coraline. 'Or a boy?'

There was a pause. 'When I was small I wore skirts and my hair was long and curled,' it said doubtfully. 'But now that you ask, it does seem to me that one day they took my skirts and gave me britches and cut my hair.'

'"Tain't something we give a mind to,' said the first of the voices.

'A boy, perhaps, then,' continued the one whose hand she was holding. 'I believe I was once a boy.' And it glowed a little more brightly in the darkness of the room behind the mirror.

'What happened to you all?' asked Coraline. 'How did you come here?'

'She left us here,' said one of the voices. 'She stole our hearts, and she stole our souls, and she took our lives away, and she left us here, and she forgot about us in the dark.'

'You poor things,' said Coraline. 'How long have you been here?'

'So very long a time,' said a voice.

'Aye. Time beyond reckoning,' said another voice.

'I walked through the scullery door,' said the voice of the one that thought it might be a boy, 'and I found myself back in the parlour. But *she* was waiting for me. She told me she was my other mamma, but I never saw my true mamma again.'

'Flee!' said the very first of the voices – another girl, Coraline fancied – 'Flee, while there's still air in your lungs and blood in your veins and warmth in your heart. Flee while you still have your mind and your soul.'

'I'm not running away,' said Coraline. 'She has my parents. I came to get them back.'

'Ah, but she'll keep you here while the days turn to dust and the leaves fall and the years pass one after the next like the tick-tick-ticking of a clock.'

'No,' said Coraline. 'She won't.'

There was silence then in the room behind the mirror.

'Peradventure,' said a voice in the darkness, 'if you could win your mama and your papa back from the beldam, you could also win free our souls.'

'Has she taken them?' asked Coraline, shocked.

'Aye. And hidden them.'

'That is why we could not leave here, when we died. She kept us, and she fed on us, until now we're nothing left of ourselves, only snakeskins and spider-husks. Find our secret hearts, young mistress.'

'And what will happen to you if I do?' asked Coraline.

The voices said nothing.

'And what is she going to do to me?' she said.

The pale figures pulsed faintly; she could imagine that they were nothing more than afterimages, like the glow left by a bright light in your eyes, after the lights go out.

'It doth not hurt,' whispered one faint voice.

'She will take your life and all you are and all you care'st for, and she will leave you with nothing but mist and fog. She'll take your joy. And one day you'll awake and your heart and your soul will have gone. A husk you'll be, a wisp you'll be, and a thing no more than a dream on waking, or a memory of something forgotten.'

'Hollow,' whispered the third voice. 'Hollow, hollow, hollow, hollow, hollow.'

'You must flee,' sighed a voice, faintly.

'I don't think so,' said Coraline. 'I tried running away, and it didn't work. She just took my parents. Can you tell me how to get out of this room?'

'If we knew then we would tell you.'

'Poor things,' said Coraline to herself.

She sat down. She took off her sweater and rolled it up and put it behind her head, as a pillow. 'She won't keep me in the dark for ever,' said Coraline. 'She brought me here to play games. "Games and challenges," the cat said. I'm not much of a challenge here in the dark.' She tried to get comfortable, twisting and bending herself to fit the cramped space behind the mirror. Her stomach rumbled. She ate her last apple, taking the tiniest bites, making it last as long as she could. When she had finished she was still hungry. Then an idea struck her, and she whispered, 'When she comes to let me out, why don't you three come with me?'

'We wish that we could,' they sighed to her, in their barely-there voices. 'But she has our hearts in her keeping. Now we belong to the dark and to the empty places. The light would shrivel us, and burn.'

'Oh,' said Coraline.

She closed her eyes, which made the darkness darker, and she rested her head on the rolled-up sweater, and she went to sleep. And as she fell asleep she thought she felt a ghost kiss her cheek, tenderly, and a small voice whisper into her ear, a voice so faint it was barely there at all, a gentle wispy nothing of a voice so hushed that Coraline could almost believe she was imagining it.

'Look through the stone,' it said to her. And then she slept.

8

THE OTHER MOTHER looked healthier than before: there was a little blush to her cheeks, and her hair was wriggling like lazy snakes on a warm day. Her black-button eyes seemed as if they had been freshly polished.

She had pushed through the mirror as if she were walking through nothing more solid than water and had stared down at Coraline. Then she had opened the door with the little silver key. She picked Coraline up, just as Coraline's real mother had when Coraline was much younger, cradling the half-sleeping child as if she were a baby.

The other mother carried Coraline into the kitchen and put her down, very gently, upon the counter-top.

Coraline struggled to wake herself up, conscious only for the moment of having been cuddled and loved, and wanting more of it; then realising where she was, and who she was with.

'There, my sweet Coraline,' said her other mother. 'I came and fetched you out of the cupboard. You needed to be taught a lesson, but we temper our justice with mercy here, we love the sinner and we hate the sin. Now, if you will be a good child who loves her mother, be compliant and fair-spoken, you and I shall understand each other perfectly and we shall love each other perfectly as well.'

Coraline scratched the sleep-grit from her eyes.

'There were other children in there,' she said. 'Old ones, from a long time ago.'

'Were there?' said the other mother. She was bustling between the pans and the fridge, bringing out eggs and cheeses, butter and a slab of sliced pink bacon.

'Yes,' said Coraline. 'There were. I think you're planning to turn me into one of them. A dead shell.'

Her other mother smiled gently. With one hand she cracked the eggs into a bowl, with the other she whisked them and whirled them. Then she dropped a pat of butter into a frying pan, where it hissed and fizzled and spun as she sliced thin slices of cheese. She poured the melted butter and the cheese into the egg mixture, and whisked it some more.

'Now, I think you're being silly, dear,' said the other mother. 'I love you. I will always love you. Nobody sensible believes in ghosts anyway. That's because they're all such liars. Smell the lovely breakfast I'm making for you.' She poured the yellow mixture into the pan. 'Cheese omelette. Your favourite.'

Coraline's mouth watered. 'You like games,' she said. 'That's what I've been told.'

The other mother's black eyes flashed. 'Everybody likes games,' was all she said.

'Yes,' said Coraline. She climbed down from the counter and sat at the kitchen table.

The bacon was sizzling and spitting under the grill. It smelled wonderful.

'Wouldn't you be happier if you won me, fair and square?' asked Coraline.

'Possibly,' said the other mother. She had a show of unconcernedness, but her fingers twitched and drummed and she licked her lips with her scarlet tongue. 'What exactly are you offering?'

'Me,' said Coraline, and she gripped her knees under the table, to stop them from shaking. 'If I lose I'll stay here with you for ever and I'll let you love me. I'll be a most dutiful daughter. I'll eat your food, and play Happy Families. And I'll let you sew your buttons into my eyes.'

Her other mother stared at her, black buttons unblinking. 'That sounds very fine,' she said. 'And if you do not lose?'

'Then you let me go. You let everyone go – my real father and mother, the dead children, everyone you've trapped here.'

The other mother took the bacon from under the grill and put it on a plate. Then she slipped the cheese omelette from the pan on to the plate, flipping it as she did so, letting it fold itself into a perfect omelette shape.

She placed the breakfast plate in front of Coraline, along with a glass of freshly squeezed orange juice and a mug of frothy hot chocolate.

'Yes,' she said. 'I think I like this game. But what kind of game shall it be? A riddle game? A test of knowledge? Or of skill?'

'An exploring game,' suggested Coraline. 'A finding-things game.'

'And what is it you think you should be finding in this hide-and-go-seek game, Coraline Jones?'

Coraline hesitated. Then, 'My parents,' said Coraline. 'And the souls of the children behind the mirror.'

The other mother smiled at this, triumphantly, and Coraline wondered if she had made the right choice. Still, it was too late to change her mind now.

'A deal,' said the other mother. 'Now eat up your breakfast, my sweet. Don't worry, it won't hurt you.'

Coraline stared at the breakfast, hating herself for giving in so easily; but she was starving.

'How do I know you'll keep your word?' asked Coraline.

'I swear it,' said the other mother. 'I swear it on my own mother's grave.'

'Does she have a grave?' asked Coraline.

'Oh yes,' said the other mother. 'I put her in there myself. And when I found her trying to crawl out, I put her back.'

'Swear on something else. So I can trust you to keep your word.'

'My right hand,' said the other mother, holding it up. She waggled the long fingers slowly, displaying the claw-like nails. 'I swear on that.'

Coraline shrugged. 'Okay,' she said. 'It's a deal.' She ate the breakfast, trying not to wolf it down. She was hungrier than she had thought.

As she ate, the other mother stared at her. It was hard to read expressions into those black-button eyes, but Coraline thought that her other mother looked hungry, too.

She drank the orange juice, but even though she knew she would like it she could not bring herself to taste the hot chocolate.

'Where should I start looking?' asked Coraline.

'Where you wish,' said her other mother, as if she did not care at all.

Coraline looked at her, and Coraline thought hard. There was no point, she decided, in exploring the garden and the grounds: they didn't exist, they weren't real. There was no abandoned tennis court in the other mother's world, no bottomless well. All that was real was the house itself.

She looked around the kitchen. She opened the oven, peered into the freezer, poked into the salad compartment of the fridge. The other mother followed her about, looking at Coraline with a smirk always hovering at the edge of her lips.

'How big are souls anyway?' asked Coraline.

The other mother sat down at the kitchen table and leaned back against the wall, saying nothing. She picked at her teeth with a long crimson-varnished fingernail, then she tapped the finger gently, tap-tap-tap, against the polished black surface of her black-button eyes.

'Fine,' said Coraline. 'Don't tell me. I don't care. It doesn't matter if you help me or not. Everyone knows that a soul is the same size as a beach ball.'

She was hoping the other mother would say something like, 'Nonsense, they're the size of ripe onions – or suitcases – or grand-father clocks,' but the other mother simply smiled, and the tap-tap-tapping of her fingernail against her eye was as steady and relentless as the drip of water droplets from the tap into the sink. And then, Coraline realised, it *was* simply the noise of the water, and she was alone in the room.

Coraline shivered. She preferred the other mother to have a loca-tion: if she were nowhere, then she could be anywhere. And, after all, it is always easier to be afraid of something you cannot see. She put her hands into her pockets and her fingers closed around the reassuring shape of the stone with the hole in it. She pulled it out of her pocket, held it in front of her as if she were holding a gun, and walked out into the hall.

There was no sound but the tap-tap of the water dripping into the metal sink.

She glanced at the mirror at the end of the hall. For a moment it clouded over, and it seemed to her that faces swam in the glass, indistinct and shapeless, and then the faces were gone, and there was nothing in the mirror but a girl who was small for her age holding something that glowed gently, like a green coal.

Coraline looked down at her hand, surprised: it was just a pebble with a hole in it, a nondescript brown stone. Then she looked back into the mirror where the stone glimmered like an emerald. A trail of green fire blew from the stone in the mirror, and drifted towards Coraline's bedroom.

'Hmm,' said Coraline.

She walked into the bedroom. The toys fluttered excitedly as she came in, as if they were pleased to see her, and a little tank rolled out of the toybox to greet her, its treads rolling over several other toys. It fell from the toybox on to the floor, tipping as it fell, and it lay on the carpet like a beetle on its back, grumbling and grinding its treads before Coraline picked it up and turned it over. The tank fled under the bed in embarrassment.

Coraline looked around the room.

She looked in the cupboards and the drawers. Then she picked up one end of the toybox and tipped all the toys in it out on to the carpet, where they grumbled and stretched and wiggled awkwardly free of each other. A grey marble rolled across the floor and clicked against the wall. None of the toys looked particularly soul-like, she thought. She picked up and examined a silver charm-bracelet from which hung tiny animal charms which chased each other around the perimeter of the bracelet, the fox never catching the rabbit, the bear never gaining on the fox.

Coraline opened her hand and looked at the stone with the hole in it, hoping for a clue but not finding one. Most of the toys that had been in the toybox had now crawled away to hide under the bed, and the few toys that were left (a green plastic soldier, the glass marble, a vivid pink yo-yo, and such) were the kind of things you find in the bottoms of toyboxes in the real world: forgotten objects, abandoned and unloved.

She was about to leave and look elsewhere. And then she remembered a voice in the darkness, a gentle whispering voice, and what it had told her to do. She raised the stone with the hole in it, and held it in front of her right eye. She closed her left eye and looked at the room through the hole in the stone.

Through the stone, the world was grey and colourless, like a pencil drawing. Everything in it was grey – no, not quite everything. Something glinted on the floor, something the colour of an ember in a nursery fireplace, the colour of a scarlet-and-orange tulip nodding in the May sun. Coraline reached out her left hand, scared that if she took her eye off it it would vanish, and she fumbled for the burning thing.

Her fingers closed about something smooth and cool. She snatched it up, and then lowered the stone with the hole in it from her eye and looked down. The grey glass marble from the bottom of the toybox sat, dully, in the pink palm of her hand. She raised the stone to her eye once more, and looked through it at the marble. Once again the marble burned and flickered with a red fire.

A voice whispered in her mind, 'Indeed, lady, it comes to me that I certainly *was* a boy, now I do think on it. Oh, but you must hurry. There are two of us still to find, and the beldam is already angry with you for uncovering me.'

If I'm going to do this, thought Coraline, I'm not going to do it in her clothes. She changed back into her pyjamas and her dressing gown and her slippers, leaving the grey sweater and the black jeans neatly folded up on the bed, the orange boots on the floor by the toy box.

She put the marble into her dressing-gown pocket and walked out into the hall.

Something stung her face and hands like sand blowing on a beach on a windy day. She covered her eyes, and pushed forward.

The sand-stings got worse, and it got harder and harder to walk, as if she were pushing into the wind on a particularly blustery day. It was a vicious wind, and a cold one.

She took a step backwards, the way she had come.

'Oh, keep going,' whispered a ghost-voice in her ear. 'For the beldam is angry.'

She stepped forward in the hallway, into another gust of wind, which stung her cheeks and face with invisible sand, sharp as needles, sharp as glass.

'Play fair,' shouted Coraline, into the wind.

There was no reply, but the wind whipped about her one more time, petulantly, and then it dropped away, and was gone. As she passed the kitchen Coraline could hear, in the sudden silence, the drip-drip of the water from the leaking tap, or perhaps the other mother's long fingernails tapping impatiently against the table. Coraline resisted the urge to look.

In a couple of strides she reached the front door, and she walked outside.

Coraline went down the steps and around the house until she reached the other Miss Spink and Miss Forcible's flat. The lamps around the door were flickering on and off almost randomly now, spelling out no words that Coraline could understand. The door was closed. She was afraid it was locked, and she pushed on it with all her strength. First it stuck, then suddenly it gave, and, with a jerk, Coraline stumbled into the dark room beyond.

Coraline closed one hand around the stone with the hole in it and walked forward into blackness. She expected to find a curtained anteroom, but there was nothing there. The room was dark. The theatre was empty. She moved ahead cautiously. Something rustled above her. She looked up into a deeper darkness, and as she did so her feet knocked against something. She reached down, picked up a torch, and clicked it on, sweeping the beam around the room.

The theatre was derelict and abandoned. Chairs were broken on the floor, and old, dusty spiders' webs draped the walls and hung from the rotten wood and the decomposing velvet hangings.

Something rustled once again. Coraline directed her light beam upwards, towards the ceiling. There were things up there, hairless, jellyish. She thought they might once have had faces, might even once have been dogs; but no dogs had wings like bats, or could hang, like spiders, like bats, upside-down.

The light startled the creatures, and one of them took to the air, its wings whirring heavily through the dust. Coraline ducked as it swooped close to her. It came to rest on a far wall, and it began to clamber, upside-down, back to the nest of the dog-bats upon the ceiling.

Coraline raised the stone to her eye and she scanned the room through it, looking for something that glowed or glinted, a telltale sign that somewhere in this room was another hidden soul. She ran the beam of the torch about the room as she searched, the thick dust in the air making the light beam seem almost solid.

There was something up on the back wall behind the ruined stage. It was greyish-white, twice the size of Coraline herself, and it was stuck to the back wall like a slug. Coraline took a deep breath. 'I'm not afraid,' she told herself. 'I'm not.' She did not believe herself, but she scrambled on to the old stage, fingers sinking into the rotting wood as she pulled herself up.

As she got closer to the thing on the wall, she saw that it was some kind of a sac, like a spider's egg-case. It twitched in the light beam. Inside the sac was something that looked like a person, but a person with two heads, with twice as many arms and legs as it should have.

The creature in the sac seemed horribly unformed and unfinished, as if two Plasticine people had been warmed and rolled together, squashed and pressed into one thing.

Coraline hesitated. She did not want to approach the thing. The dog-bats dropped, one by one, from the ceiling, and began to circle the room, coming close to her but never touching her.

Perhaps there are no souls hidden in here, she thought. Perhaps I can just leave and go somewhere else. She took a last look through the hole in the stone: the abandoned theatre was still a bleak grey, but now there was a brown glow, as rich and bright as polished cherrywood, coming from inside the sac. Whatever was glowing was being held in one of the hands of the thing on the wall.

Coraline walked slowly across the damp stage, trying to make as little noise as she could, afraid that, if she disturbed the thing in the sac, it would open its eyes, and see her, and then . . .

But there was nothing that she could think of that was as scary as having it look at her. Her heart pounded in her chest. She took another step forward.

She had never been so scared, but still she walked forward until she reached the sac. Then she pushed her hand into the sticky, clinging whiteness of the stuff on the wall. It crackled softly, like a tiny fire, as she pushed, and it clung to her skin and clothes like a spider's web clings, like white candy-floss. She pushed her hand into it, and she reached upward until she touched a cold hand, which was, she could feel, closed around another glass marble. The creature's skin felt slippery, as if it had been covered in jelly. Coraline tugged at the marble.

At first nothing happened; it was held tight in the creature's grasp. Then, one by one, the fingers loosened their grip, and the marble slipped into her hand. She pulled her arm back through the sticky webbing, relieved that the thing's eyes had not opened. She shone the light on its faces: they resembled, she decided, the younger versions of Miss Spink and Miss Forcible, but twisted and squeezed together, like two lumps of wax that had melted and melded together into one ghastly object.

Without warning, one of the creature's hands made a grab for Coraline's arm. Its fingernails scraped her skin, but it was too slippery to grip, and Coraline pulled away successfully. And then the eyes opened – four black buttons glinting and staring down at her – and two voices that sounded like no voice that Coraline had ever heard began to speak to her. One of them wailed and whispered, the other buzzed like a fat and angry bluebottle at a windowpane, but the voices said, as one person, '*Thief! Give it back! Stop! Thief!*'

The air became alive with dog-bats. Coraline began to back away. She realised then that, terrifying though the thing on the wall was, the thing that had once been the other Misses Spink and Forcible, it was attached to the wall by its web, encased in its cocoon. It could not follow her.

The dog-bats flapped and fluttered about her, but they did

nothing to hurt Coraline. She climbed down from the stage and shone the torch about the old theatre looking for the way out.

'Flee, miss,' wailed a girl's voice in her head. 'Flee, now. You have two of us. Flee this place while your blood still flows.'

Coraline dropped the marble into her pocket beside the other. She spotted the door, ran to it, and pulled on it until it opened.

9

OUTSIDE, THE WORLD had become a formless, swirling mist with no shapes or shadows behind it, while the house itself seemed to have twisted and stretched. It appeared to Coraline that it was crouching and staring down at her, as if it were not really a house but only the idea of a house – and the person who had had the idea, she was certain, was not a good person. There was sticky web-stuff clinging to her arm, and she wiped it off as best she could. The grey windows of the house slanted at strange angles.

The other mother was waiting for her, standing on the grass with her arms folded. Her black-button eyes were expressionless, but her lips were pressed tightly together in a cold fury.

When she saw Coraline she reached out one long white hand, and she crooked a finger. Coraline walked towards her. The other mother said nothing.

'I've found two,' said Coraline. 'One soul still to go.'

The expression on the other mother's face did not change. She might not have heard what Coraline said.

'Well, I just thought you'd want to know,' said Coraline.

'Thank you, Coraline,' said the other mother coldly, and her voice did not just come from her mouth. It came from the mist, and the fog, and the house, and the sky. She said, 'You know that I love you.'

And, despite herself, Coraline nodded. It was true: the other

mother loved her. But she loved Coraline as a miser loves money, or a dragon loves its gold. In the other mother's button eyes, Coraline knew that she was a possession, nothing more. A tolerated pet, whose behaviour was no longer amusing.

'I don't want your love,' said Coraline. 'I don't want anything from you.'

'Not even a helping hand?' asked the other mother. 'You have been doing so well, after all. I thought you might want a little hint, to help you with the rest of your treasure hunt.'

'I'm doing fine on my own,' said Coraline.

'Yes,' said the other mother. 'But if you wanted to get into the flat in the front – the empty one – to look around, you would find the door locked, and then where would you be?'

'Oh.' Coraline pondered this for a moment. Then she said, 'Is there a key?'

The other mother stood there in the paper-grey fog of the flattening world. Her black hair drifted about her head, as if it had a mind and a purpose all of its own. She coughed, suddenly, in the back of her throat, and then she opened her mouth.

The other mother reached up her hand and removed a small, brass, front-door key from her tongue.

'Here,' she said. 'You'll need this to get in.'

She tossed the key, casually, towards Coraline, who caught it, one-handed, before she could think about whether she wanted it or not. The key was still slightly damp.

A chill wind blew about them, and Coraline shivered and looked away. When she looked back she was alone.

Uncertainly, she walked round to the front of the house and stood in front of the door to the empty flat. Like all the doors, it was painted bright green.

'She does not mean you well,' whispered a ghost-voice in her ear. 'We do not believe that she would help you. It must be a trick.'

Coraline said, 'Yes, you're right, I expect.' Then she put the key in the lock, and turned it.

Silently the door swung open, and silently Coraline walked inside.

The flat had walls the colour of old milk. The wooden boards of the floor were uncarpeted and dusty with the marks and patterns of old carpets and rugs on them.

There was no furniture in there, only places where furniture had once been. Nothing decorated the walls; there were discoloured rectangles on the walls to show where paintings or photographs had once hung. It was so silent that Coraline imagined that she could hear the motes of dust drifting through the air.

She found herself to be quite worried that something would jump out at her, so she began to whistle. She thought it might make it harder for things to jump out at her, if she was whistling.

First she walked through the empty kitchen. Then she walked through an empty bathroom, containing only a cast-iron bath, and, in the bath, a dead spider the size of a small cat. The last room she looked at had, she supposed, once been a bedroom; she could imagine that the rectangular dust-shadow on the floorboards had once been a bed. Then she saw something, and smiled, grimly. Set into the floorboards was a large metal ring. Coraline knelt and took the cold ring in her hands, and she tugged upward, as hard as she could.

Terribly slowly, stiffly, heavily, a hinged square of floor lifted: it was a trapdoor. It lifted, and through the opening Coraline could see only darkness. She reached down, and her hand found a cold switch. She flicked it without much hope that it would work, but somewhere below her a bulb lit, and a thin yellow light came up from the hole in the floor. She could see steps, heading down, but nothing else.

Coraline put her hand into her pocket and took out the stone with the hole in it. She looked through it at the cellar but saw nothing. She put the stone back into her pocket.

Up through the hole in the floor came the smell of damp clay, and something else, an acrid tang like sour vinegar.

Coraline let herself down into the hole, looking nervously at the trapdoor. It was so heavy that if it fell she was sure she would be trapped down in the darkness for ever. She put up a hand and touched it, but it stayed in position. And then she turned towards the darkness below, and she walked down the steps. Set into the wall at the bottom of the steps was another light switch, metal and rusting. She pushed it until it clicked down, and a naked bulb hanging from a wire from the low ceiling came on. It did not give out enough light even for Coraline to make out the things that had been painted on to the flaking cellar walls. The paintings seemed crude. There were eyes, she could see that, and things that might have been grapes. And other things, below them. Coraline could not be sure that they were paintings of people.

There was a pile of rubbish in one corner of the room: cardboard boxes filled with mildewed papers, and decaying curtains in a heap beside them.

Coraline's slippers crunched across the cement floor. The bad smell was worse now. She was ready to turn and leave, when she saw the foot sticking out from beneath the pile of curtains.

She took a deep breath (the smells of sour wine and mouldy bread filled her head) and pulled away the damp cloth to reveal something more or less the size and shape of a person.

In that dim light, it took her several seconds to recognise it for what it was: the thing was pale and swollen, like a grub, with thin, stick-like arms and feet. It had almost no features on its face, which had puffed and swollen like risen bread dough.

The thing had two large black buttons where its eyes should have been.

Coraline made a noise, a sound of revulsion and horror, and, as if it had heard her and awakened, the thing began to sit up. Coraline stood there, frozen. The thing turned its head until both its black-button eyes were pointed straight at her. A mouth opened in the mouthless face, strands of pale stuff sticking to the lips, and a voice that no longer even faintly resembled her father's whispered, 'Coraline.'

'Well,' said Coraline to the thing that had once been her other father, 'at least you didn't jump out at me.'

The creature's twig-like hands moved to its face and pushed the pale clay about, making something like a nose. It said nothing.

'I'm looking for my parents,' said Coraline. 'Or a stolen soul, from one of the other children. Are they down here?'

'There is nothing down here,' said the pale thing, indistinctly. 'Nothing but dust and damp and forgetting.' The thing was white, and huge, and swollen. Monstrous, thought Coraline, but also miserable. She raised the stone with the hole in it to her eye, and looked through it. Nothing. The pale thing was telling her the truth.

'Poor thing,' she said. 'I bet she made you come down here as a punishment for telling me too much.'

The thing hesitated, then it nodded. Coraline wondered how she could ever have imagined that this grub-like thing resembled her father.

'I'm so sorry,' she said.

'She's not best pleased,' said the thing that was once the other father. 'Not best pleased at all. You've put her quite out of sorts. And when she gets out of sorts, she takes it out on everybody else. It's her way.'

Coraline patted its hairless head. Its skin was tacky, like warm bread dough. 'Poor thing,' she said. 'You're just a thing she made and then threw away.'

The thing nodded vigorously; as it nodded, the left button-eye fell off and clattered on to the concrete floor. The thing looked around vacantly with its one eye, as if it had lost her. Finally it saw her, and, as if making a great effort, it opened its mouth once more and said in a wet, urgent voice, 'Run, child. Leave this place. She wants me to hurt you, to keep you here for ever, so that you can never finish the game, and she will win. She is pushing me so hard to hurt you. I cannot fight her.'

'You *can*,' said Coraline. 'Be brave.'

She looked around: the thing that had once been the other father was between her and the steps up and out of the cellar. She started edging along the wall, heading towards the steps. The thing twisted bonelessly until its one eye was again facing her. It seemed to be getting bigger now, and more awake. 'Alas,' it said. 'I cannot.'

And it lunged across the cellar towards her then, its toothless mouth opened wide.

Coraline had a single heartbeat in which to react. She could only think of two things to do. Either she could scream, and try to run away, and be chased around a badly lit cellar by the huge grub-thing – be chased until it caught her. Or she could do something else.

So she did something else.

As the thing reached her, Coraline put out her hand and closed it around the thing's remaining button-eye, and she tugged, as hard as she knew how.

For a moment nothing happened. Then the button came away and flew from her hand, clicking against the brickwork before it fell to the cellar floor.

The thing froze in place. It threw its pale head back blindly, and opened its mouth horribly wide, and it roared its anger and frustration. Then, all in a rush, the thing swept towards the place where Coraline had been standing.

But Coraline was not standing there any longer. She was already tiptoeing, as quietly as she could, up the steps that would take her away from the dim cellar with the crude paintings on the walls. She could not take her eyes from the floor beneath her, though, across which a pale thing flopped and writhed, hunting for her. Then, as if it was being told what to do, the creature stopped moving, and its blind head tipped to one side.

It's listening for me, thought Coraline. I must be extra quiet. She took another step up and her foot slipped on the step, and the thing heard her.

Its head tipped towards her. For a moment it swayed and seemed to be gathering its wits. Then, fast as a serpent, it slithered for the steps, and began to flow up them, towards her. Coraline turned and ran wildly up the last half-dozen steps, and she pushed herself up and on to the floor of the dusty bedroom. Without pausing, she pulled the heavy trapdoor towards her, and let go of it. It crashed down with a thump just as something large banged against it. The trapdoor shook and rattled in the floor, but it stayed where it was.

Coraline took a deep breath. If there had been any furniture in that flat, even a chair, she would have pulled it on to the trapdoor, but there was nothing.

She walked out of that flat as fast as she could, without actually ever running, and she locked the front door behind her. She left the door-key under the mat. Then she walked down on to the drive.

Coraline had half-expected that the other mother would be

77

standing there waiting for her to come out, but the world was silent and empty.

Coraline wanted to go home.

She hugged herself, and told herself that she was brave, and she almost believed herself, and then she walked around to the side of the house, in the grey mist that wasn't a mist, and she made for the stairs, to go up.

10

CORALINE WALKED UP the steps outside the building to the top-most flat where, in her world, the crazy old man upstairs lived. She had gone up there once with her real mother, when her mother was collecting for charity. They had stood in the open doorway, waiting for the crazy old man with the big moustache to find the envelope that Coraline's mother had left, and the flat had smelled of strange foods and pipe tobacco and odd, sharp, cheesy-smelling things which Coraline could not name. She had not wanted to go any further inside than that.

'I'm an explorer,' said Coraline out loud, but her words sounded muffled and dead on the misty air. She had made it out of the cellar, hadn't she?

And she had. But if there was one thing that Coraline was certain of, it was that this flat would be worse.

She reached the top of the steps. The topmost flat had once been the attic of the house, but that was long ago.

She knocked on the green-painted door. It swung open, and she walked in.

We have eyes and we have nerveses
We have tails, we have teeth,
You'll all get what you deserveses
When we rise from underneath,

whispered a dozen or more tiny voices, in that dark flat with the roof so low where it met the walls that Coraline could almost reach up and touch it.

Red eyes stared at her. Little pink feet scurried away as she came close. Darker shadows slipped through the shadows at the edges of things.

It smelt much worse in here than in the real crazy old man upstairs's flat. That smelled of food (unpleasant food, to Coraline's mind, but she knew that was a matter of taste: she did not like spices, herbs or exotic things). This place smelled as if all the exotic foods in the world had been left out to go rotten.

'Little girl,' said a rustling voice in a far room.

'Yes,' said Coraline. *I'm not frightened*, she told herself, and as she thought it she knew that it was true. There was nothing here that frightened her. These things – even the thing in the cellar – were illusions, things made by the other mother in a ghastly parody of the real people and real things on the other end of the corridor. She couldn't truly make anything, decided Coraline. She could only twist and copy and distort things that already existed.

And then Coraline found herself wondering why the other mother would have placed a snowglobe on the drawing-room mantelpiece; a place that, in her world, was quite bare.

And once she had asked herself the question, she began to understand the answer.

Then the voice came again, and her train of thought was gone.

'Come here, little girl. I know what you want, little girl.' It was a rustling voice, scratchy and dry. It made Coraline think of some kind of enormous dead insect. Which was silly, she knew. How could a dead thing, especially a dead insect, have a voice?

She walked through several rooms with low, slanting ceilings until she came to the final room. It was a bedroom, and the other crazy old man upstairs sat at the far end of the room, in the near-darkness, bundled up in his coat and hat. As Coraline entered he began to talk. 'Nothing's changed, little girl,' he said, his voice sounding like the noise dry leaves make as they rustle across a pavement. 'And what if you do everything you swore you would? What then?

Nothing's changed. You'll go home. You'll be bored. You'll be ignored. No one will listen to you, not really listen to you. You're too clever and too quiet for them to understand. They don't even get your name right.

'Stay here with us,' said the voice from the figure at the end of the room. 'We will listen to you and play with you and laugh with you. Your other mother will build whole worlds for you to explore, and tear them down every night when you are done. Every day will be better and brighter than the one that went before. Remember the toy-box? How much better would a world be built just like that, and all for you?'

'And will there be grey, wet days where I just don't know what to do and there's nothing to read or to watch and nowhere to go and the day drags on forever?' asked Coraline.

From the shadows, the man said, 'Never.'

'And will there be awful meals, with food made from recipes, with garlic and tarragon and broad beans in?' asked Coraline.

'Every meal will be a thing of joy,' whispered the voice from under the old man's hat. 'Nothing will pass your lips that does not entirely delight you.'

'And could I have Day-glo green gloves to wear, and yellow wellington boots in the shape of frogs?' asked Coraline.

'Frogs, ducks, rhinos, octopuses – whatever you desire. The world will be built new for you every morning. If you stay here, you can have whatever you want.'

Coraline sighed. 'You really don't understand, do you?' she said. 'I don't *want* whatever I want. Nobody does. Not really. What kind of fun would it be if I just got everything I ever wanted? Just like that, and it didn't *mean* anything. What then?'

'I don't understand,' said the whispery voice.

'Of course you don't understand,' she said, raising the stone with the hole in it to her eye. 'You're just a bad copy she made of the crazy old man upstairs.'

There was a glow coming from the raincoat of the man, at about chest height. Through the hole in the stone the glow twinkled and shone blue-white as any star. She wished she had a stick or something to poke him with; she had no wish to get any closer to the shadowy man at the end of the room.

'Not even that any more,' said the dead, whispery voice.

Coraline took a step closer to the man, and he fell apart. Black rats leapt from the sleeves and from under the coat and hat, a score or more of them, red eyes shining in the dark. They chittered and they fled. The coat fluttered and fell heavily to the floor. The hat rolled into one corner of the room.

Coraline reached out her hand and pulled the coat open. It was empty, although it was greasy to the touch. There was no sign of the final glass marble in it. She scanned the room, squinting through the hole in the stone, and caught sight of something that twinkled and burned like a star, at floor level, by the doorway. It was being carried in the forepaws of the largest black rat. As she looked, it slipped away.

The other rats watched her from the corners of the room as she ran after it.

Now, rats can run faster than people, especially over short distances. But a large black rat holding a marble in its two front paws is no match for a determined girl (even if she is small for her age) moving at a run. Smaller black rats ran back and forth across her path, trying to distract her, but she ignored them all, keeping her eyes fixed on the one with the marble, who was heading straight out of the flat, towards the front door.

They reached the steps on the outside of the building.

Coraline had time to observe that the house itself was continuing to change, becoming less distinct, and flattening out, even as she raced down the stairs. It reminded her of a photograph of a house now, not the thing itself. Then she was simply racing pell-mell down the steps in pursuit of the rat, with no room in her mind for anything else, certain she was gaining on it. She was running fast – too fast, she discovered, as she came to the bottom of one flight of steps, and her foot skidded and twisted and she went crashing on to the concrete landing.

Her left knee was scraped and skinned, and the palm of one hand she had thrown out to stop herself was a mess of scraped skin and grit. It hurt a little, and it would, she knew, soon hurt much more. She picked the grit out of the palm and climbed to her feet and, as fast as she could, knowing that she had lost and it was already too late, she went down the final set of steps to ground level.

She looked around for the rat, but it was gone, and the marble with it.

Her hand stung where the skin had been scraped, and there was blood trickling down her ripped pyjama-leg from her knee. It was as bad as the summer that her mother had taken the training wheels off Coraline's bicycle; but then, back then, in with all the cuts and scrapes (her knees had had scabs on top of scabs) she had a feeling of achievement. She was learning something, doing something she had not known how to do before. Now she felt nothing but cold loss. She had failed the ghost-children. She had failed her parents. She had failed herself, failed everything.

She closed her eyes and wished that the earth would swallow her up.

There was a cough.

She opened her eyes, and saw the rat. It was lying on the brick path at the bottom of the steps, with a surprised look on its face – which was now several centimetres away from the rest of it. Its whiskers were stiff, its eyes were wide open, its teeth visible and yellow and sharp. A collar of wet blood glistened at its neck.

Beside the decapitated rat, a smug expression on its face, was the black cat. It rested one paw on the grey glass marble.

'I think I once mentioned,' said the cat, 'that I don't like rats at the best of times. It looked like you needed this one, however. I hope you don't mind my getting involved.'

'I think,' said Coraline, trying to catch her breath, 'I think you may . . . have said . . . something of the sort.'

The cat lifted its paw from the marble, which rolled towards Coraline. She picked it up. In her mind, a final voice whispered to her, urgently.

'She has lied to you. She will never give you up, now she has you. She will no more give any of us up than she can change her nature.' The hairs on the back of Coraline's neck prickled, and Coraline knew that the girl's voice told the truth. She put the marble in her dressing-gown pocket with the others.

She had all three marbles, now.

All she needed to do was to find her parents.

And, Coraline realised, that was easy. She knew exactly where her parents were. If she had stopped to think, she might have known where they were all along. The other mother could not create. She could only transform, and twist, and change.

And the mantelpiece in the drawing room back home was quite empty. But, knowing that, she knew something else, as well.

'The other mother. She plans to break her promise. She won't let us go,' said Coraline.

'I wouldn't put it past her,' admitted the cat. 'Like I said, there's no guarantee she'll play fair.' And then he raised his head. 'Hello . . . did you see that?'

'What?'

'Look behind you,' said the cat.

The house had flattened out even more. It no longer looked like a photograph – more like a drawing, a crude, charcoal scribble of a house drawn on grey paper.

'Whatever's happening,' said Coraline, 'thank you for helping with the rat. I suppose I'm almost there, aren't I? So you go off into the mist or wherever you go, and I'll, well, I hope I get to see you at home. If she lets me go home.'

The cat's fur was on end, and its tail was bristling like a chimney-sweep's brush.

'What's wrong?' asked Coraline.

'They've gone,' said the cat. 'They aren't there any more. The ways in and out of this place. They just went flat.'

'Is that bad?'

The cat lowered its tail, swishing it from side to side angrily. It made a low growling noise in the back of its throat. It walked in a circle, until it was facing away from Coraline, and then it began to walk backwards, stiffly, one step at a time, until it was pushing up against Coraline's leg. She put down a hand to stroke it, and could feel how hard its heart was beating. It was trembling, like a dead leaf in a storm.

'You'll be fine,' said Coraline. 'Everything's going to be fine. I'll take you home.'

The cat said nothing.

'Come on, cat,' said Coraline. She took a step back towards the steps, but the cat stayed where it was, looking miserable and, oddly, much smaller.

'If the only way out is past her,' said Coraline, 'then that's the way we're going to go.' She went back to the cat, bent down and picked it up. The cat did not resist. It simply trembled. She supported its bottom with one hand and rested its front legs on her shoulder. The cat was heavy, but not too heavy to carry. It licked at the palm of her hand, where the blood from the scrape was welling up.

Coraline walked up the steps one at a time, heading back to her own flat. She was aware of the marbles clicking in her pocket, aware of the stone with the hole in it, aware of the cat pressing itself against her.

She got to her front door – now just a small-child's scrawl of a door – and she pushed her hand against it, half-expecting that her hand would rip through it, revealing nothing behind it but blackness and a scattering of stars.

But the door swung open, and Coraline went through.

11

ONCE INSIDE, IN her flat, or rather, in the flat that was not hers, Coraline was pleased to see that it had not transformed into the empty drawing that the rest of the house seemed to have become. It had depth and shadows, and someone who stood in the shadows waiting for Coraline to return.

'So you're back,' said the other mother. She did not sound pleased. 'And you brought vermin with you.'

'No,' said Coraline. 'I brought a friend.' She could feel the cat stiffening under her hands, as if it were anxious to be away. Coraline wanted to hold on to it like a teddy bear, for reassurance, but she knew that cats hate to be squeezed, and she suspected that frightened cats were liable to bite and scratch if provoked in any way, even if they were on your side.

'You know I love you,' said the other mother, flatly.

'You have a very funny way of showing it,' said Coraline. She walked down the hallway, then turned into the drawing room, steady step by steady step, pretending that she could not feel the other mother's blank black eyes on her back. Her grandmother's formal furniture was still there, and the painting on the wall of the strange fruit (but now the fruit in the painting had been eaten, and all that remained in the bowl was the browning core of an apple, several plum and peach stones, and the stem of what had formerly been a bunch of grapes). The lion-pawed table raked the carpet with its clawed wooden feet, as if it were impatient for something. At the end of the room, in the corner, stood the wooden door, which had once, in another place, opened on to a plain brick wall. Coraline tried not to stare at it. The window showed nothing but mist.

This was it, Coraline knew. The moment of truth. The unravelling time.

The other mother had followed her in. Now she stood in the centre of the room, between Coraline and the mantelpiece, and looked down at Coraline with black-button eyes. It was funny, Coraline thought. The other mother did not look anything at all like her own mother. She wondered how she had ever been deceived into imagining a resemblance. The other mother was huge – her head almost brushed the ceiling of the room – and very pale, the colour of a spider's belly. Her hair writhed and twined about her head, and her teeth were sharp as knives . . .

'Well?' said the other mother, sharply. 'Where are they?'

Coraline leaned against an armchair, adjusted the cat with her left hand, put her right hand into her pocket, and pulled out the three glass marbles. They were a frosted grey, and they clinked together in the palm of her hand. The other mother reached her white fingers out for them, but Coraline slipped them back into her pocket. She knew it was true, then. The other mother had no intention of letting her go, or of keeping her word. It had been an entertainment, and nothing more. 'Hold on,' she said. 'We aren't finished yet, are we?'

The other mother looked daggers, but she smiled sweetly. 'No,' she said. 'I suppose not. After all, you still need to find your parents, don't you?'

'Yes,' said Coraline. I must not look at the mantelpiece, she thought. I must not even think about it.

'Well?' said the other mother. 'Produce them. Would you like to look in the cellar again? I have some other interesting things hidden down there, you know.'

'No,' said Coraline. 'I know where my parents are.' The cat was heavy in her arms. She moved it forward, unhooking its claws from her shoulder as she did so.

'Where?'

'It stands to reason,' said Coraline. 'I've looked everywhere you'd hide them. They aren't in the house.'

The other mother stood very still, giving nothing away, lips tightly closed. She might have been a wax statue. Even her hair had stopped moving.

'So,' Coraline continued, both hands wrapped firmly around the black cat, 'I know where they have to be. You've hidden them in the passageway between the houses, haven't you? They are behind that door.' She nodded her head towards the door in the corner.

The other mother remained statue-still, but a hint of a smile crept back on to her face. 'Oh, they are, are they?'

'Why don't you open it?' said Coraline. 'They'll be there, all right.'

It was her only way home, she knew. But it all depended on the other mother needing to gloat, needing not only to win but to show that she had won.

The other mother reached her hand slowly into her apron pocket and produced the black iron key. The cat stirred uncomfortably in Coraline's arms, as if it wanted to get down. *Just stay there for a few moments longer*, she thought at it, wondering if it could hear her. *I'll get us both home. I said I would. I promise.* She felt the cat relax ever-so-slightly in her arms.

The other mother walked over to the door and pushed the key into the lock.

She turned the key.

Coraline heard the mechanism clunk heavily. She was already starting, as quietly as she could, step by step, to back away towards the mantelpiece.

The other mother pushed down on the door handle and pulled open the door, revealing a corridor behind it, dark and empty. 'There,' she said, waving her hands at the corridor. The expression of delight on her face was a very bad thing to see. 'You're wrong! You *don't* know where your parents are, do you? They aren't there.' She turned and looked at Coraline. 'Now,' she said, 'you're going to stay here for ever and always.'

'No,' said Coraline. 'I'm not.' And, hard as she could, she threw the black cat towards the other mother. It yowled and landed on the other mother's head, claws flailing, teeth bared, fierce and angry. Fur on end, it looked half again as big as it was in real life.

Without waiting to see what would happen, Coraline reached up to the mantelpiece, closed her hand around the snow-globe, then pushed it deep into the pocket of her dressing gown.

The cat made a deep, ululating yowl and sank its teeth into the other mother's cheek. She was flailing at it. Blood ran from the cuts on her white face – not red blood, but a deep, tarry black stuff. Coraline ran for the door.

She pulled the key out of the lock.

'Leave her! Come on!' she shouted to the cat. It hissed, and swiped its scalpel-sharp claws at the other mother's face in one wild rake which left black ooze trickling from several gashes on her nose. Then it sprang down towards Coraline. 'Quickly!' she said. The cat ran towards her, and they both stepped into the dark corridor.

It was colder in the corridor, like stepping down into a cellar on a warm day. The cat hesitated for a moment, then, seeing the other mother was coming towards them, it ran to Coraline and stopped by her legs.

Coraline began to pull the door closed.

It was heavier than she imagined a door could be, and pulling it closed was like trying to close a door against a high wind. And then she felt something from the other side starting to pull against her.

Shut! she thought. Then she said, out loud, 'Come on, *please.*' And she felt the door begin to move, to pull closed, to give against the phantom wind.

Suddenly she was aware of other people in the corridor with her. She could not turn her head to look at them, but she knew them without having to look. 'Help me, please,' she said. 'All of you.'

The other people in the corridor – three children, two adults – were somehow too insubstantial to touch the door. But their hands closed about hers, as she pulled on the big iron door handle, and suddenly she felt strong.

'Never let up, miss! Hold strong! Hold strong!' whispered a voice in her mind.

'Pull, girl, pull!' whispered another.

And then a voice that sounded like her mother's – her own mother, her real, wonderful, maddening, infuriating, glorious mother, just said, 'Well done, Coraline,' and that was enough.

The door started to slip closed, easily as anything.

'No!' screamed a voice from beyond the door, and it no longer sounded even faintly human.

Something snatched at Coraline, reaching through the closing gap between the door and the doorpost. Coraline jerked her head out of the way, but the door began to open once more.

'We're going to go home,' said Coraline. 'We are. Help me.' She ducked the snatching fingers.

They moved through her, then: ghost-hands lent her strength that she no longer possessed. There was a final moment of resistance, as if something were caught in the door, and then, with a crash, the wooden door banged closed.

Something dropped from Coraline's head height to the floor. It landed with a sort of a scuttling thump.

'Come on!' said the cat. 'This is not a good place to be in. Quickly.'

Coraline turned her back on the door and began to run, as fast as was practical, through the dark corridor, dragging her hand along the wall to make sure she didn't bump into anything or get turned around in the darkness.

It was an uphill run, and it seemed to her that it went on for a longer distance than anything could possibly go. The wall she was touching seemed warm and yielding now, and, she realised, it felt as if it was covered in a fine downy fur. It moved, as if it were taking a breath. She snatched her hand away from it.

Winds howled in the dark.

She was scared she would bump into something, and she put out her hand for the wall once more. This time what she touched felt hot and wet, as if she had put her hand in somebody's mouth, and she pulled it back with a small wail.

Her eyes had adjusted to the dark. She could half-see, as faintly glowing patches ahead of her, two adults, three children. She could hear the cat, too, padding in the dark in front of her.

And there was something else, which suddenly scuttled between her feet, nearly sending Coraline flying. She caught herself before she went down, using her own momentum to keep moving. She knew that if she fell in that corridor she might never get up again. Whatever that corridor was was older by far than the other mother. It was deep, and slow, and it knew that she was there . . .

Then daylight appeared, and she ran towards it, puffing and wheezing. 'Almost there,' she called encouragingly, but in the light she discovered that the wraiths had gone, and she was alone. She did not have time to wonder what had happened to them. Panting for breath, she staggered through the door and slammed it behind her with the loudest, most satisfying bang you can imagine.

Coraline locked the door with the key, and put the key back into her pocket.

The black cat was huddled in the farthest corner of the room, the pink tip of its tongue showing, its eyes wide. Coraline went over to it, and crouched down.

'I'm sorry,' she said. 'I'm sorry I threw you at her. But it was the only way to distract her enough to get us all out. She would never have kept her word, would she?'

The cat looked up at her, then it rested its head on her hand, licking her fingers with its sandpapery tongue. It began to purr.

'Then we're friends?' said Coraline.

She sat down on one of her grandmother's uncomfortable armchairs, and the cat sprang up into her lap and made itself comfortable. The light that came through the picture window was daylight, real golden late-afternoon daylight, not a white mist-light. The sky was a robin's-egg blue, and Coraline could see trees and, beyond the trees, green hills, which faded on the horizon into purples and greys. The sky had never seemed so *sky*; the world had never seemed so *world*.

Coraline stared at the leaves on the trees and at the patterns of light and shadow on the cracked bark of the trunk of the beech tree outside the window, then she looked down at her lap, at the way that the rich sunlight brushed every hair on the cat's head, turning each white whisker to gold.

Nothing, she thought, had ever been so *interesting*.

And, caught up in the interestingness of the world, Coraline barely noticed that she had wriggled down and curled, cat-like, in her grandmother's uncomfortable armchair, nor did she notice when she fell into a deep and dreamless sleep.

12

HER MOTHER SHOOK her gently awake.
 'Coraline?' she said. 'Darling, what a funny place to fall asleep. And really, this room is only for best. We looked all over the house for you.'

Coraline stretched and blinked. 'I'm sorry,' she said. 'I fell asleep.'

'I can see that,' said her mother. 'And wherever did the cat come from? He was waiting by the front door when I came in. Shot out like a bullet as I opened it.'

'Probably had things to do,' said Coraline. Then she hugged her mother, so tightly that her arms began to ache. Her mother hugged Coraline back.

'Dinner in fifteen minutes,' said her mother. 'Don't forget to wash your hands. And just *look* at those pyjama bottoms. What did you do to your poor knee?'

'I tripped,' said Coraline. She went into the bathroom, and she washed her hands and cleaned her bloody knee. She put ointment on her cuts and scrapes.

She went into her bedroom – her real bedroom, her true bedroom. She pushed her hands into the pockets of her dressing gown, and she pulled out three marbles, a stone with a hole in it, the black key, and an empty snow-globe.

She shook the snow-globe and watched the glittery snow swirl through the water to fill the empty world. She put it down and watched the snow fall, covering the place where the little couple had once stood.

Coraline took a piece of string from her toybox and she strung the black key on to it. Then she knotted the string and hung it around her neck.

'There,' she said. She put on some clothes, and hid the key under her T-shirt. It was cold against her skin. The stone went into her pocket.

Coraline walked down the hallway to her father's study. He had his back to her, but she knew, just on seeing him, that his eyes, when he turned around, would be her father's kind grey eyes, and she crept over and kissed him on the back of his balding head.

'Hello, Coraline,' he said. Then he looked round and smiled at her. 'What was that for?'

'Nothing,' said Coraline. 'I just miss you sometimes. That's all.'

'Oh good,' he said. He put the computer to sleep, stood up, and then, for no reason at all, he picked Coraline up, which he had not done for such a long time, not since he had started pointing out to her she was much too old to be carried, and he carried her into the kitchen.

Dinner that night was pizza, and even though it was home-made by her father (so the crust was alternately thick and doughy and raw, or too thin and burnt), and even though he had put slices of green pepper on it, along with little meatballs and, of all things, pineapple chunks, Coraline ate the entire slice she had been given.

Well, she ate everything except for the pineapple chunks.

And soon enough it was bedtime.

Coraline kept the key around her neck, but she put the grey marbles beneath her pillow; and in bed that night, Coraline dreamed a dream.

She was at a picnic, under an old oak tree, in a green meadow. The sun was high in the sky and, while there were distant fluffy white clouds on the horizon, the sky above her head was a deep, untroubled blue.

There was a white-linen cloth laid on the grass, with bowls piled high with food – she could see salads and sandwiches, nuts and fruit, jugs of lemonade and water and thick chocolate milk. Coraline sat on one side of the tablecloth while three other children took a side each. They were dressed in the oddest clothes.

The smallest of them, sitting on Coraline's left, was a boy with red-velvet knee-britches and a frilly white shirt. His face was dirty, and he was piling his plate high with boiled new potatoes and with what looked like cold, whole, cooked trout. 'This is the finest of picnics, lady,' he said to her.

'Yes,' said Coraline. 'I think it is. I wonder who organised it.'

'Why, I rather think you did, miss,' said a tall girl, sitting opposite Coraline. She wore a brown, rather shapeless dress, and had a brown bonnet on her head which tied beneath her chin. 'And we are more grateful for it and for all than ever words can say.' She was eating slices of bread and jam, deftly cutting the bread from a large golden-brown loaf with a huge knife, then spooning on the purple jam with a wooden spoon. She had jam all around her mouth.

'Aye. This is the finest food I have eaten in centuries,' said the girl on Coraline's right. She was a very pale child, dressed in what seemed to be spiders' webs, with a circle of glittering silver set in her blonde hair. Coraline could have sworn that the girl had two wings – like dusty silver butterfly wings, not bird wings – coming out of her back. The girl's plate was piled high with pretty flowers. She smiled at Coraline, as if it had been a very long time since she had smiled and she had almost, but not quite, forgotten how. Coraline found herself liking this girl immensely.

And then, in the way of dreams, the picnic had ended and they were playing in the meadow, running and shouting and tossing a glittering ball from one to another. Coraline knew it was a dream then, because none of them ever got tired or winded or out of breath. She wasn't even sweating. They just laughed and ran in a game that was partly tag, partly piggy-in-the-middle, and partly just a magnificent romp.

Three of them ran along the ground, while the pale girl fluttered a little over their heads, swooping down on butterfly wings to grab the ball and swinging up again into the sky before she tossed the ball to one of the other children.

And then, without a word about it being spoken, the game was over and the four of them went back to the picnic cloth, where the lunch had been cleared away, and there were four bowls waiting for them, three of ice-cream, one of honeysuckle flowers piled high.

They ate with relish.

'Thank you for coming to my party,' said Coraline. 'If it is mine.'

'The pleasure is ours, Coraline Jones,' said the winged girl, nibbling another honeysuckle blossom. 'If there were but something we could do for you, to thank you, and to reward you.'

'Aye,' said the boy with the red-velvet britches and the dirty face. He put out his hand and held Coraline's hand with his own. It was warm now.

'It's a very fine thing you did for us, miss,' said the tall girl. She now had a smear of chocolate ice-cream all around her lips.

'I'm just pleased it's all over,' said Coraline.

Was it her imagination, or did a shadow cross the faces of the other children at the picnic?

The winged girl, the circlet in her hair glittering like a star, rested her fingers for a moment on the back of Coraline's hand. 'It is over and done with for *us*,' she said. 'This is our staging post. From here, we three will set out for uncharted lands, and what comes after no one alive can say . . .' She stopped talking.

'There's a *but*, isn't there?' said Coraline. 'I can feel it. Like a rain cloud.'

The boy on her left tried to smile bravely, but his lower lip began to tremble and he bit it with his upper teeth and said nothing. The girl in the brown bonnet shifted uncomfortably and said, 'Yes, miss.'

'But I got you three back,' said Coraline. 'I got Mum and Dad back. I shut the door. I locked it. What more was I meant to do?'

The boy squeezed Coraline's hand with his. She found herself remembering when it had been her, trying to reassure him, when he was little more than a cold memory in the darkness.

'Well, can't you give me a clue?' asked Coraline. 'Isn't there *something* you can tell me?'

'The beldam swore by her good right hand,' said the tall girl, 'but she lied.'

'M-my governess,' said the boy, 'used to say that nobody is ever given more to shoulder than he or she can bear.' He shrugged as he said this, as if he had not yet made his own mind up whether or not it was true.

'We wish you luck,' said the winged girl. 'Good fortune and wisdom and courage – although you have already shown that you have all three of these blessings, and in abundance.'

'She hates you,' blurted out the boy. 'She hasn't lost anything for so long. Be wise. Be brave. Be tricky.'

'But it's not *fair*,' said Coraline, in her dream, angrily. 'It's just not *fair*. It should be over.'

The boy with the dirty face stood up and hugged Coraline tightly. 'Take comfort in this,' he whispered. 'Th'art alive. Thou livest.'

And in her dream Coraline saw that the sun had set and the stars were twinkling in the darkening sky.

Coraline stood in the meadow, and she watched as the three children (two of them walking, one flying) went away from her, across the grass, silver in the light of the huge moon.

The three of them came to a small wooden bridge over a stream. They stopped there, and turned and waved, and Coraline waved back.

And what came after was darkness.

Coraline woke in the early hours of the morning, convinced she had heard something moving, but unsure what it was.

She waited.

Something made a rustling noise outside her bedroom door. She wondered if it was a rat. The door rattled. Coraline clambered out of bed.

'Go away,' said Coraline, sharply. 'Go away or you'll be sorry.'

There was a pause, then the whatever-it-was scuttled away down the hall. There was something odd and irregular about its footsteps, if they *were* footsteps. Coraline found herself wondering if it was perhaps a rat with an extra leg . . .

'It isn't over, is it?' she said to herself.

Then she opened the bedroom door. The grey, pre-dawn light showed her the whole of the corridor, completely deserted.

She went towards the front door, sparing a hasty glance back at the wardrobe-door mirror hanging on the wall at the other end of the hallway, seeing nothing but her own pale face staring back at her, looking sleepy and serious. Gentle, reassuring snores came from her parents' room, but the door was closed. All the doors off the corridor were closed. Whatever the scuttling thing was, it had to be here somewhere.

Coraline opened the front door and looked at the grey sky. She wondered how long it would be until the sun came up, wondered whether her dream had been a true thing while knowing in her heart that it had been. Something she had taken to be part of the shadows under the hall couch detached itself from beneath the couch and made a mad, scrabbling rush on its long white legs, heading for the front door.

Coraline's mouth dropped open in horror and she stepped out of the way as the thing clicked and scuttled past her and out of the house, running crab-like on its too-many tapping, clicking, scurrying feet.

She knew what it was, and she knew what it was after. She had seen it too many times in the last few days, reaching and clutching and snatching and popping blackbeetles obediently into the other mother's mouth. Five-footed, crimson-nailed, the colour of bone.

It was the other mother's right hand.

It wanted the black key.

13

CORALINE'S PARENTS NEVER seemed to remember anything about their time in the snow-globe. At least, they never said any-thing about it, and Coraline never mentioned it to them.

Sometimes, she wondered whether they had ever noticed that they had lost two days in the real world, and came to the eventual conclusion that they had not. Then again, there are some people who keep track of every day and every hour, and there are people who don't, and Coraline's parents were solidly in the second camp.

Coraline had placed the marbles beneath her pillow before she went to sleep that first night home in her own room once more. She went back to bed, after she saw the other mother's hand, although there was not much time left for sleeping, and she rested her head back on the pillow.

Something scrunched gently as she did do.

She sat up and lifted the pillow. The fragments of the glass marbles that she saw looked like the remains of eggshells one finds beneath trees in springtime: like empty, broken robins' eggs, or even more delicate, wrens' eggs, perhaps.

Whatever had been inside the glass spheres had gone. Coraline thought of the three children waving goodbye to her in the moon-light, waving before they crossed that silver stream.

She gathered up the eggshell-thin fragments with care and placed them in a small blue box which had once held a bracelet that her

grandmother had given her when she was a little girl. The bracelet was long-lost, but the box remained.

Miss Spink and Miss Forcible came back from visiting Miss Spink's niece, and Coraline went down to their flat for tea. It was a Monday. On Wednesday Coraline would go back to school: a whole new school year would begin.

Miss Forcible insisted on reading Coraline's tea leaves.

'Well, looks like everything's mostly shipshape and Bristol fashion, lovey,' said Miss Forcible.

'Sorry?' said Coraline.

'Everything is coming up roses,' said Miss Forcible. 'Well, almost everything. I'm not sure what *that* is.' She pointed to a clump of tea leaves sticking to the side of the cup.

Miss Spink tutted and reached for the cup. 'Honestly, Miriam. Give it over here. Let me see . . .'

She blinked through her thick spectacles. 'Oh dear. No, I have no idea what that signifies. It looks almost like a hand.'

Coraline looked. The clump of leaves did look a little like a hand, reaching for something.

Hamish the Scottie dog was hiding under Miss Forcible's chair, and he wouldn't come out.

'I think he was in some sort of fight,' said Miss Spink. 'He has a deep gash in his side, poor dear. We'll take him to the vet later this afternoon. I wish I knew what could have done it.'

Something, Coraline knew, would have to be done.

That final week of the holidays, the weather was magnificent, as if the summer itself were trying to make up for the miserable weather they had been having by giving them some bright and glorious days before it ended.

The crazy old man upstairs called down to Coraline when he saw her coming out of Miss Spink and Miss Forcible's flat.

'Hey! Hi! You! Caroline!' he shouted over the railing.

'It's Coraline,' she said. 'How are the mice?'

'Something has frightened them,' said the old man, scratching his moustache. 'I think maybe there is a weasel in the house. Something is about. I heard it in the night. In my country we would have put down a trap for it, maybe put down a little meat or hamburger, and when the creature comes to feast, then – bam! – it would be caught and never bother us more. The mice are so scared they will not even pick up their little musical instruments.'

'I don't think it wants meat,' said Coraline. She put her hand up and touched the black key that hung about her neck. Then she went inside.

She bathed herself, and kept the key round her neck the whole time she was in the bath. She never took it off any more.

Something scratched at her bedroom window after she went to bed. Coraline was almost asleep, but she slipped out of bed and pulled open the curtains. A white hand with crimson fingernails leapt from the window-ledge on to a drainpipe and was immediately out of sight. There were deep gouges in the glass on the other side of the window.

Coraline slept uneasily that night, waking from time to time to plot and plan and ponder, then falling back into sleep, never quite certain where her pondering ended and the dream began, one ear always open for the sound of something scratching at her window-pane or at her bedroom door.

In the morning Coraline said to her mother, 'I'm going to have a picnic with my dolls today. Can I borrow a sheet – an old one, one you don't need any longer – as a tablecloth?'

'I don't think we have one of those,' said her mother. She opened the kitchen drawer that held the napkins and the tablecloths, and she prodded about in it. 'Hold on. Will this do?'

It was a folded-up disposable paper tablecloth covered with red flowers, left over from some picnic they had been on several years before.

'That's perfect,' said Coraline.

'I didn't think you played with your dolls any more,' said Mrs Jones.

'I don't,' admitted Coraline. 'They're protective coloration.'

'Well, be back in time for lunch,' said her mother. 'Have a good time.'

Coraline filled a cardboard box with dolls and several plastic dolls' tea-cups. She filled a jug with water.

Then she went outside. She walked down to the road, just as if she were going to the shops. Before she reached the supermarket she cut over a fence into some wasteland, and along an old drive, then she crawled under a hedge. She had to go under the hedge in two journeys in order not to spill the water from the jug.

It was a long, roundabout looping journey, but at the end of it Coraline was satisfied that she had not been followed.

She came out behind the dilapidated old tennis court. She crossed over it to the meadow where the long grass swayed. She found the planks on the edge of the meadow. They were astonishingly heavy – almost too heavy for a girl to lift, even using all her strength, but she managed. She didn't have any choice. She pulled the planks out of the way, one by one, grunting and sweating with the effort, revealing a deep, round, brick-lined hole in the ground. It smelled of damp and the dark. The bricks were greenish and slippery.

She spread out the tablecloth and laid it carefully over the top of the well. She put a plastic dolls' cup every twenty centimetres or so, at the edge of the well, and she weighed each cup down with water from the jug.

She put a doll in the grass beside each cup, making it look as much like a dolls' tea party as she could. Then she retraced her steps, back under the hedge, along the dusty yellow drive, around the back of the shops, back to her house.

She reached up and took the key from around her neck. She dangled it from the string, as if the key were just something she liked to play with. Then she knocked on the door of Miss Spink and Miss Forcible's flat.

Miss Spink opened the door.

'Hello, dear,' she said.

'I don't want to come in,' said Coraline. 'I just wanted to find out how Hamish was doing.'

Miss Spink sighed. 'The vet says that Hamish is a brave little soldier,' she said. 'Luckily, the cut doesn't seem to be infected. We cannot imagine what could have done it. The vet says some animal, he thinks, but has no idea what. Mister Bobo says he thinks it might have been a weasel.'

'Mister Bobo?'

'The man in the top flat. Mister Bobo. Fine old circus family I believe. Romanian or Slovenian or Livonian, or one of those countries. Bless me, I can never remember them any more.'

It had never occurred to Coraline that the crazy old man upstairs actually had a name, she realised. If she'd known his name was Mr Bobo she would have said it every chance she got. How often do you get to say a name like 'Mister Bobo' aloud?

'Oh,' said Coraline to Miss Spink. 'Mister Bobo. Right. Well,' she said, a little louder, 'I'm going to go and play with my dolls now, over by the old tennis court, round the back.'

'That's nice, dear,' said Miss Spink. Then she added, confidentially, 'Make sure you keep an eye out for the old well. Mister Lovat, who was here before your time, said that he thought it might go down for half a mile or more.'

Coraline hoped that the hand had not heard this last remark, and she changed the subject. 'This key?' said Coraline, loudly. 'Oh, it's just some old key from our house. It's part of my game. That's why I'm carrying it around with me on this piece of string. Well, goodbye now.'

'What an extraordinary child,' said Miss Spink to herself as she closed the door.

Coraline ambled across the meadow towards the old tennis court, dangling and swinging the black key on its piece of string as she walked.

Several times she thought she saw something the colour of bone in the undergrowth. It was keeping pace with her, about ten metres away.

She tried to whistle, but nothing happened, so she sang out loud instead, a song her father had made up for her when she was a little baby and which had always made her laugh. It went:

Oh . . . My twitchy witchy girl
I think you are so nice,

I give you bowls of porridge
And I give you bowls of ice-
cream.
I give you lots of kisses,
And I give you lots of hugs,
But I never give you sandwiches
with bugs
in.

That was what she sang as she sauntered through the woods, and her voice hardly trembled at all.

The dolls' tea party was where she had left it. She was relieved that it was not a windy day, for everything was still in its place, every water-filled plastic cup weighed down the paper tablecloth as it was meant to. She breathed a sigh of relief.

Now was the hardest part.

'Hello, dolls,' she said brightly. 'It's teatime!'

She walked close to the paper tablecloth. 'I brought the lucky key,' she told the dolls. 'To make sure we have a good picnic.'

And then, as carefully as she could, she leaned over and gently placed the key on the tablecloth. She was still holding on to the string. She held her breath, hoping that the cups of water at the edges of the well would weigh the cloth down, letting it take the weight of the key without collapsing into the well.

The key sat in the middle of the paper picnic cloth. Coraline let go of the string and took a step back. Now it was all up to the hand.

She turned to her dolls.

'Who would like a piece of cherry cake?' she asked. 'Jemima? Pinky? Primrose?' and she served each doll a slice of invisible cake on an invisible plate, chattering happily as she did so.

From the corner of her eye she saw something bone white scamper from one tree trunk to another, closer and closer. She forced herself not to look at it.

'Jemima!' said Coraline. 'What a bad girl you are! You've dropped your cake! Now I'll have to go over and get you a whole new slice!' And she walked around the tea party until she was on the other side of it to the hand. She pretended to clean up spilled cake and then to get Jemima another piece.

And then, in a skittering, chittering rush, it came. The hand, running high on its fingertips, scrabbled through the tall grass and up on to a tree stump. It stood there for a moment, like a crab tasting the air, and then it made one triumphant, nail-clacking leap on to the centre of the paper tablecloth.

Time slowed for Coraline. The white fingers closed around the black key . . .

And then the weight and the momentum of the hand sent the plastic dolls' cups flying, and the paper tablecloth and the key and the other mother's right hand went tumbling down into the darkness of the well.

Coraline counted slowly under her breath. She got up to forty before she heard a muffled splash coming from a long way below.

Someone had once told her that if you look up at the sky from the bottom of a mineshaft, even in the brightest daylight, you see a night sky and stars. Coraline wondered if the hand could see stars from where it was.

She hauled the heavy planks back on to the well, covering it as carefully as she could. She didn't want anything to fall in. She didn't want anything ever to get out. Then she put her dolls and the cups back in the cardboard box she had carried them out in. Something caught her eye while she was doing this, and she straightened up in time to see the black cat stalking towards her, its tail held high and curling at the tip like a question mark. It was the first time she had seen the cat in several days, since they had returned together from the other mother's place.

The cat walked over to her and jumped up on to the planks that covered the well. Then, slowly, it winked one eye at her.

It sprang down into the long grass in front of her and rolled over on to its back, wiggling about ecstatically.

Coraline scratched and tickled the soft fur on its belly, and the cat purred contentedly. When it had had enough it rolled over on to its front once more and walked back towards the tennis court, like a tiny patch of midnight in the midday sun.

Coraline went back to the house.

Mr Bobo was waiting for her in the driveway. He clapped her on the shoulder.

'The mice tell me that all is good,' he said. 'They say that you are our saviour, Caroline.'

'It's Coraline, Mister Bobo,' said Coraline. 'Not Caroline. Coraline.'

'Coraline,' said Mr Bobo, repeating her name to himself with wonderment and respect. 'Very good, Coraline. The mice say that I must tell you that as soon as they are ready to perform in public, you will come up to watch them as the first audience of all. They will play *tumpty umpty* and *toodle oodle*, and they will dance and do a thousand tricks. That is what they say.'

'I would like that very much,' said Coraline. 'When they're ready.'

She knocked at Miss Spink and Miss Forcible's door. Miss Spink let her in and Coraline went into their parlour. She put her box of dolls down on the floor. Then she put her hand into her pocket and pulled out the stone with the hole in it.

'Here you go,' she said. 'I don't need it any more. I'm very grateful. I think it may have saved my life, and saved some other people's deaths.'

She gave them both tight hugs, although her arms barely stretched around Miss Spink, and Miss Forcible smelled like the raw garlic she had been cutting. Then Coraline picked up her box of dolls and went out.

'What an extraordinary child,' said Miss Spink. No one had hugged her like that since she had retired from the theatre.

That night Coraline lay in bed, all bathed, teeth cleaned, with her eyes open, staring up at the ceiling.

It was warm enough that, now the hand was gone, she had opened her bedroom window wide. She had insisted to her father that the curtains not be entirely closed.

Her new school clothes were laid out carefully on her chair for her to put on when she woke.

Normally, on the night before the first day of term, Coraline was apprehensive and nervous. But, she realised, there was nothing left about school that could scare her any more.

She fancied she could hear sweet music on the night air: the kind of music that can only be played on the tiniest silver trombones and trumpets and bassoons, on piccolos and tubas so delicate and small that their keys could only be pressed by the tiny pink fingers of white mice.

Coraline imagined that she was back again in her dream, with the two girls and the boy under the oak tree in the meadow, and she smiled.

As the first stars came out Coraline finally allowed herself to drift into sleep, while the gentle upstairs music of the mouse circus spilled out on to the warm evening air, telling the world that the summer was almost over.

The Case of the Four and Twenty Blackbirds

I SAT IN MY office, nursing a glass of hooch and idly cleaning my automatic. Outside the rain fell steadily, like it seems to do most of the time in our fair city, whatever the tourist board says. Heck, I didn't care. I'm not on the tourist board. I'm a private dick, and one of the best, although you wouldn't have known it; the office was crumbling, the rent was unpaid, and the hooch was my last.

Things are tough all over.

To cap it all the only client I'd had all week never showed up on the street corner where I'd waited for him. He said it was going to be a big job, but now I'd never know: he kept a prior appointment in the morgue.

So when the dame walked into my office I was sure my luck had changed for the better.

"What are you selling, lady?"

She gave me a look that would have induced heavy breathing in a pumpkin, and which shot my heartbeat up to three figures. She had long blonde hair and a figure that would have made Thomas Aquinas forget his vows. I forgot all mine about never taking cases from dames.

"What would you say to some of the green stuff?" she asked in a husky voice, getting straight to the point.

"Continue, sister." I didn't want her to know how bad I needed the dough, so I held my hand in front of my mouth; it doesn't help if a client sees you salivate.

She opened her purse and flipped out a photograph. Glossy eight by ten. "Do you recognize that man?"

In my business you know who people are. "Yeah."

"He's dead."

"I know that too, sweetheart. It's old news. It was an accident."

Her gaze went so icy you could have chipped it into cubes and cooled a cocktail with it. "My brother's death was no accident."

I raised an eyebrow—you need a lot of arcane skills in my business—and said, "Your brother, eh?" Funny, she hadn't struck me as the type that had brothers.

"I'm Jill Dumpty."

"So your brother was Humpty Dumpty?"

"And he didn't fall off that wall, Mr. Horner. He was pushed."

Interesting, if true. Dumpty had his finger in most of the crooked pies in town; I could think of five guys who would have preferred to see him dead than alive without trying. Without trying too hard, anyway.

"You seen the cops about this?"

"Nah. The King's Men aren't interested in anything to do with his death. They say they did all they could do in trying to put him together again after the fall."

I leaned back in my chair.

"So what's it to you. Why do you need me?"

"I want you to find the killer, Mr. Horner. I want him brought to justice. I want him to fry like an egg. Oh—and one other *little* thing," she added lightly. "Before he died Humpty had a small manila envelope full of photographs he was meant to be sending me. Medical photos. I'm a trainee nurse, and I need them to pass my finals."

I inspected my nails, then looked up at her face, taking in a handful of waist and several curves on the way up. She was a looker, although her cute nose was a little on the shiny side. "I'll take the case. Seventy-five a day and two hundred bonus for results."

She smiled; my stomach twisted around once and went into orbit. "You get another two hundred if you get me those photographs. I want to be a nurse real bad." Then she dropped three fifties on my desktop.

I let a devil-may-care grin play across my rugged face. "Say, sister, how about letting me take you out for dinner? I just came into some money."

She gave an involuntary shiver of anticipation and muttered something about having a thing about midgets, so I knew I was onto a good thing. Then she gave me a lopsided smile that would have made Albert Einstein drop a decimal point. "First find my brother's killer, Mr. Horner. And my photographs. *Then* we can play."

She closed the door behind her. Maybe it was still raining but I didn't notice. I didn't care.

There are parts of town the tourist board doesn't mention. Parts of town where the police travel in threes if they travel at all. In my line of work you get to visit them more than is healthy. Healthy is never.

He was waiting for me outside Luigi's. I slid up behind him, my rubber-soled shoes soundless on the shiny wet sidewalk.

"Hiya, Cock."

He jumped and spun around; I found myself gazing up into the muzzle of a .45. "Oh, Horner." He put the gun away. "Don't call me Cock. I'm Bernie Robin to you, short-stuff, and don't you forget it."

"Cock Robin is good enough for me, Cock. Who killed Humpty Dumpty?"

He was a strange-looking bird, but you can't be choosy in my profession. He was the best underworld lead I had.

"Let's see the color of your money."

I showed him a fifty.

"Hell," he muttered. "It's green. Why can't they make puce or mauve money for a change?" He took it though. "All I know is that the Fat Man had his finger in a lot of pies."

"So?"

"One of those pies had four and twenty blackbirds in it."

"Huh?"

"Do I hafta spell it out for you? I . . . ughh—" He crumpled to the sidewalk, an arrow protruding from his back. Cock Robin wasn't going to be doing any more chirping.

* * *

117

Sergeant O'Grady looked down at the body, then he looked down at me. "Faith and begorrah, to be sure," he said. "If it isn't Little Jack Horner himself."

"I didn't kill Cock Robin, Sarge."

"And I suppose that the call we got down at the station telling us you were going to be rubbing the late Mr. Robin out—here, tonight—was just a hoax?"

"If I'm the killer, where are my arrows?" I thumbed open a pack of gum and started to chew. "It's a frame."

He puffed on his meerschaum and then put it away, and idly played a couple of phrases of the *William Tell* overture on his oboe. "Maybe. Maybe not. But you're still a suspect. Don't leave town. And, Horner . . ."

"Yeah?"

"Dumpty's death was an accident. That's what the coroner said. That's what I say. Drop the case."

I thought about it. Then I thought of the money, and the girl. "No dice, Sarge."

He shrugged. "It's your funeral." He said it like it probably would be.

I had a funny feeling he could be right.

"You're out of your depth, Horner. You're playing with the big boys. And it ain't healthy."

From what I could remember of my school days he was correct. Whenever I played with the big boys I always wound up having the stuffing beaten out of me. But how did O'Grady—how *could* O'Grady have known that? Then I remembered something else.

O'Grady was the one that used to beat me up the most.

It was time for what we in the profession call legwork. I made a few discreet inquiries around town, but found out nothing about Dumpty that I didn't know already.

Humpty Dumpty was a bad egg. I remembered him when he was new in town, a smart young animal trainer with a nice line in training mice to run up clocks. He went to the bad pretty fast though; gambling, drink, women, it's the same story all over. A bright young kid thinks that the streets of Nurseryland are paved with gold, and by the time he finds out otherwise it's much too late.

Dumpty started off with extortion and robbery on a small scale—he trained up a team of spiders to scare little girls away from their curds and whey, which he'd pick up and sell on the black market. Then he moved on to blackmail—the nastiest game. We crossed paths once, when I was hired by this young society kid—let's call him Georgie Porgie—to recover some compromising snaps of him kissing the girls and making them cry. I got the snaps, but I learned it wasn't healthy to mess with the Fat Man. And I don't make the same mistakes twice. Hell, in my line of work I can't afford to make the same mistakes once.

It's a tough world out there. I remember when Little Bo Peep first came to town . . . but you don't want to hear my troubles. If you're not dead yet, you've got troubles of your own.

I checked out the newspaper files on Dumpty's death. One minute he was sitting on a wall, the next he was in pieces at the bottom. All the King's Horses and all the King's Men were on the scene in minutes, but he needed more than first aid. A medic named Foster was called—a friend of Dumpty's from his Gloucester days—although I don't know of anything a doc can do when you're dead.

Hang on a second—*Dr. Foster!*

I got that old feeling you get in my line of work. Two little brain cells rub together the right way and in seconds you've got a twenty-four-karat cerebral fire on your hands.

You remember the client who didn't show—the one I'd waited for all day on the street corner? An accidental death. I hadn't bothered to check it out—I can't afford to waste time on clients who aren't going to pay for it.

Three deaths, it seemed. Not one.

I reached for the telephone and rang the police station. "This is Horner," I told the desk man. "Lemme speak to Sergeant O'Grady."

There was a crackling and he came on the line. "O'Grady speaking."

"It's Horner."

"Hi, Little Jack." That was just like O'Grady. He'd been kidding me about my size since we were kids together. "You finally figured out that Dumpty's death was accidental?"

"Nope. I'm now investigating three deaths. The Fat Man's, Bernie Robin's, and Dr. Foster's."

"Foster the plastic surgeon? His death was an accident."

"Sure. And your mother was married to your father."

There was a pause. "Horner, if you phoned me up just to talk dirty, I'm not amused."

"Okay, wise guy. If Humpty Dumpty's death was an accident and so was Dr. Foster's, tell me just one thing.

"Who killed Cock Robin?" I don't ever get accused of having too much imagination, but there's one thing I'd swear to. I could *hear* him grinning over the phone as he said: "You did, Horner. And I'm staking my badge on it."

The line went dead.

My office was cold and lonely, so I wandered down to Joe's Bar for some companionship and a drink or three.

Four and twenty blackbirds. A dead doctor. The Fat Man. Cock Robin . . . Heck, this case had more holes in it than Swiss cheese and more loose ends than a torn string vest. And where did the juicy Miss Dumpty come into it? Jack and Jill—we'd make a great team. When this was all over perhaps we could go off together to Louie's little place on the hill, where no one's interested in whether you got a marriage license or not. The Pail of Water, that was the name of the joint.

I called the bartender over. "Hey, Joe."

"Yeah, Mr. Horner?" He was polishing a glass with a rag that had seen better days as a shirt.

"Did you ever meet the Fat Man's sister?"

He scratched at his cheek. "Can't say as I did. His sister . . . huh? Hey—the Fat Man didn't have a sister."

"You sure of that?"

"Sure I'm sure. It was the day my sister had her first kid—I told the Fat Man I was an uncle. He gave me this look and says, 'Ain't no way I'll ever be an uncle, Joe. Got no sisters or brothers, nor no other kinfolk neither.'"

If the mysterious Miss Dumpty wasn't his sister, who *was* she?

"Tell me, Joe. Didja ever see him in here with a dame—about so high, shaped like this?" My hands described a couple of parabolas. "Looks like a blonde love goddess."

He shook his head. "Never saw him with any dames. Recently he was hanging around with some medical guy, but the only thing he ever cared about was those crazy birds and animals of his."

I took a swig of my drink. It nearly took the roof of my mouth off. "Animals? I thought he'd given all that up."

"Naw—couple weeks back he was in here with a whole bunch of blackbirds he was training to sing 'Wasn't that a dainty dish to set before *mmm mmm.*'"

"*Mmm mmm?*"

"Yeah. I got no idea who."

I put my drink down. A little of it spilt on the counter, and I watched it strip the paint. "Thanks, Joe. You've been a big help." I handed him a ten-dollar bill. "For information received," I said—adding, "Don't spend it all at once."

In my profession it's making little jokes like that that keeps you sane.

I had one contact left. Ma Hubbard. I found a pay phone and called her number.

"Old Mother Hubbard's Cupboard—Cake Shop and licensed Soup Kitchen."

"It's Horner, Ma."

"Jack? It ain't safe for me to talk to you."

"For old time's sake, sweetheart. You owe me a favor." Some two-bit crooks had once knocked off the Cupboard, leaving it bare. I'd tracked them down and returned the cakes and soup.

"Okay. But I don't like it."

"*You* know everything that goes on around here on the food front, Ma. What's the significance of a pie with four and twenty trained blackbirds in it?"

She whistled long and low. "You really don't know?"

"I wouldn't be asking you if I did."

"You should read the Court pages of the papers next time, sugar. Jeez. You are out of your depth."

"C'mon, Ma. Spill it."

"It so happens that that particular dish was set before the King a few weeks back. . . . Jack? Are you still there?"

"I'm still here, ma'am," I said quietly. "All of a sudden a lot of things are starting to make sense." I put down the phone.

It was beginning to look like Little Jack Horner had pulled out a plum from this pie.

It was raining, steady and cold. I phoned a cab.

Quarter of an hour later one lurched out of the darkness.

"You're late."

"So complain to the tourist board."

I climbed in the back, wound down the window, and lit a cigarette.

And I went to see the Queen.

The door to the private part of the palace was locked. It's the part that the public don't get to see. But I've never been public, and the little lock hardly slowed me up. The door to the private apartments with the big red heart on it was unlocked, so I knocked and walked straight in.

The Queen of Hearts was alone, standing in front of the mirror, holding a plate of jam tarts with one hand, powdering her nose with the other. She turned, saw me, and gasped, dropping the tarts.

"Hey, Queenie," I said. "Or would you feel more comfortable if I called you Jill?"

She was still a good-looking slice of dame, even without the blonde wig.

"Get out of here!" she hissed.

"I don't think so, toots." I sat down on the bed. "Let me spell a few things out for you."

"Go ahead." She reached behind her for a concealed alarm button. I let her press it. I'd cut the wires on my way in—in my profession there's no such thing as being too careful.

"Let me spell a few things out for you."

"You just said that."

"I'll tell this my way, lady."

I lit a cigarette, and a thin plume of blue smoke drifted heavenward, which was where I was going if my hunch was wrong. Still, I've learned to trust hunches.

"Try this on for size. Dumpty—the Fat Man—wasn't your brother. He wasn't even your friend. In fact he was blackmailing you. He knew about your nose."

She turned whiter than a number of corpses I've met in my time in the business. Her hand reached up and cradled her freshly powdered nose.

"You see, I've known the Fat Man for many years, and many years ago he had a lucrative concern in training animals and birds to do certain unsavory things. And that got me to thinking. . . . I had a client recently who didn't show, due to his having been stiffed first. Dr. Foster, of Gloucester, the plastic surgeon. The official version of his death was that he'd just sat too close to a fire and melted.

"But just suppose he was killed to stop him telling something that he knew. I put two and two together and hit the jackpot. Let me reconstruct a scene for you: You were out in the garden—probably hanging out some clothes—when along came one of Dumpty's trained pie blackbirds and *pecked off your nose.*

"So there you were, standing in the garden, your hand in front of your face, when along came the Fat Man with an offer you couldn't refuse. He could introduce you to a plastic surgeon who could fix you up with a nose as good as new, for a price. And no one need ever know. Am I right so far?"

She nodded dumbly, then, finding her voice, muttered, "Pretty much. But I ran back into the parlor after the attack, to eat some bread and honey. That was where he found me."

"Fair enough." The color was starting to come back into her cheeks now. "So you had the operation from Foster, and no one was going to be any the wiser. Until Dumpty told you that he had photos of the op. You had to get rid of him. A couple of days later you were out walking in the palace grounds. There was Humpty, sitting on a wall, his back to you, gazing out into the distance. In a fit of madness, you pushed. And Humpty Dumpty had a great fall."

"But now you were in big trouble. Nobody suspected you of his murder, but where were the photographs? Foster didn't have them, although he smelled a rat and had to be disposed of—before he could see me. But you didn't know how much he'd told me, and you still didn't have the snapshots, so you took me on to find out. And that was your mistake, sister."

Her lower lip trembled, and my heart quivered. "You won't turn me in, will you?"

"Sister, you tried to frame me this afternoon. I don't take kindly to that."

With a shaking hand she started to unbutton the top button of her blouse. "Perhaps we could come to some sort of arrangement?"

I shook my head. "Sorry, your majesty. Mrs. Horner's little boy Jack was always taught to keep his hands off royalty. It's a pity, but that's how it is." To be on the safe side I looked away, which was a mistake. A cute little ladies' pistol was in her hands and pointing at me before you could sing a song of sixpence. The shooter may have been small, but I knew it packed enough of a wallop to take me out of the game permanently.

This dame was *lethal.*

"Put that gun down, your majesty." Sergeant O'Grady strolled through the bedroom door, his police special clutched in his ham-like fist.

"I'm sorry I suspected you, Horner," he said drily. "You're lucky I did, though, sure and begorrah. I had you tailed here and I overheard the whole thing."

"Hi, Sarge, thanks for stopping by. But I hadn't finished my explanation. If you'll take a seat I'll wrap it up."

He nodded brusquely, and sat down near the door. His gun hardly moved.

I got up from the bed and walked over to the Queen. "You see, toots, what I didn't tell you was who *did* have the snaps of your nose job. Humpty did, when you killed him."

A charming frown crinkled her perfect brow. "I don't understand. . . . I had the body searched."

"Sure, afterward. But the first people to get to the Fat Man were the King's Men. The cops. And one of them pocketed the envelope. When any fuss had died down the blackmail would have started again. Only this time you wouldn't have known who to kill. And I owe you an apology." I bent down to tie my shoelaces.

"Why?"

"I accused you of trying to frame me this afternoon. You didn't. That arrow was the property of a boy who was the best archer in my school—I should have recognized that distinctive fletching anywhere. Isn't that right," I said, turning back to the door, "'Sparrow' O'Grady?"

Under the guise of tying my shoelaces I had already palmed a couple of the Queen's jam tarts, and, flinging one of them upward, I neatly smashed the room's only lightbulb.

It only delayed the shooting a few seconds, but a few seconds was all I needed, and as the Queen of Hearts and Sergeant "Sparrow" O'Grady cheerfully shot each other to bits, I split.

In my business, you have to look after number one.

Munching on a jam tart I walked out of the palace grounds and into the street. I paused by a trash can, to try to burn the manila envelope of photographs I had pulled from O'Grady's pocket as I walked past him, but it was raining so hard they wouldn't catch.

When I got back to my office I phoned the tourist board to complain. They said the rain was good for the farmers, and I told them what they could do with it.

They said that things are tough all over.

And I said, "Yeah."

TROLL BRIDGE

THEY PULLED UP most of the railway tracks in the early sixties, when I was three or four. They slashed the train services to ribbons. This meant that there was nowhere to go but London, and the little town where I lived became the end of the line.

My earliest reliable memory: eighteen months old, my mother away in hospital having my sister, and my grandmother walking with me down to a bridge, and lifting me up to watch the train below, panting and steaming like a black iron dragon.

Over the next few years they lost the last of the steam trains, and with them went the network of railways that joined village to village, town to town.

I didn't know that the trains were going. By the time I was seven they were a thing of the past.

We lived in an old house on the outskirts of the town. The fields opposite were empty and fallow. I used to climb the fence and lie in the shade of a small bulrush patch, and read; or if I were feeling more adventurous I'd explore the grounds of the empty manor beyond the fields. It had a weed-clogged ornamental pond, with a low wooden bridge over it. I never saw any groundsmen or caretakers in my forays through the gardens and woods, and I never attempted to enter the manor. That would have been courting disaster, and, besides, it was a matter of faith for me that all empty old houses were haunted.

It is not that I was credulous, simply that I believed in all things dark and dangerous. It was part of my young creed that the night was full of ghosts and witches, hungry and flapping and dressed completely in black.

The converse held reassuringly true: daylight was safe. Daylight was always safe.

A ritual: on the last day of the summer school term, walking home from school, I would remove my shoes and socks and, carrying them in my hands, walk down the stony flinty lane on pink and tender feet. During the summer holiday I would put shoes on only under duress. I would revel in my freedom from footwear until school term began once more in September.

When I was seven I discovered the path through the wood. It was summer, hot and bright, and I wandered a long way from home that day.

I was exploring. I went past the manor, its windows boarded up and blind, across the grounds, and through some unfamiliar woods. I scrambled down a steep bank, and I found myself on a shady path that was new to me and overgrown with trees; the light that penetrated the leaves was stained green and gold, and I thought I was in fairyland.

A little stream trickled down the side of the path, teeming with tiny, transparent shrimps. I picked them up and watched them jerk and spin on my fingertips. Then I put them back.

I wandered down the path. It was perfectly straight, and overgrown with short grass. From time to time I would find these really terrific rocks: bubbly, melted things, brown and purple and black. If you held them up to the light you could see every color of the rainbow. I was convinced that they had to be extremely valuable, and stuffed my pockets with them.

I walked and walked down the quiet golden-green corridor, and saw nobody.

I wasn't hungry or thirsty. I just wondered where the path was going. It traveled in a straight line, and was perfectly flat. The path never changed, but the countryside around it did. At first I was walking along the bottom of a ravine, grassy banks climbing steeply

130

on each side of me. Later, the path was above everything, and as I walked I could look down at the treetops below me, and the roofs of the occasional distant houses. My path was always flat and straight, and I walked along it through valleys and plateaus, valleys and plateaus. And eventually, in one of the valleys, I came to the bridge.

It was built of clean red brick, a huge curving arch over the path. At the side of the bridge were stone steps cut into the embankment, and, at the top of the steps, a little wooden gate.

I was surprised to see any token of the existence of humanity on my path, which I was by now convinced was a natural formation, like a volcano. And, with a sense more of curiosity than anything else (I had, after all, walked hundreds of miles, or so I was convinced, and might be *anywhere*), I climbed the stone steps, and went through the gate.

I was nowhere.

The top of the bridge was paved with mud. On each side of it was a meadow. The meadow on my side was a wheatfield; the other field was just grass. There were the caked imprints of huge tractor wheels in the dried mud. I walked across the bridge to be sure: no trip-trap, my bare feet were soundless.

Nothing for miles; just fields and wheat and trees.

I picked a stalk of wheat, and pulled out the sweet grains, peeling them between my fingers, chewing them meditatively.

I realized then that I was getting hungry, and went back down the stairs to the abandoned railway track. It was time to go home. I was not lost; all I needed to do was follow my path home once more.

There was a troll waiting for me, under the bridge.

"I'm a troll," he said. Then he paused, and added, more or less as an afterthought, "Fol rol de ol rol."

He was huge: his head brushed the top of the brick arch. He was more or less translucent: I could see the bricks and trees behind him, dimmed but not lost. He was all my nightmares given flesh. He had huge strong teeth, and rending claws, and strong, hairy hands. His hair was long, like one of my sister's little plastic gonks, and his eyes bulged. He was naked, and his penis hung from the bush of gonk hair between his legs.

"I heard you, Jack," he whispered, in a voice like the wind. "I heard you trip-trapping over my bridge. And now I'm going to eat your life."

I was only seven, but it was daylight, and I do not remember being scared. It is good for children to find themselves facing the elements of a fairy tale—they are well-equipped to deal with these.

"Don't eat me," I said to the troll. I was wearing a stripy brown T-shirt and brown corduroy trousers. My hair also was brown, and I was missing a front tooth. I was learning to whistle between my teeth, but wasn't there yet.

"I'm going to eat your life, Jack," said the troll.

I stared the troll in the face. "My big sister is going to be coming down the path soon," I lied, "and she's far tastier than me. Eat her instead."

The troll sniffed the air, and smiled. "You're all alone," he said. "There's nothing else on the path. Nothing at all." Then he leaned down, and ran his fingers over me: it felt like butterflies were brushing my face—like the touch of a blind person. Then he snuffled his fingers, and shook his huge head. "You don't have a big sister. You've only a younger sister, and she's at her friend's today."

"Can you tell all that from smell?" I asked, amazed.

"Trolls can smell the rainbows, trolls can smell the stars," it whispered, sadly. "Trolls can smell the dreams you dreamed before you were ever born. Come close to me and I'll eat your life."

"I've got precious stones in my pocket," I told the troll. "Take them, not me. Look." I showed him the lava jewel rocks I had found earlier.

"Clinker," said the troll. "The discarded refuse of steam trains. Of no value to me."

He opened his mouth wide. Sharp teeth. Breath that smelled of leaf mold and the underneaths of things. "Eat. Now."

He became more and more solid to me, more and more real; and the world outside became flatter, began to fade.

"Wait." I dug my feet into the damp earth beneath the bridge, wiggled my toes, held on tightly to the real world. I stared into his big eyes. "You don't want to eat my life. Not yet. I—I'm only seven. I haven't *lived* at all yet. There are books I haven't read yet. I've never been on an airplane. I can't whistle yet—not really. Why don't you let me go? When I'm older and bigger and more of a meal I'll come back to you."

The troll stared at me with eyes like headlamps.

Then it nodded.

"When you come back, then," it said. And it smiled.

I turned around and walked back down the silent straight path where the railway lines had once been.

After a while I began to run.

I pounded down the track in the green light, puffing and blowing, until I felt a stabbing ache beneath my rib cage, the pain of stitch; and, clutching my side, I stumbled home.

The fields started to go, as I grew older. One by one, row by row, houses sprang up with roads named after wildflowers and respectable authors. Our home—an aging, tattered Victorian house—was sold, and torn down; new houses covered the garden.

They built houses everywhere.

I once got lost in the new housing estate that covered two meadows I had once known every inch of. I didn't mind too much that the fields were going, though. The old manor house was bought by a multinational, and the grounds became more houses.

It was eight years before I returned to the old railway line, and when I did, I was not alone.

I was fifteen; I'd changed schools twice in that time. Her name was Louise, and she was my first love.

I loved her gray eyes, and her fine light brown hair, and her gawky way of walking (like a fawn just learning to walk which sounds really dumb, for which I apologize): I saw her chewing gum, when I was thirteen, and I fell for her like a suicide from a bridge.

The main trouble with being in love with Louise was that we were best friends, and we were both going out with other people.

I'd never told her I loved her, or even that I fancied her. We were buddies.

I'd been at her house that evening: we sat in her room and played

Rattus Norvegicus, the first Stranglers LP. It was the beginning of punk, and everything seemed so exciting: the possibilities, in music as in everything else, were endless. Eventually it was time for me to go home, and she decided to accompany me. We held hands, innocently, just pals, and we strolled the ten-minute walk to my house.

The moon was bright, and the world was visible and colorless, and the night was warm.

We got to my house. Saw the lights inside, and stood in the driveway, and talked about the band I was starting. We didn't go in.

Then it was decided that I'd walk *her* home. So we walked back to her house.

She told me about the battles she was having with her younger sister, who was stealing her makeup and perfume. Louise suspected that her sister was having sex with boys. Louise was a virgin. We both were.

We stood in the road outside her house, under the sodium-yellow streetlight, and we stared at each other's black lips and pale yellow faces.

We grinned at each other.

Then we just walked, picking quiet roads and empty paths. In one of the new housing estates, a path led us into the woodland, and we followed it.

The path was straight and dark, but the lights of distant houses shone like stars on the ground, and the moon gave us enough light to see. Once we were scared, when something snuffled and snorted in front of us. We pressed close, saw it was a badger, laughed and hugged and kept on walking.

We talked quiet nonsense about what we dreamed and wanted and thought.

And all the time I wanted to kiss her and feel her breasts, and hold her, and be held by her.

Finally I saw my chance. There was an old brick bridge over the path, and we stopped beneath it. I pressed up against her. Her mouth opened against mine.

Then she went cold and stiff, and stopped moving.

"Hello," said the troll.

I let go of Louise. It was dark beneath the bridge, but the shape of the troll filled the darkness.

"I froze her," said the troll, "so we can talk. Now: I'm going to eat your life."

My heart pounded, and I could feel myself trembling.

"No."

"You said you'd come back to me. And you have. Did you learn to whistle?"

"Yes."

"That's good. I never could whistle." It sniffed, and nodded. "I am pleased. You have grown in life and experience. More to eat. More for me."

I grabbed Louise, a taut zombie, and pushed her forward. "Don't take me. I don't want to die. Take *her*. I bet she's much tastier than me. And she's two months older than I am. Why don't you take her?"

The troll was silent.

It sniffed Louise from toe to head, snuffling at her feet and crotch and breasts and hair.

Then it looked at me.

"She's an innocent," it said. "You're not. I don't want her. I want you."

I walked to the opening of the bridge and stared up at the stars in the night.

"But there's so much I've never done," I said, partly to myself. "I mean, I've never. Well, I've never had sex. And I've never been to America. I haven't . . ." I paused. " I haven't *done* anything. Not yet."

The troll said nothing.

"I could come back to you. When I'm older."

The troll said nothing.

"I *will* come back. Honest I will."

"Come back to me?" said Louise. "Why? Where are you going?"

I turned around. The troll had gone, and the girl I had thought I loved was standing in the shadows beneath the bridge.

"We're going home," I told her. "Come on."

We walked back, and never said anything.

She went out with the drummer in the punk band I started, and,

135

much later, married someone else. We met once, on a train, after she was married, and she asked me if I remembered that night.

I said I did.

"I really liked you, that night, Jack," she told me. "I thought you were going to kiss me. I thought you were going to ask me out. I would have said yes. If you had."

"But I didn't."

"No," she said. "You didn't." Her hair was cut very short. It didn't suit her.

I never saw her again. The trim woman with the taut smile was not the girl I had loved, and talking to her made me feel uncomfortable.

I moved to London, and then, some years later, I moved back again, but the town I returned to was not the town I remembered: there were no fields, no farms, no little flint lanes; and I moved away as soon as I could, to a tiny village ten miles down the road.

I moved with my family—I was married by now, with a toddler— into an old house that had once, many years before, been a railway station. The tracks had been dug up, and the old couple who lived opposite us used the ground where the tracks had been to grow vegetables.

I was getting older. One day I found a gray hair; on another, I heard a recording of myself talking, and I realized I sounded just like my father.

I was working in London, doing A&R for one of the major record companies. I was commuting into London by train most days, coming back some evenings.

I had to keep a small flat in London; it's hard to commute when the bands you're checking out don't even stagger onto the stage until midnight. It also meant that it was fairly easy to get laid, if I wanted to, which I did.

I thought that Eleanora—that was my wife's name; I should have mentioned that before, I suppose—didn't know about the other women; but I got back from a two-week jaunt to New York one winter's day, and when I arrived at the house it was empty and cold.

She had left a letter, not a note. Fifteen pages, neatly typed, and every word of it was true. Including the PS, which read: *You really don't love me. And you never did.*

I put on a heavy coat, and I left the house and just walked, stunned and slightly numb.

There was no snow on the ground, but there was a hard frost, and the leaves crunched under my feet as I walked. The trees were skeletal black against the harsh gray winter sky.

I walked down the side of the road. Cars passed me, traveling to and from London. Once I tripped on a branch, half hidden in a heap of brown leaves, ripping my trousers, cutting my leg.

I reached the next village. There was a river at right angles to the road, and a path I'd never seen before beside it, and I walked down the path, and stared at the partly frozen river. It gurgled and plashed and sang.

The path led off through fields; it was straight and grassy.

I found a rock, half buried, on one side of the path. I picked it up, brushed off the mud. It was a melted lump of purplish stuff, with a strange rainbow sheen to it. I put it into the pocket of my coat and held it in my hand as I walked, its presence warm and reassuring.

The river meandered away across the fields, and I walked on in silence.

I had walked for an hour before I saw houses—new and small and square—on the embankment above me.

And then I saw the bridge, and I knew where I was: I was on the old railway path, and I'd been coming down it from the other direction.

There were graffiti painted on the side of the bridge: BARRY LOVES SUSAN and the omnipresent NF of the National Front.

I stood beneath the bridge in the red brick arch, stood among the ice-cream wrappers, and the crisp packets, and watched my breath steam in the cold afternoon air.

The blood had dried into my trousers.

Cars passed over the bridge above me; I could hear a radio playing loudly in one of them.

"Hello?" I said quietly, feeling embarrassed, feeling foolish. "Hello?"

There was no answer. The wind rustled the crisp packets and the leaves.

"I came back. I said I would. And I did. Hello?"

Silence.

I began to cry then, stupidly, silently, sobbing under the bridge.

A hand touched my face, and I looked up.

"I didn't think you'd come back," said the troll.

He was my height now, but otherwise unchanged. His long gonk hair was unkempt and had leaves in it, and his eyes were wide and lonely.

I shrugged, then wiped my face with the sleeve of my coat. "I came back."

Three kids passed above us on the bridge, shouting and running.

"I'm a troll," whispered the troll in a small, scared voice. "Fol rol de ol rol."

He was trembling.

I held out my hand and took his huge clawed paw in mine. I smiled at him. "It's okay," I told him. "Honestly. It's okay."

The troll nodded.

He pushed me to the ground, onto the leaves and the wrappers, and lowered himself on top of me. Then he raised his head, and opened his mouth, and ate my life with his strong sharp teeth.

When he was finished, the troll stood up and brushed himself down. He put his hand into the pocket of his coat and pulled out a bubbly, burnt lump of clinker rock.

He held it out to me.

"This is yours," said the troll.

I looked at him: wearing my life comfortably, easily, as if he'd been wearing it for years. I took the clinker from his hand, and sniffed it. I could smell the train from which it had fallen, so long ago. I gripped it tightly in my hairy hand.

"Thank you," I said.

"Good luck," said the troll.

"Yeah. Well. You too."

The troll grinned with my face.

138

It turned its back on me and began to walk back the way I had come, toward the village, back to the empty house I had left that morning; and it whistled as it walked.

I've been here ever since. Hiding. Waiting. Part of the bridge.

I watch from the shadows as the people pass: walking their dogs, or talking, or doing the things that people do. Sometimes people pause beneath my bridge, to stand, or piss, or make love. And I watch them, but say nothing; and they never see me.

Fol rol de ol rol.

I'm just going to stay here, in the darkness under the arch. I can hear you all out there, trip-trapping, trip-trapping over my bridge.

Oh yes, I can hear you.

But I'm not coming out.

DON'T ASK JACK

NOBODY KNEW WHERE the toy had come from, which great-grandparent or distant aunt had owned it before it was given to the nursery.

It was a box, carved and painted in gold and red. It was undoubtedly attractive and, or so the grown-ups maintained, quite valuable—perhaps even an antique. The latch, unfortunately, was rusted shut, and the key had been lost, so the Jack could not be released from his box. Still, it was a remarkable box, heavy and carved and gilt.

The children did not play with it. It sat at the bottom of the huge old wooden toy box, which was the same size and age as a pirate's treasure chest, or so the children thought. The Jack-in-the-Box was buried beneath dolls and trains, clowns and paper stars and old conjuring tricks, and crippled marionettes with their strings irrevocably tangled, with dressing-up clothes (here the tatters of a long-ago wedding dress, there a black silk hat crusted with age and time) and costume jewelry, broken hoops and tops and hobbyhorses. Under them all was Jack's box.

The children did not play with it. They whispered among themselves, alone in the attic nursery. On gray days when the wind howled about the house and rain rattled the slates and pattered down the eaves they told each other stories about Jack, although they had never seen him. One claimed that Jack was an evil wizard, placed in the box as punishment for crimes too awful to describe; another (I am certain that it must have been one of the girls) maintained that Jack's box was Pandora's box, and he had been placed in the box as guardian to prevent the bad things inside it from coming out once more. They would not even touch the box, if they could help it, although when, as happened from time to time, an adult would comment on the absence of that sweet old Jack-in-the-Box, and retrieve it from the chest, and place it in a position of honor on the mantelpiece, then the children would pluck up their courage and, later, hide it away once more in the darkness.

The children did not play with the Jack-in-the-Box. And when they grew up and left the great house, the attic nursery was closed up and almost forgotten.

Almost, but not entirely. For each of the children, separately, remembered walking alone in the moon's blue light, on his or her own bare feet, up to the nursery. It was almost like sleepwalking, feet soundless on the wood of the stairs, on the threadbare nursery carpet. Remembered opening the treasure chest, pawing through the dolls and the clothes and pulling out the box.

And then the child would touch the catch, and the lid would open, slow as a sunset, and the music would begin to play, and Jack came out. Not with a pop and a bounce: he was no spring-heeled Jack. But deliberately, intently, he would rise from the box and motion to the child to come closer, closer, and smile.

And there in the moonlight, he told them each things they could never quite remember, things they were never able entirely to forget.

The oldest boy died in the Great War. The youngest, after their parents died, inherited the house, although it was taken from him when he was found in the cellar one night with cloths and paraffin and matches, trying to burn the great house to the ground. They took him to the madhouse, and perhaps he is there still.

The other children, who had once been girls and now were women, declined, each and every one, to return to the house in which they had grown up; and the windows of the house were boarded up, and the doors were all locked with huge iron keys, and the sisters visited it as often as they visited their eldest brother's grave, or

144

the sad thing that had once been their younger brother, which is to say, never.

Years have passed, and the girls are old women, and owls and bats have made their homes in the old attic nursery; rats build their nests among the forgotten toys. The creatures gaze uncuriously at the faded prints on the wall, and stain the remnants of the carpet with their droppings.

And deep within the box within the box, Jack waits and smiles, holding his secrets. He is waiting for the children. He can wait forever.

How to Sell
the Ponti Bridge

M Y FAVORITE ROGUES' CLUB is the oldest and still the most exclusive in all the Seven Worlds. It was formed by a loose association of rogues, cheats, scoundrels, and confidence men almost seventy thousand years ago. It has been copied many times in many places (there was one started quite recently, within the last five hundred years at any rate, in the City of London), but none of the other clubs matches the original Rogues' Club, in the city of Lost Carnadine, for atmosphere. No other club has quite so select a membership.

And the membership of the Lost Carnadine Rogues' Club is particularly select. You will understand the kind of person who makes it to membership if I tell you that I myself have seen, walking or sitting or eating or talking, in its many rooms, such notables as Daraxius Lo (who sold the Kzem a frogbat on a holy day), Prottle (who sold the palace of the King of Vandaria to the King of Vandaria), and the self-styled Lord Niff (who, I have heard it whispered, was the original inventor of the fox twist, the cheat that broke the bank at the Casino Grande). In addition, I have seen Rogues of interuniversal renown fail to gain admittance to even discuss their membership with the secretary—on one memorable day I passed a famous financier, in company with the head of the Hy-Brasail mafia and a preeminent prime minister on their way down the back stairs with the blackest of expressions upon their faces, having obviously been told not even to think about returning. No, the ones who make it into the Rogues' Club are a high bunch. I am sure that you will have heard of each of them. Not under those names, of course, but the touch is distinctive, is it not?

I myself gained membership by means of a brilliant piece of creative scientific research, something that revolutionized the thinking of a whole generation. It was my disdain for regular methodology and, as I have said, creative research that gained me membership, and when I am in that part of the cosmos I make a point of stopping off for an evening, taking in some sparkling conversation, drinking the club's fine wines, and basking in the presence of my moral equals.

It was late in the evening and the log fire was burning low in the grate, and a handful of us sat and drank one of the fine dark wines of Spidireen in an alcove in the great hall. "Of course," one of my new friends was saying, "there are some scams that no self-respecting rogue would ever touch, they are so old and classless and tired. For example, selling a tourist the Ponti Bridge."

"It's the same with Nelson's Column, or the Eiffel Tower, or the Brooklyn Bridge, back on my homeworld," I told them. "Sad little con games, with as much class as a back-alley game of Find the Lady. But look on the good side: Nobody who sold the Ponti Bridge would ever get membership in a club like this."

"No?" said a quiet voice from the corner of the room. "How strange. I do believe it was the time I sold the Ponti Bridge that gained me membership in this club." A tall gentleman, quite bald and most exquisitely dressed, got up from the chair in which he had been sitting, and walked over to us. He was sipping the inside of an imported rhûm fruit, and smiling, I think at the effect that he had created. He walked over to us, pulled up a cushion, and sat down. "I don't believe we've met," he said.

My friends introduced themselves (the gray-haired deft woman, Gloathis; the short, quiet dodger Redcap) as did I.

He smiled wider. "Your fame precedes each of you. I am honored. You may call me Stoat."

"Stoat?" said Gloathis. "The only Stoat I ever heard of was the man who pulled the Derana Kite job, but that was . . . what, over a hundred years ago. What am I thinking? You adopted the name as a tribute, I presume."

"You are a wise woman," said Stoat. "It would be impossible for me to be the same man." He leaned forward on his cushion. "You were talking about the sale of the Ponti Bridge?"

"Indeed we were."

"And you were all of the opinion that selling the Ponti Bridge is a measly scam, unworthy of a member of this club? And perhaps you are right. Let us examine the ingredients of a good scam." He ticked off the points on the fingers of his left hand as he spoke. "*Firstly*, the scam must be credible. *Secondly*, it must be simple—the more complex the more chance of error. *Thirdly*, when the sucker is stung he must be stung in such a way as to prevent him from ever turning to the law. *Fourthly*, the mainspring of any elegant con is human greed and human vanity. *Lastly*, it must involve trust—confidence, if you will."

"Surely," said Gloathis.

"So you are telling me that the sale of the Ponti Bridge—or any other major landmark not yours to sell—cannot have these characteristics? Gentlemen. Lady. Let me tell you my story.

"I had arrived in Ponti some years ago almost penniless. I had but thirty gold crowns, and I needed a million. Why? I am afraid that is another story. I took stock of myself—I had the gold crowns and some smart robes. I was fluent in the aristocratic Ponti dialect, and I am, I pride myself, quite brilliant. Still, I could think of nothing that would bring me the kind of money I had to have in the time by which I needed it. My mind, usually teeming and coruscating with fine schemes, was a perfect blank. So, trusting to my gods to bring me inspiration, I went on a guided tour of the city. . . ."

Ponti lies to the south and to the east, a free city and port at the foot of the Mountains of Dawn. Ponti is a sprawling city, on either side of the Bay of Dawn, a beautiful natural harbor. Spanning the bay is the bridge, which was built of jewels, of mortar, and of magic nearly two thousand years ago. There were jeers when it was first planned and begun, for none credited that a structure almost half a mile across

151

could ever be successfully completed, or would stand for long once erected, but the bridge was completed, and the jeers turned to gasps of awe and civic pride. It spanned the Bay of Dawn, a perfect structure that flashed and shone and glinted in myriad rainbow colors beneath the noon sun.

The tour guide paused at the foot of it. "As you can see, ladies and gentlemen, if you will examine closely, the bridge is built entirely of precious stones—rubies, diamonds, sapphires, emeralds, chryolanths, carbuncles, and such—and they are bound together with a transparent mortar which was crafted by the twin sages Hrolgar and Hrylthfgur out of a primal magic. The jewels are all real—make no mistake about that—and were gathered from all five corners of the world by Emmidus, King of Ponti at the time."

A small boy near the front of the group turned to his mother and announced loudly, "We did him in school. He's called Emmidus the Last, because there weren't any more after him. And they told us—"

The tour guide interrupted smoothly. "The young man is quite correct. King Emmidus bankrupted the city-state obtaining the jewels, and thus set the scene for our current beneficent Ruling Enclave to appear."

The small boy's mother was now twisting his ear, which cheered the tour guide up immensely. "I'm sure you've heard that confidence tricksters are always trying to play tourists for mugs by telling them that they are representing the Ruling Enclave, and that as the owners of the bridge they are entitled to sell it. They get a hefty deposit, then scarper. To clarify matters," he said, as he said five times each day, and he and the tourists chuckled together, "the bridge is definitely not for sale." It was a good line. It always got a laugh.

His party started to make its way across the bridge. Only the small boy noticed that one of their number had remained behind—a tall man, quite bald. He stood at the foot of the bridge, lost in contemplation. The boy wanted to point this out to everybody, but his ear hurt, and so he said nothing.

The man at the foot of the bridge smiled abruptly. "Not for sale, eh?" he said aloud. Then he turned and walked back to the city.

* * *

They were playing a game not unlike tennis with large heavy-strung racquets and jeweled skulls for balls. The skulls were so satisfying in the way they thunked when hit cleanly, in the way they curved in great looping parabolas across the marble court. The skulls had never sat on human necks; they had been obtained, at great loss of life and significant expense, from a demon race in the highlands, and, afterward jeweled (emeralds and sweet rubies set in a lacy silver filigree in the eye sockets and about the jawbone) in Carthus's own workshops.

It was Carthus's serve.

He reached for the next skull in the pile and held it up to the light, marveling at the craftsmanship, in the way that the jewels, when struck by the light at a certain angle, seemed to glow with an inner luminescence. He could have told you the exact value and the probable provenance of each jewel—perhaps the very mine from which it had been dug. The skulls were also beautiful: bone the color of milky mother-of-pearl, translucent and fine. Each had cost him more than the value of the jewels set in its elegant bony face. The demon race had now been hunted to the verge of extinction, and the skulls were well-nigh irreplaceable.

He lobbed the skull over the net. Aathia struck it neatly back at him, forcing him to run to meet it (his footsteps echoing on the cold marble floor) and—*thunk*—hit it back to her.

She almost reached it in time. Almost, but not quite: the skull eluded her racquet and fell toward the stone floor and then, only an inch or so above the ground, it stopped, bobbing slightly, as if immersed in liquid or a magnetic field.

It was magic, of course, and Carthus had paid most highly for it. He could afford to.

"My point, lady," he called, bowing low.

Aathia—his partner in all but love—said nothing. Her eyes glinted like chips of ice, or like the jewels that were the only things she loved. Carthus and Aathia, jewel merchants. They made a strange pair.

There was a discreet cough from behind Carthus. He turned to

153

see a white-tuniced slave holding a parchment scroll. "Yes?" said Carthus. He wiped the sweat from his face with the back of his hand.

"A message, lord. The man who left it said that it was urgent."

Carthus grunted. "Who's it from?"

"I have not opened it. I was told it was for your eyes and the eyes of the Lady Aathia, and for no other."

Carthus stared at the parchment scroll but made no move to take it. He was a big man with a fleshy face, sandy receding hair, and a worried expression. His business rivals—and there were many, for Ponti had become, over the years, the center of the wholesale jewel business—had learned that his expression held no clue to his inner feelings. In many cases it had cost them money to learn this.

"Take the message, Carthus," said Aathia, and when he did not, she walked around the net herself and plucked the scroll from the slave's fingers. "Leave us."

The slave's bare feet were soundless on the chill marble floor.

Aathia broke the seal with her sleeve knife and unrolled the parchment. Her eyes flicked over it once, fast, then again at a slower pace. She whistled. "Here . . ." Carthus took it and read it through.

"I—I really don't know what to make of it," he said in a high, petulant voice. With his racquet he rubbed absentmindedly at the small crisscross scar on his right cheek. The pendant that hung about his neck, proclaiming him one of the High Council of the Ponti Jewel Merchants' Guild, stuck briefly to his sweaty skin, and then swung free. "What do you think, my flower?"

"I am not your 'flower.'"

"Of course not, lady."

"Better, Carthus. We'll make a real citizen of you yet. Well, for a start, the name is obviously false. 'Glew Croll' indeed! There are more men named Glew Croll in Ponti than there are diamonds in your storehouses. The address is obviously rented accommodation in the Undercliffs. There was no ring mark on the wax seal. It's as if he has gone out of his way to maintain anonymity."

"Yes. I can see all that. But what about this 'business opportunity' he talks about? And if it is, as he implies, Ruling Enclave business, why would it be carried on with the secrecy he requests?"

154

She shrugged. "The Ruling Enclave has never been averse to secrecy. And, reading between the lines, it would appear that there is a great deal of wealth involved."

Carthus was silent. He reached down to the skull pile, leaned his racquet against it, and placed the scroll beside it. He picked up a large skull. He caressed it gently with his blunt, stubby fingers. "You know," he said, as if speaking to the skull, "this could be my chance to get one up on the the rest of the bleeders on the Guild High Council. Dead-blood aristocratic half-wits."

"There speaks the son of a slave," said Aathia. "If it wasn't for my name you would never have made council membership."

"Shut up." His expression was vaguely worried, which meant nothing at all. "I can show them. I'm going to show them. You'll see."

He hefted the skull in his right hand as if testing the weight of it, reveling in and computing the value of the bone, the jewels, the fine-worked silver. Then he spun around, suprisingly fast for one so big, and threw the skull with all his might at a far pillar, well beyond the field of play. It seemed to hang in the air forever and then, with a painful slowness, it hit the pillar and smashed into a thousand fragments. The almost-musical tinkling sounds it made as it did so were very beautiful.

"I'll go and change and meet this Glew Croll then," muttered Carthus. He walked out of the room, carrying the scroll with him. Aathia stared at him as he left, then she clapped her hands, summoning a slave to clear up the mess.

The caves that honeycomb the rock on the north side of the Bay of Dawn, down into the bay, beneath the bridge, are known as the Undercliffs. Carthus took his clothes off at the door, handing them to his slave, and walked down the narrow stone steps. His flesh gave an involuntary shiver as he entered the water (kept a little below blood temperature in the aristocratic manner, but still chill after the heat of the day), and he swam down the corridor into an anteroom. Reflected light glimmered across the walls. On the water floated four other men and two women. They lounged on large wooden floats, elegantly carved into the shapes of waterbirds and fish.

Carthus swam over to an empty float—a dolphin—and hauled his bulk up onto it. Like the other six he wore nothing but the Jewelers' Guild High Council pendant. All the High Council members, bar one, were there.

"Where's the president?" he asked of no one in particular.

A skeletal woman with flawless white skin pointed to one of the inner rooms. Then she yawned and twisted her body, a rippling twist, at the end of which she was off the float—hers was carved into the shape of a giant swan—and into the water. Carthus envied and hated her: that twist had been one of the twelve so-called noble dives. He knew that, despite having practiced for years, he could not hope to emulate her.

"Effete bitch," he muttered beneath his breath. Still, it was reassuring to see other council members here. He wondered if any of them knew anything he didn't.

There was a splashing behind him, and he turned. Wommet, the council president, was clutching Carthus's float. They bowed to each other, then Wommet (a small hunchback, whose ever so many times great-grandfather had made his fortune finding for King Emmidus the jewels that had bankrupted Ponti, and had thus laid the foundations for the Ruling Enclave's two-thousand-year rule) said, "He will speak to you next, Messire Carthus. Down the corridor on the left. It's the first room you come to."

The other council members, on their floats, looked at Carthus blankly. They were aristocrats of Ponti, and so they hid their envy and their irritation that Carthus was going in before them, although they did not hide it as well as they thought they did; and, somewhere deep inside, Carthus smiled.

He suppressed the urge to ask the hunchback what this business was all about, and he slipped off his float. The warmed seawater stung his eyes.

The room in which Grew Croll waited was up several rock steps, and was dry and dark and smoky. One lamp burned fitfully on the table in the center of the room. There was a robe on the chair, and Carthus slipped it on. A man stood in the shadows beyond the lamplight, but even in the murk Carthus could see that he was tall and completely bald.

"I bid you good day," said a cultured voice.

156

"And on your house and kin also," responded Carthus.

"Sit down, sit down. As you have undoubtedly inferred from the message I sent you, this is Ruling Enclave business. Now, before another word is said, I must ask you to read and sign this oath of secrecy. Take all the time you need." He pushed a paper across the table: it was a comprehensive oath, pledging Carthus to secrecy about all matters discussed during their meeting on pain of the Ruling Enclave's "extreme displeasure"—a polite euphemism for death. Carthus read it over twice. "It—it isn't anything illegal, is it?"

"Sir!" The cultured voice was offended. Carthus shrugged his great shoulders and signed. The paper was taken from his fingers and placed in a trunk at the far end of the hall. "Very good. We can get down to business then. Something to drink? Smoke? Inhale? No? Very well."

A pause.

"As you may have already surmised, Glew Croll is not my name. I am a junior administrative member of the Ruling Enclave." (Carthus grunted, his suspicions confirmed, and he scratched his ear.) "Messire Carthus, what do you know of the Bridge of Ponti?"

"Same as everyone. National landmark. Tourist attraction. Very impressive if you like that sort of thing. Built of jewels and magic. Jewels aren't all of the highest quality, although there's a rose diamond at the summit as big as a baby's fist, and reportedly flawless. . . ."

"Very good. Have you heard the term 'magical half-life'?"

Carthus hadn't. Not that he could recall. "I've heard the term," he said, "but I'm not a magician, obviously, and . . ."

"A magical half-life, messire, is the nigromantic term for the length of time a magician, warlock, witch, or whatever's magic lasts after his or her death. A simple hedge witch's conjurations and so on will often vanish and be done with on the moment of her death. At the other end of the scale you have such phenomena as the Sea Serpent Sea, in which the purely magical sea serpents still frolic and bask almost nine thousand years after the execution of Cilimwai Lah, their creator."

"Right. That. Yes, I knew that."

"Good. Then you will understand the import when I tell you that the half-life of the Ponti Bridge—according to the wisest of our natural philosophers—is little more than two thousand years. Soon, perhaps very soon, messire, it will begin to crumble and collapse."

The fat jeweler gasped. "But that's terrible. If the news got around . . ." He trailed off, weighing up the implications.

"Precisely. There would be panic. Trouble. Unrest. The news cannot be allowed to leak out until we are ready, hence this secrecy."

"I think I will have that drink now, please," said Carthus.

"Very wise." The bald nobleman unstoppered a crystal flagon and poured clear blue wine into a goblet. He passed it across the table and continued. "Any jeweler—and there are only seven in Ponti and perhaps two others elsewhere who could cope with the volume—who was permitted to demolish and keep the materials of the Ponti Bridge would regain whatever he paid for it in publicity alone, leaving aside the value of the jewels. It is my task to talk to the city's most prestigious wholesale jewelers about this matter.

"The Ruling Enclave has a number of concerns. As you can imagine, if the jewels were all released at once in Ponti, they would soon be almost worthless. In exchange for entire ownership of the bridge, the jeweler would have to undertake to build a structure beneath it, and as the bridge crumbles he or she would collect the jewels, and would undertake to sell no more than half a percent of them within the city walls. You, as the senior partner in Carthus and Aathia, are one of the people I have been appointed to discuss this matter with."

The jeweler shook his head. It seemed almost too good to be true—*if* he could get it. "Anything else?" he asked. His voice was casual. He sounded uninterested.

"I am but a humble servant of the Enclave," said the bald man. "They, for their part, will wish to make a profit on this. Each of you will submit a tender for the bridge, via myself, to the Ruling Enclave. There is to be no conferring among you jewelers. The Enclave will choose the best offer and then, in open and formal session, the winner will be announced and then—and only then—will the winner pay any money into the city treasury. Most of the winning bid, as I understand things, will go toward the building of another bridge (out of significantly more mundane materials, I suspect) and to pay-ing for a ferry for the citizens while there is no bridge."

"I see."

The tall man stared at Carthus. To the jeweler it seemed as if those hard eyes were boring into his soul. "You have exactly five days to submit your tender, Carthus. Let me warn you of two things. Firstly, if there is any indication of collaboration between any of you jewelers, you will earn the Enclave's extreme displeasure. Secondly, if *anybody* finds out about the spell fatigue, then we will not waste time in find-ing out which of you jewelers opened his mouth too wide and not too well. The High Council of the Ponti Jewelers' Guild will be replaced with another council, and your businesses will be annexed by the city—perhaps to be offered as prizes in the next Autumn Games. Do I make my meaning plain?"

Carthus's voice was gravel in his throat. "Yes."

"Go then. Your tender in five days, remember. Send another in."

Carthus left the room as if in a dream, croaked "He wants you now," to the nearest High Council member in the anteroom, and was relieved to find himself outside in the sunlight and the fresh air. Far above him the jeweled heights of the Ponti Bridge stood, as they had stood, glinting and twinkling and shining down on the town, for the last two thousand years.

He squinted: Was it his imagination, or were the jewels less bright, the structure less permanent, the whole glorious bridge subtly less magnificent than before? Was the air of permanence that hung about the bridge beginning to fade away?

Carthus began to calculate the value of the bridge in terms of jewel weight and volume. He wondered how Aathia would treat him if he presented her with the rose diamond from the summit; and the High Council would not view him as a nouveau riche upstart, not him, not if he was the man who bought the Ponti Bridge.

Oh, they would all treat him better. There was no doubt of that.

One by one, the man who called himself Glew Croll saw the jewel merchants. Each reacted in his or her own way—shock or laughter, sorrow or gloom—at the news of the spell fatigue in the binding of the Ponti Bridge. And, beneath the sneers or the dismay, each of them began to judge profits and balance sheets, mentally judge and guess possible tenders, activate spies in rival jewelers' houses.

Carthus himself told no one anything, not even his beloved, unattainable Aathia. He locked himself in his study and wrote tenders, tore them up, wrote tenders once again. The rest of the jewelers were similarly occupied.

The fire had burned out in the Rogues' Club, leaving only a few red embers in a bed of gray ash, and dawn was painting the sky silver. Gloathis, Redcap, and I had listened to the man called Stoat all night. It was at this point in his narrative that he leaned back on his cushion, and he grinned.

"So there you have it, friends," he said. "A perfect scam. Eh?"

I glanced at Gloathis and Redcap, and was relieved to see that they looked as blank as I felt.

"I'm sorry," said Redcap. "I just don't see . . ."

"You don't see, eh? And what about you, Gloathis? Do you see? Or are your eyes covered with mud?"

Gloathis looked serious. She said, "Well . . . you obviously convinced them all that you were a representative of the Ruling Enclave—and having them all meet in the anteroom was an inspired idea. But I fail to see the profit in this for you. You've said that you need a million, but none of them is going to pay anything to you. They are waiting for a public announcement that will never come, and then the chance to pay their money into the public treasury. . . ."

"You think like a mug," said Stoat. He looked at me and raised an eyebrow. I shook my head. "And you call yourself rogues."

Redcap looked exasperated. "I just don't see the profit in it! You've spent your thirty gold coins on renting the offices and sending the messages. You've told them you're working for the Enclave, and they will pay everything to the Enclave. . . ."

It was hearing Redcap spell it out that did it. I saw it all, and I understood, and as I understood I could feel the laughter welling up inside me. I tried to keep it inside, and the effort almost choked me. "Oh, priceless, priceless," was all I could say for some moments. My

160

friends stared at me, irritated. Stoat said nothing, but he waited.

I got up, leaned in to Stoat, and whispered in his ear. He nodded once, and I began to chortle once again.

"At least one of you has some potential," said Stoat. Then he stood up. He drew his robes around him and swept off down the torch-lined corridors of the Lost Carnadine Rogues' Club, vanishing into the shadows. I stared after him as he left. The other two were looking at me.

"I don't understand," said Redcap.

"What did he do?" begged Gloathis.

"Call yourself rogues?" I asked. "I worked it out for myself. Why can't you two simply . . . Oh, very well. After the jewelers left his office he let them stew for a few days, letting the tension build and build. Then, secretly, he arranged to see each of the jewelers at different times and in different places—probably lowlife taverns.

"And in each tavern he would greet the jeweler and point out the one thing that he—or they—had overlooked. The tenders would be submitted to the Enclave through my friend. He could arrange for the jeweler he was talking to—Carthus, say—to put in the winning tender.

"For of course, he *was* open to bribery."

Gloathis slapped her forehead. "I'm such an oaf! I should have seen it! He could easily have raked in a million gold coins' worth of bribes from that lot. And once the last jeweler paid him, he'd vanish. The jewelers couldn't complain—if the Enclave thought they'd tried to bribe someone they thought to be an Enclave official, they'd be lucky to keep their right arms, let alone their lives and businesses. What a perfect con."

And there was silence in the Hall of the Lost Carnadine Rogues' Club. We were lost in contemplation of the brilliance of the man who sold the Ponti Bridge.

OCTOBER IN THE CHAIR

OCTOBER WAS IN the chair, so it was chilly that evening, and the leaves were red and orange and tumbled from the trees that circled the grove. The twelve of them sat around a campfire roasting huge sausages on sticks, which spat and crackled as the fat dripped onto the burning applewood, and drinking fresh apple cider, tangy and tart in their mouths.

April took a dainty bite from her sausage, which burst open as she bit into it, spilling hot juice down her chin. "Beshrew and suck ordure on it," she said.

Squat March, sitting next to her, laughed, low and dirty, and then pulled out a huge, filthy handkerchief. "Here you go," he said.

April wiped her chin. "Thanks," she said. "The cursed bag of innards burned me. I'll have a blister there tomorrow."

September yawned. "You are *such* a hypochondriac," he said, across the fire. "And such *language*." He had a pencil-thin mustache and was balding in the front, which made his forehead seem high and wise.

"Lay off her," said May. Her dark hair was cropped short against her skull, and she wore sensible boots. She smoked a small brown cigarillo that smelled heavily of cloves. "She's sensitive."

"Oh puh*lease*," said September. "Spare me."

October, conscious of his position in the chair, sipped his apple cider, cleared his throat, and said, "Okay. Who wants to begin?" The chair he sat in was carved from one large block of oakwood, inlaid

165

with ash, with cedar, and with cherrywood. The other eleven sat on tree stumps equally spaced about the small bonfire. The tree stumps had been worn smooth and comfortable by years of use.

"What about the minutes?" asked January. "We always do minutes when I'm in the chair."

"But you aren't in the chair now, are you, dear?" said September, an elegant creature of mock solicitude.

"What about the minutes?" repeated January. "You can't ignore them."

"Let the little buggers take care of themselves," said April, one hand running through her long blonde hair. "And I think September should go first."

September preened and nodded. "Delighted," he said.

"Hey," said February. "Hey-hey-hey-hey-hey-hey-hey. I didn't hear the chairman ratify that. Nobody starts till October says who starts, and then nobody else talks. Can we have maybe the tiniest semblance of order here?" He peered at them, small, pale, dressed entirely in blues and grays.

"It's fine," said October. His beard was all colors, a grove of trees in autumn, deep brown and fire orange and wine red, an untrimmed tangle across the lower half of his face. His cheeks were apple red. He looked like a friend; like someone you had known all your life. "September can go first. Let's just get it rolling."

September placed the end of his sausage into his mouth, chewed daintily, and drained his cider mug. Then he stood up and bowed to the company and began to speak.

"Laurent DeLisle was the finest chef in all of Seattle, at least, Laurent DeLisle thought so, and the Michelin stars on his door confirmed him in his opinion. He was a remarkable chef, it is true—his minced lamb brioche had won several awards; his smoked quail and white truffle ravioli had been described in the *Gastronome* as 'the tenth wonder of the world.' But it was his wine cellar . . . ah, his wine cellar . . . that was his source of pride and his passion.

"I understand that. The last of the white grapes are harvested in me, and the bulk of the reds: I appreciate fine wines, the aroma, the taste, the aftertaste as well.

"Laurent DeLisle bought his wines at auctions, from private wine lovers, from reputable dealers: he would insist on a pedigree for each wine, for wine frauds are, alas, too common, when the bottle is selling for perhaps five, ten, a hundred thousand dollars, or pounds, or euros.

"The treasure—the jewel—the rarest of the rare and the *ne plus ultra* of his temperature-controlled wine cellar was a bottle of 1902 Château Lafitte. It was on the wine list at one hundred and twenty thousand dollars, although it was, in true terms, priceless, for it was the last bottle of its kind."

"Excuse me," said August politely. He was the fattest of them all, his thin hair combed in golden wisps across his pink pate.

September glared down at his neighbor. "Yes?"

"Is this the one where some rich dude buys the wine to go with the dinner, and the chef decides that the dinner the rich dude ordered isn't good enough for the wine, so he sends out a different dinner, and the guy takes one mouthful, and he's got, like, some rare allergy and he just dies like that, and the wine never gets drunk after all?"

September said nothing. He looked a great deal.

"Because if it is, you told it before. Years ago. Dumb story then. Dumb story now." August smiled. His pink cheeks shone in the firelight.

September said, "Obviously pathos and culture are not to everyone's taste. Some people prefer their barbecues and beer, and some of us like—"

February said, "Well, I hate to say this, but he kind of does have a point. It has to be a new story."

September raised an eyebrow and pursed his lips. "I'm done," he said abruptly. He sat down on his stump.

They looked at one another across the fire, the months of the year.

June, hesitant and clean, raised her hand and said, "I have one about a guard on the X-ray machines at LaGuardia Airport, who could read all about people from the outlines of their luggage on the screen, and one day she saw a luggage X-ray so beautiful that she fell in love with the person, and she had to figure out which person in

167

the line it was, and she couldn't, and she pined for months and months. And when the person came through again she knew it this time, and it was the man, and he was a wizened old Indian man and she was pretty and black and, like, twenty-five, and she knew it would never work out and she let him go, because she could also see from the shapes of his bags on the screen that he was going to die soon."

October said, "Fair enough, young June. Tell that one."

June stared at him, like a spooked animal. "I just did," she said.

October nodded. "So you did," he said, before any of the others could say anything. And then he said, "Shall we proceed to my story, then?"

February sniffed. "Out of order there, big fella. The man in the chair only tells his story when the rest of us are through. Can't go straight to the main event."

May was placing a dozen chestnuts on the grate above the fire, deploying them into patterns with her tongs. "Let him tell his story if he wants to," she said. "God knows it can't be worse than the one about the wine. And I have things to be getting back to. Flowers don't bloom by themselves. All in favor?"

"You're taking this to a formal vote?" February said. "I cannot believe this. I cannot believe this is happening." He mopped his brow with a handful of tissues, which he pulled from his sleeve.

Seven hands were raised. Four people kept their hands down— February, September, January, and July. ("I don't have anything personal on this," said July apologetically. "It's purely procedural. We shouldn't be setting precedents.")

"It's settled then," said October. "Is there anything anyone would like to say before I begin?"

"Um. Yes. Sometimes," said June, "sometimes I think somebody's watching us from the woods, and then I look and there isn't anybody there. But I still think it."

April said, "That's because you're crazy."

"Mm," said September to everybody. "That's our April. She's sensitive, but she's still the cruelest."

"Enough," said October. He stretched in his chair. He cracked a cobnut with his teeth, pulled out the kernel, and threw the fragments of shell into the fire, where they hissed and spat and popped, and he began.

There was a boy, October said, who was miserable at home, although they did not beat him. He did not fit well, not his family, his town, nor even his life. He had two brothers, who were twins, older than he was, and who hurt him or ignored him, and were popular. They played football: some games one twin would score more and be the hero, and some games the other would. Their little brother did not play football. They had a name for their brother. They called him the Runt.

They had called him the Runt since he was a baby, and at first their mother and father had chided them for it.

The twins said, "But he *is* the runt of the litter. Look at *him*. Look at *us*." The boys were six when they said this. Their parents thought it was cute. A name like the Runt can be infectious, so pretty soon the only person who called him Donald was his grandmother, when she telephoned him on his birthday, and people who did not know him.

Now, perhaps because names have power, he was a runt: skinny and small and nervous. He had been born with a runny nose, and it had not stopped running in a decade. At mealtimes, if the twins liked the food, they would steal his; if they did not, they would contrive to place their food on his plate and he would find himself in trouble for leaving good food uneaten.

Their father never missed a football game, and would buy an ice cream afterward for the twin who had scored the most, and a consolation ice cream for the other twin, who hadn't. Their mother described herself as a newspaperwoman, although she mostly sold advertising space and subscriptions: she had gone back to work fulltime once the twins were capable of taking care of themselves.

The other kids in the boy's class admired the twins. They had called him Donald for several weeks in first grade, until the word trickled down that his brothers called him the Runt. His teachers rarely called him anything at all, although among themselves they could sometimes be heard to say that it was a pity the youngest Covay boy didn't have the pluck or the imagination or the life of his brothers.

The Runt could not have told you when he first decided to run away, nor when his daydreams crossed the border and became plans. By the time that he admitted to himself he was leaving he had a large Tupperware container hidden beneath a plastic sheet behind the garage containing three Mars bars, two Milky Ways, a bag of nuts, a small bag of licorice, a flashlight, several comics, an unopened packet of beef jerky, and thirty-seven dollars, most of it in quarters. He did not like the taste of beef jerky, but he had read that explorers had survived for weeks on nothing else; and it was when he put the packet of beef jerky into the Tupperware box and pressed the lid down with a pop that he knew he was going to have to run away.

He had read books, newspapers, and magazines. He knew that if you ran away you sometimes met bad people who did bad things to you; but he had also read fairy tales, so he knew that there were kind people out there, side by side with the monsters.

The Runt was a thin ten-year-old, small, with a runny nose and a blank expression. If you were to try and pick him out of a group of boys, you'd be wrong. He'd be the other one. Over at the side. The one your eye slipped over.

All through September he put off leaving. It took a really bad Friday, during the course of which both of his brothers sat on him (and the one who sat on his face broke wind and laughed uproariously), for him to decide that whatever monsters were waiting out in the world would be bearable, perhaps even preferable.

Saturday, his brothers were meant to be looking after him, but soon they went into town to see a girl they liked. The Runt went around the back of the garage and took the Tupperware container out from beneath the plastic sheeting. He took it up to his bedroom. He emptied his schoolbag onto his bed, filled it with his candies and comics and quarters and the beef jerky. He filled an empty soda bottle with water.

The Runt walked into town and got on the bus. He rode west, ten-dollars-in-quarters' worth of west, to a place he didn't know, which he thought was a good start, then he got off the bus and walked. There was no sidewalk now, so when cars came past he would edge over into the ditch, to safety.

The sun was high. He was hungry, so he rummaged in his bag and pulled out a Mars bar. After he ate it he found he was thirsty, and he drank almost half of the water from his soda bottle before he realized he was going to have to ration it. He had thought that once he got out of the town he would see springs of fresh water everywhere, but there were none to be found. There was a river, though, that ran beneath a wide bridge.

The Runt stopped halfway across the bridge to stare down at the brown water. He remembered something he had been told in school: that, in the end, all rivers flowed into the sea. He had never been to the seashore. He clambered down the bank and followed the river. There was a muddy path along the side of the riverbank, and an occasional beer can or plastic snack packet to show that people had been that way before, but he saw no one as he walked.

He finished his water.

He wondered if they were looking for him yet. He imagined police cars and helicopters and dogs, all trying to find him. He would evade them. He would make it to the sea.

The river ran over some rocks, and it splashed. He saw a blue heron, its wings wide, glide past him, and he saw solitary end-of-season dragonflies, and sometimes small clusters of midges, enjoying the Indian summer. The blue sky became dusk gray, and a bat swung down to snatch insects from the air. The Runt wondered where he would sleep that night.

Soon the path divided, and he took the branch that led away from the river, hoping it would lead to a house or to a farm with an empty barn. He walked for some time, as the dusk deepened, until at the end of the path he found a farmhouse, half tumbled down and unpleasant looking. The Runt walked around it, becoming increasingly certain as he walked that nothing could make him go inside, and then he climbed over a broken fence to an abandoned pasture, and settled down to sleep in the long grass with his schoolbag for his pillow.

He lay on his back, fully dressed, staring up at the sky. He was not in the slightest bit sleepy.

"They'll be missing me by now," he told himself. "They'll be worried."

171

He imagined himself coming home in a few years' time. The delight on his family's faces as he walked up the path to home. Their welcome. Their love. . . .

He woke some hours later, with the bright moonlight in his face. He could see the whole world—as bright as day, like in the nursery rhyme, but pale and without colors. Above him, the moon was full, or almost, and he imagined a face looking down at him, not unkindly, in the shadows and shapes of the moon's surface.

A voice said, "Where do you come from?"

He sat up, not scared, not yet, and looked around him. Trees. Long grass. "Where are you? I don't see you."

Something he had taken for a shadow moved, beside a tree on the edge of the pasture, and he saw a boy of his own age.

"I'm running away from home," said the Runt.

"Whoa," said the boy. "That must have taken a whole lot of guts."

The Runt grinned with pride. He didn't know what to say.

"You want to walk a bit?" said the boy.

"Sure," said the Runt. He moved his schoolbag so it was next to the fence post, so he could always find it again.

They walked down the slope, giving a wide berth to the old farmhouse.

"Does anyone live there?" asked the Runt.

"Not really," said the other boy. He had fair, fine hair that was almost white in the moonlight. "Some people tried a long time back, but they didn't like it, and they left. Then other folk moved in. But nobody lives there now. What's your name?"

"Donald," said the Runt. And then, "But they call me the Runt. What do they call you?"

The boy hesitated. "Dearly," he said.

"That's a cool name."

Dearly said, "I used to have another name, but I can't read it anymore."

They squeezed through a huge iron gateway, rusted part open, part closed, and they were in the little meadow at the bottom of the slope.

"This place is cool," said the Runt.

There were dozens of stones of all sizes in the small meadow. Tall stones, bigger than either of the boys, and small ones, just the right size for sitting on. There were some broken stones. The Runt knew what sort of a place this was, but it did not scare him. It was a loved place.

"Who's buried here?" he asked.

"Mostly okay people," said Dearly. "There used to be a town over there. Past those trees. Then the railroad came and they built a stop in the next town over, and our town sort of dried up and fell in and blew away. There's bushes and trees now, where the town was. You can hide in the trees and go into the old houses and jump out."

The Runt said, "Are they like that farmhouse up there? The houses?" He didn't want to go in them, if they were.

"No," said Dearly. "Nobody goes in them, except for me. And some animals, sometimes. I'm the only kid around here."

"I figured," said the Runt.

"Maybe we can go down and play in them," said Dearly.

"That would be pretty cool," said the Runt.

It was a perfect early October night: almost as warm as summer, and the harvest moon dominated the sky. You could see everything.

"Which one of these is yours?" asked the Runt.

Dearly straightened up proudly and took the Runt by the hand. He pulled him to an overgrown corner of the field. The two boys pushed aside the long grass. The stone was set flat into the ground, and it had dates carved into it from a hundred years before. Much of it was worn away, but beneath the dates it was possible to make out the words

DEARLY DEPARTED
WILL NEVER BE FORG

"Forgotten, I'd wager," said Dearly.

"Yeah, that's what I'd say too," said the Runt.

They went out of the gate, down a gully, and into what remained of the old town. Trees grew through houses, and buildings had fallen in on themselves, but it wasn't scary. They played hide-and-seek. They explored. Dearly showed the Runt some pretty cool places, including

173

a one-room cottage that he said was the oldest building in that whole part of the county. It was in pretty good shape, too, considering how old it was.

"I can see pretty good by moonlight," said the Runt. "Even inside. I didn't know that it was so easy."

"Yeah," said Dearly. "And after a while you get good at seeing even when there ain't any moonlight."

The Runt was envious.

"I got to go to the bathroom," said the Runt. "Is there somewhere around here?"

Dearly thought for a moment. "I don't know," he admitted. "I don't do that stuff anymore. There are a few outhouses still standing, but they may not be safe. Best just to do it in the woods."

"Like a bear," said the Runt.

He walked out the back, into the woods that pushed up against the wall of the cottage, and went behind a tree. He'd never done that before, in the open air. He felt like a wild animal. When he was done he wiped himself off with fallen leaves. Then he went back out the front. Dearly was sitting in a pool of moonlight, waiting for him.

"How did you die?" asked the Runt.

"I got sick," said Dearly. "My maw cried and carried on something fierce. Then I died."

"If I stayed here with you," said the Runt, "would I have to be dead, too?"

"Maybe," said Dearly. "Well, yeah. I guess."

"What's it like? Being dead?"

"I don't mind it," admitted Dearly. "Worst thing is not having anyone to play with."

"But there must be lots of people up in that meadow," said the Runt. "Don't they ever play with you?"

"Nope," said Dearly. "Mostly, they sleep. And even when they walk, they can't be bothered to just go and see stuff and do things. They can't be bothered with me. You see that tree?"

It was a beech tree, its smooth gray bark cracked with age. It sat in what must once have been the town square, ninety years before.

"Yeah," said the Runt.

"You want to climb it?"

"It looks kind of high."

"It is. Real high. But it's easy to climb. I'll show you."

It was easy to climb. There were handholds in the bark, and the boys went up the big beech like a couple of monkeys or pirates or warriors. From the top of the tree one could see the whole world. The sky was starting to lighten, just a hair, in the east.

Everything waited. The night was ending. The world was holding its breath, preparing to begin again.

"This was the best day I ever had," said the Runt.

"Me too," said Dearly. "What you going to do now?"

"I don't know," said the Runt.

He imagined himself going on across the world, all the way to the sea. He imagined himself growing up and growing older, bringing himself up by his bootstraps. Somewhere in there he would become fabulously wealthy. And then he would go back to the house with the twins in it, and he would drive up to their door in his wonderful car, or perhaps he would turn up at a football game (in his imagination the twins had neither aged nor grown) and look down at them in a kindly way. He would buy them all—the twins, his parents—a meal at the finest restaurant in the city, and they would tell him how badly they had misunderstood him and mistreated him. They apologized and wept, and through it all he said nothing. He let their apologies wash over him. And then he would give each of them a gift, and afterward he would leave their lives once more, this time for good.

It was a fine dream.

In reality, he knew, he would keep walking, and be found tomorrow or the day after that, and go home and be yelled at, and everything would be the same as it ever was, and day after day, hour after hour until the end of time he'd still be the Runt, only now they'd be mad at him for having dared to walk away.

"I have to go to bed soon," said Dearly. He started to climb down the big beech tree.

Climbing down the tree was harder, the Runt found. You couldn't see where you were putting your feet and had to feel around for somewhere to put them. Several times he slipped and slid, but Dearly went down ahead of him and would say things like "A little to the right, now," and they both made it down just fine.

The sky continued to lighten, and the moon was fading, and it was harder to see. They clambered back through the gully. Sometimes the Runt wasn't sure that Dearly was there at all, but when he got to the top, he saw the boy waiting for him.

They didn't say much as they walked up to the meadow filled with stones. The Runt put his arm over Dearly's shoulder, and they walked in step up the hill.

"Well," said Dearly. "Thanks for coming over."

"I had a good time," said the Runt.

"Yeah," said Dearly. "Me too."

Down in the woods somewhere a bird began to sing.

"If I wanted to stay—?" said the Runt, all in a burst. Then he stopped. *I might never get another chance to change it,* thought the Runt. He'd never get to the sea. They'd never let him.

Dearly didn't say anything, not for a long time. The world was gray. More birds joined the first.

"I can't do it," said Dearly eventually. "But they might."

"Who?"

"The ones in there." The fair boy pointed up the slope to the tumbledown farmhouse with the jagged, broken windows, silhouetted against the dawn. The gray light had not changed it.

The Runt shivered. "There's people in there?" he said. "I thought you said it was empty."

"It ain't empty," said Dearly. "I said nobody lives there. Different things." He looked up at the sky. "I got to go now," he added. He squeezed the Runt's hand. And then he just wasn't there any longer.

The Runt stood in the little graveyard all on his own, listening to the birdsong on the morning air. Then he made his way up the hill. It was harder by himself.

He picked up his schoolbag from the place he had left it. He ate his last Milky Way and stared at the tumbledown building. The empty windows of the farmhouse were like eyes, watching him.

It was darker inside there. Darker than anything.

He pushed his way through the weed-choked yard. The door to

the farmhouse was mostly crumbled away. He stopped at the doorway, hesitating, wondering if this was wise. He could smell damp, and rot, and something else underneath. He thought he heard something move, deep in the house, in the cellar, maybe, or the attic. A shuffle, maybe. Or a hop. It was hard to tell.

Eventually, he went inside.

Nobody said anything. October filled his wooden mug with apple cider when he was done, and drained it, and filled it again.

"It was a story," said December. "I'll say that for it." He rubbed his pale blue eyes with a fist. The fire was almost out.

"What happened next?" asked June nervously. "After he went into the house?"

May, sitting next to her, put her hand on June's arm. "Better not to think about it," she said.

"Anyone else want a turn?" asked August. There was silence. "Then I think we're done."

"That needs to be an official motion," pointed out February.

"All in favor?" said October. There was a chorus of "ayes." "All against?" Silence. "Then I declare this meeting adjourned."

They got up from the fireside, stretching and yawning, and walked away into the wood, in ones and twos and threes, until only October and his neighbor remained.

"Your turn in the chair next time," said October.

"I know," said November. He was pale and thin lipped. He helped October out of the wooden chair. "I like your stories. Mine are always too dark."

"I don't think so," said October. "It's just that your nights are longer. And you aren't as warm."

"Put it like that," said November, "and I feel better. I suppose we can't help who we are."

"That's the spirit," said his brother. And they touched hands as they walked away from the fire's orange embers, taking their stories with them back into the dark.

For Ray Bradbury

CHIVALRY

MRS. WHITAKER FOUND the Holy Grail; it was under a fur coat.

Every Thursday afternoon Mrs. Whitaker walked down to the post office to collect her pension, even though her legs were no longer what they were, and on the way back home she would stop in at the Oxfam Shop and buy herself a little something.

The Oxfam Shop sold old clothes, knickknacks, oddments, bits and bobs, and large quantities of old paperbacks, all of them donations: secondhand flotsam, often the house clearances of the dead. All the profits went to charity.

The shop was staffed by volunteers. The volunteer on duty this afternoon was Marie, seventeen, slightly overweight, and dressed in a baggy mauve jumper which looked like she had bought it from the shop.

Marie sat by the till with a copy of *Modern Woman* magazine, filling out a "Reveal Your Hidden Personality" questionnaire. Every now and then, she'd flip to the back of the magazine and check the relative points assigned to an A), B), or C) answer before making up her mind how she'd respond to the question.

Mrs. Whitaker puttered around the shop.

They still hadn't sold the stuffed cobra, she noted. It had been there for six months now, gathering dust, glass eyes gazing balefully at the clothes racks and the cabinet filled with chipped porcelain and chewed toys.

Mrs. Whitaker patted its head as she went past.

She picked out a couple of Mills & Boon novels from a bookshelf—*Her Thundering Soul* and *Her Turbulent Heart*, a shilling each—and gave careful consideration to the empty bottle of Mateus Rosé with a decorative lampshade on it before deciding she really didn't have anywhere to put it.

She moved a rather threadbare fur coat, which smelled badly of mothballs. Underneath it was a walking stick and a water-stained copy of *Romance and Legend of Chivalry* by A. R. Hope Moncrieff, priced at five pence. Next to the book, on its side, was the Holy Grail. It had a little round paper sticker on the base, and written on it, in felt pen, was the price: 30p.

Mrs. Whitaker picked up the dusty silver goblet and appraised it through her thick spectacles.

"This is nice," she called to Marie.

Marie shrugged.

"It'd look nice on the mantelpiece."

Marie shrugged again.

Mrs. Whitaker gave fifty pence to Marie, who gave her ten pence change and a brown paper bag to put the books and the Holy Grail in. Then she went next door to the butcher's and bought herself a nice piece of liver. Then she went home.

The inside of the goblet was thickly coated with a brownish-red dust. Mrs. Whitaker washed it out with great care, then left it to soak for an hour in warm water with a dash of vinegar added.

Then she polished it with metal polish until it gleamed, and she put it on the mantelpiece in her parlor, where it sat between a small soulful china basset hound and a photograph of her late husband, Henry, on the beach at Frinton in 1953.

She had been right: It did look nice.

For dinner that evening she had the liver fried in breadcrumbs with onions. It was very nice.

The next morning was Friday; on alternate Fridays Mrs. Whitaker and Mrs. Greenberg would visit each other. Today it was Mrs. Greenberg's turn to visit Mrs. Whitaker. They sat in the parlor and ate macaroons and drank tea. Mrs. Whitaker took one sugar in her tea, but Mrs. Greenberg took sweetener, which she always carried in her handbag in a small plastic container.

"That's nice," said Mrs. Greenberg, pointing to the Grail. "What is it?"

"It's the Holy Grail," said Mrs. Whitaker. "It's the cup that Jesus drunk out of at the Last Supper. Later, at the Crucifixion, it caught His precious blood when the centurion's spear pierced His side."

Mrs. Greenberg sniffed. She was small and Jewish and didn't hold with unsanitary things. "I wouldn't know about that," she said, "but it's very nice. Our Myron got one just like that when he won the swimming tournament, only it's got his name on the side."

"Is he still with that nice girl? The hairdresser?"

"Bernice? Oh yes. They're thinking of getting engaged," said Mrs. Greenberg.

"That's nice," said Mrs. Whitaker. She took another macaroon.

Mrs. Greenberg baked her own macaroons and brought them over every alternate Friday: small sweet light-brown biscuits with almonds on top.

They talked about Myron and Bernice, and Mrs. Whitaker's nephew Ronald (she had had no children), and about their friend Mrs. Perkins who was in hospital with her hip, poor dear.

At midday Mrs. Greenberg went home, and Mrs. Whitaker made herself cheese on toast for lunch, and after lunch Mrs. Whitaker took her pills: the white and the red and two little orange ones.

The doorbell rang.

Mrs. Whitaker answered the door. It was a young man with shoulder-length hair so fair it was almost white, wearing gleaming silver armor, with a white surcoat.

"Hello," he said.

"Hello," said Mrs. Whitaker.

"I'm on a quest," he said.

"That's nice," said Mrs. Whitaker noncommitally.

"Can I come in?" he asked.

Mrs. Whitaker shook her head. "I'm sorry, I don't think so," she said.

"I'm on a quest for the Holy Grail," the young man said. "Is it here?"

"Have you got any identification?" Mrs. Whitaker asked. She knew that it was unwise to let unidentified strangers into your home when you were elderly and living on your own. Handbags get emptied, and worse than that.

The young man went back down the garden path. His horse, a huge gray charger, big as a shire horse, its head high and its eyes intelligent, was tethered to Mrs. Whitaker's garden gate. The knight fumbled in the saddlebag and returned with a scroll.

It was signed by Arthur, King of All Britons, and charged all persons of whatever rank or station to know that here was Galaad, Knight of the Table Round, and that he was on a Right High and Noble Quest. There was a drawing of the young man below that. It wasn't a bad likeness.

Mrs. Whitaker nodded. She had been expecting a little card with a photograph on it, but this was far more impressive.

"I suppose you had better come in," she said.

They went into her kitchen. She made Galaad a cup of tea, then she took him into the parlor.

Galaad saw the Grail on her mantelpiece, and dropped to one knee. He put down the teacup carefully on the russet carpet. A shaft of light came through the net curtains and painted his awed face with golden sunlight and turned his hair into a silver halo.

"It is truly the Sangrail," he said very quietly. He blinked his pale blue eyes three times, very fast, as if he were blinking back tears.

He lowered his head as if in silent prayer.

Galaad stood up again and turned to Mrs. Whitaker. "Gracious lady, keeper of the Holy of Holies, let me now depart this place with the Blessed Chalice, that my journeyings may be ended and my geas fulfilled."

"Sorry?" said Mrs. Whitaker.

Galaad walked over to her and took her old hands in his. "My quest is over," he told her. "The Sangrail is finally within my reach."

Mrs. Whitaker pursed her lips. "Can you pick your teacup and saucer up, please?" she said.

Galaad picked up his teacup apologetically.

"No. I don't think so," said Mrs. Whitaker. "I rather like it there.

It's just right, between the dog and the photograph of my Henry."

"Is it gold you need? Is that it? Lady, I can bring you gold. . . ."

"No," said Mrs. Whitaker. "I don't want any gold, thank *you*. I'm simply not interested."

She ushered Galaad to the front door. "Nice to meet you," she said.

His horse was leaning its head over her garden fence, nibbling her gladioli. Several of the neighborhood children were standing on the pavement, watching it.

Galaad took some sugar lumps from the saddlebag, and showed the braver of the children how to feed the horse, their hands held flat. The children giggled. One of the older girls stroked the horse's nose.

Galaad swung himself up onto the horse in one fluid movement. Then the horse and the knight trotted off down Hawthorne Crescent.

Mrs. Whitaker watched them until they were out of sight, then sighed and went back inside.

The weekend was quiet.

On Saturday Mrs. Whitaker took the bus into Maresfield to visit her nephew Ronald, his wife, Euphonia, and their daughters, Clarissa and Dillian. She took them a currant cake she had baked herself.

On Sunday morning Mrs. Whitaker went to church. Her local church was St. James the Less, which was a little more "Don't think of this as a church, think of it as a place where like-minded friends hang out and are joyful" than Mrs. Whitaker felt entirely comfortable with, but she liked the vicar, the Reverend Bartholomew, when he wasn't actually playing the guitar.

After the service, she thought about mentioning to him that she had the Holy Grail in her front parlor, but decided against it.

On Monday morning Mrs. Whitaker was working in the back garden. She had a small herb garden she was extremely proud of: dill, vervain, mint, rosemary, thyme, and a wild expanse of parsley. She was down on her knees, wearing thick green gardening gloves, weeding, and picking out slugs and putting them in a plastic bag.

Mrs. Whitaker was very tenderhearted when it came to slugs. She would take them down to the back of her garden, which bordered on the railway line, and throw them over the fence.

She cut some parsley for the salad. There was a cough behind her. Galaad stood there, tall and beautiful, his armor glinting in the morning sun. In his arms he held a long package, wrapped in oiled leather.

"I'm back," he said.

"Hello," said Mrs. Whitaker. She stood up, rather slowly, and took off her gardening gloves. "Well," she said, "now you're here, you might as well make yourself useful."

She gave him the plastic bag full of slugs and told him to tip the slugs out over the back of the fence.

He did.

Then they went into the kitchen.

"Tea? Or lemonade?" she asked.

"Whatever you're having," Galaad said.

Mrs. Whitaker took a jug of her homemade lemonade from the fridge and sent Galaad outside to pick a sprig of mint. She selected two tall glasses. She washed the mint carefully and put a few leaves in each glass, then poured the lemonade.

"Is your horse outside?" she asked.

"Oh yes. His name is Grizzel."

"And you've come a long way, I suppose."

"A very long way."

"I see," said Mrs. Whitaker. She took a blue plastic basin from under the sink and half filled it with water. Galaad took it out to Grizzel. He waited while the horse drank and brought the empty basin back to Mrs. Whitaker.

"Now," she said, "I suppose you're still after the Grail."

"Aye, still do I seek the Sangrail," he said. He picked up the leather package from the floor, put it down on her tablecloth, and unwrapped it. "For it, I offer you this."

It was a sword, its blade almost four feet long. There were words and symbols traced elegantly along the length of the blade. The hilt was worked in silver and gold, and a large jewel was set in the pommel.

"It's very nice," said Mrs. Whitaker doubtfully.

"This," said Galaad, "is the sword Balmung, forged by Wayland Smith in the dawn times. Its twin is Flamberge. Who wears it is unconquerable in war, and invincible in battle. Who wears it is incapable of a cowardly act or an ignoble one. Set in its pommel is the sardonyx Bircone, which protects its possessor from poison slipped into wine or ale, and from the treachery of friends."

Mrs. Whitaker peered at the sword. "It must be very sharp," she said, after a while.

"It can slice a falling hair in twain. Nay, it could slice a sunbeam," said Galaad, proudly.

"Well, then, maybe you ought to put it away," said Mrs. Whitaker.

"Don't you want it?" Galaad seemed disap-pointed.

"No, thank you," said Mrs. Whitaker. It occurred to her that her late husband, Henry, would have quite liked it. He would have hung it on the wall in his study next to the stuffed carp he had caught in Scotland, and pointed it out to visitors.

Galaad rewrapped the oiled leather around the sword Balmung and tied it up with white cord.

He sat there, disconsolate.

Mrs. Whitaker made him some cream cheese and cucumber sandwiches for the journey back and wrapped them in greaseproof paper. She gave him an apple for Grizell. He seemed very pleased with both gifts.

She waved them both good-bye.

That afternoon she took the bus down to the hospital to see Mrs. Perkins, who was still in with her hip, poor love. Mrs. Whitaker took her some home-made fruitcake, although she had left out the walnuts from the recipe, because Mrs. Perkins's teeth weren't what they used to be.

She watched a little television that evening, and had an early night.

On Tuesday the postman called. Mrs. Whitaker was up in the box-room at the top of the house, doing a spot of tidying, and, taking each step slowly and carefully, she didn't make it downstairs in time. The postman had left her a message which said that he'd tried to

187

deliver a packet, but no one was home.

Mrs. Whitaker sighed.

She put the message into her handbag and went down to the post office.

The package was from her niece Shirelle in Sydney, Australia. It contained photographs of her husband, Wallace, and her two daughters, Dixie and Violet, and a conch shell packed in cotton wool.

Mrs. Whitaker had a number of ornamental shells in her bedroom. Her favorite had a view of the Bahamas done on it in enamel. It had been a gift from her sister, Ethel, who had died in 1983.

She put the shell and the photographs in her shopping bag. Then, seeing that she was in the area, she stopped in at the Oxfam Shop on her way home.

"Hullo Mrs. W.," said Marie.

Mrs. Whitaker stared at her. Marie was wearing lipstick (possibly not the best shade for her, nor particularly expertly applied, but, thought Mrs. Whitaker, that would come with time) and a rather smart skirt. It was a great improvement.

"Oh. Hello, dear," said Mrs. Whitaker.

"There was a man in here last week, asking about that thing you bought. The little metal cup thing. I told him where to find you. You don't mind, do you?"

"No, dear," said Mrs. Whitaker. "He found me."

"He was really dreamy. Really, really dreamy," sighed Marie wistfully. "I could of gone for him.

"And he had a big white horse and all," Marie concluded. She was standing up straighter as well, Mrs. Whitaker noted approvingly.

On the bookshelf Mrs. Whitaker found a new Mills & Boon novel—*Her Majestic Passion*—although she hadn't yet finished the two she had bought on her last visit.

She picked up the copy of *Romance and Legend of Chivalry* and opened it. It smelled musty. EX LIBRIS FISHER was neatly handwritten at the top of the first page in red ink.

She put it down where she had found it.

When she got home, Galaad was waiting for her. He was giving the neighborhood children rides on Grizell's back, up and down the street.

"I'm glad you're here," she said. "I've got some cases that need moving."

She showed him up to the boxroom in the top of the house. He moved all the old suitcases for her, so she could get to the cupboard at the back.

It was very dusty up there.

She kept him up there most of the afternoon, moving things around while she dusted.

Galaad had a cut on his cheek, and he held one arm a little stiffly.

They talked a little while she dusted and tidied. Mrs. Whitaker told him about her late husband, Henry; and how the life insurance had paid the house off; and how she had all these things, but no one really to leave them to, no one but Ronald really, and his wife only liked modern things. She told him how she had met Henry during the war, when he was in the ARP and she hadn't closed the kitchen blackout curtains all the way; and about the sixpenny dances they went to in the town; and how they'd gone to London when the war had ended, and she'd had her first drink of wine.

Galaad told Mrs. Whitaker about his mother, Elaine, who was flighty and no better than she should have been and something of a witch to boot; and his grandfather King Pelles, who was well-meaning although at best a little vague; and of his youth in the Castle of Bliant on the Joyous Isle; and his father, whom he knew as "Le Chevalier Mal Fet," who was more or less completely mad, and was in reality Lancelot du Lac, greatest of knights, in disguise and bereft of his wits; and of Galaad's days as a young squire in Camelot.

At five o'clock Mrs. Whitaker surveyed the box-room and decided that it met with her approval; then she opened the window so the room could air, and they went downstairs to the kitchen, where she put on the kettle.

Galaad sat down at the kitchen table.

He opened the leather purse at his waist and took out a round white stone. It was about the size of a cricket ball.

"My lady," he said, "this is for you, an you give me the Sangrail."

Mrs. Whitaker picked up the stone, which was heavier than it looked, and held it up to the light. It was milkily translucent, and

189

deep inside it flecks of silver glittered and glinted in the late-afternoon sunlight. It was warm to the touch.

Then, as she held it, a strange feeling crept over her: Deep inside she felt stillness and a sort of peace. *Serenity,* that was the word for it; she felt serene.

Reluctantly she put the stone back on the table.

"It's very nice," she said.

"That is the Philosopher's Stone, which our forefather Noah hung in the Ark to give light when there was no light; it can transform base metals into gold; and it has certain other properties," Galaad told her proudly. "And that isn't all. There's more. Here." From the leather bag he took an egg and handed it to her.

It was the size of a goose egg and was a shiny black, mottled with scarlet and white. When Mrs. Whitaker touched it, the hairs on the back of her neck prickled. Her immediate impression was one of incredible heat and freedom. She heard the crackling of distant fires, and for a fraction of a second she seemed to feel herself far above the world, swooping and diving on wings of flame.

She put the egg down on the table, next to the Philosopher's Stone.

"That is the Egg of the Phoenix," said Galaad. "From far Araby it comes. One day it will hatch out into the Phoenix bird itself; and when its time comes, the bird will build a nest of flame, lay its egg, and die, to be reborn in flame in a later age of the world."

"I thought that was what it was," said Mrs. Whitaker.

"And, last of all, lady," said Galaad, "I have brought you this."

He drew it from his pouch, and gave it to her. It was an apple, apparently carved from a single ruby, on an amber stem.

A little nervously, she picked it up. It was soft to the touch—deceptively so: Her fingers bruised it, and ruby-colored juice from the apple ran down Mrs. Whitaker's hand.

The kitchen filled—almost imperceptibly, magically—with the smell of summer fruit, of raspberries and peaches and strawberries and red currants. As if from a great way away she heard distant voices raised in song and far music on the air.

"It is one of the apples of the Hesperides," said Galaad quietly. "One bite from it will heal any illness or wound, no matter how deep;

a second bite restores youth and beauty; and a third bite is said to grant eternal life."

Mrs. Whitaker licked the sticky juice from her hand. It tasted like fine wine.

There was a moment, then, when it all came back to her—how it was to be young: to have a firm, slim body that would do whatever she wanted it to do; to run down a country lane for the simple unladylike joy of running; to have men smile at her just because she was herself and happy about it.

Mrs. Whitaker looked at Sir Galaad, most comely of all knights, sitting fair and noble in her small kitchen.

She caught her breath.

"And that's all I have brought for you," said Galaad. "They weren't easy to get, either."

Mrs. Whitaker put the ruby fruit down on her kitchen table. She looked at the Philosopher's Stone, and the Egg of the Phoenix, and the Apple of Life.

Then she walked into her parlor and looked at the mantelpiece: at the little china basset hound, and the Holy Grail, and the photograph of her late husband, Henry, shirtless, smiling and eating an ice cream in black and white almost forty years away.

She went back into the kitchen. The kettle had begun to whistle. She poured a little steaming water into the teapot, swirled it around, and poured it out. Then she added two spoonfuls of tea and one for the pot and poured in the rest of the water. All this she did in silence.

She turned to Galaad then, and she looked at him.

"Put that apple away," she told Galaad firmly. "You shouldn't offer things like that to old ladies. It isn't proper."

She paused, then. "But I'll take the other two," she continued, after a moment's thought. "They'll look nice on the mantelpiece. And two for one's fair, or I don't know what is."

Galaad beamed. He put the ruby apple into his leather pouch. Then he went down on one knee, and kissed Mrs. Whitaker's hand.

"Stop that," said Mrs. Whitaker. She poured them both cups of tea, after getting out the very best china, which was only for special occasions.

They sat in silence, drinking their tea.

When they had finished their tea they went into the parlor.

Galaad crossed himself, and picked up the Grail.

Mrs. Whitaker arranged the Egg and the Stone where the Grail had been. The Egg kept tipping on one side, and she propped it up against the little china dog.

"They do look very nice," said Mrs. Whitaker.

"Yes," agreed Galaad. "They look very nice."

"Can I give you anything to eat before you go back?" she asked.

He shook his head.

"Some fruitcake," she said. "You may not think you want any now, but you'll be glad of it in a few hours' time. And you should probably use the facilities. Now, give me that, and I'll wrap it up for you."

She directed him to the small toilet at the end of the hall, and went into the kitchen, holding the Grail. She had some old Christmas wrapping paper in the pantry, and she wrapped the Grail in it, and tied the package with twine. Then she cut a large slice of fruitcake and put it in a brown paper bag, along with a banana and a slice of processed cheese in silver foil.

Galaad came back from the toilet. She gave him the paper bag, and the Holy Grail. Then she went up on tiptoes and kissed him on the cheek.

"You're a nice boy," she said. "You take care of yourself."

He hugged her, and she shooed him out of the kitchen, and out of the back door, and she shut the door behind him. She poured herself another cup of tea, and cried quietly into a Kleenex, while the sound of hoofbeats echoed down Hawthorne Crescent.

On Wednesday Mrs. Whitaker stayed in all day.

On Thursday she went down the post office to collect her pension. Then she stopped in at the Oxfam Shop.

The woman on the till was new to her. "Where's Marie?" asked Mrs. Whitaker.

The woman on the till, who had blue-rinsed gray hair and blue spectacles that went up into diamanté points, shook her head and shrugged her shoulders. "She went off with a young man," she said. "On a horse. *Tch.* I ask you. I'm meant to be down in the Heathfield shop this afternoon. I had to get my Johnny to run me up here, while we find someone else."

"Oh," said Mrs. Whitaker. "Well, it's nice that she's found herself a young man."

"Nice for her, maybe," said the lady on the till, "but some of us were meant to be in Heathfield this afternoon."

On a shelf near the back of the shop Mrs. Whitaker found a tarnished old silver container with a long spout. It had been priced at sixty pence, according to the little paper label stuck to the side. It looked a little like a flattened, elongated teapot.

She picked out a Mills & Boon novel she hadn't read before. It was called *Her Singular Love*. She took the book and the silver container up to the woman on the till.

"Sixty-five pee, dear," said the woman, picking up the silver object, staring at it. "Funny old thing, isn't it? Came in this morning." It had writing carved along the side in blocky old Chinese characters and an elegant arching handle. "Some kind of oil can, I suppose."

"No, it's not an oil can," said Mrs. Whitaker, who knew exactly what it was. "It's a lamp."

There was a small metal finger ring, unornamented, tied to the handle of the lamp with brown twine.

"Actually," said Mrs. Whitaker, "on second thoughts, I think I'll just have the book."

She paid her five pence for the novel, and put the lamp back where she had found it, in the back of the shop. After all, Mrs. Whitaker reflected, as she walked home, it wasn't as if she had anywhere to put it.

THE PRICE

TRAMPS AND VAGABONDS have marks they make on gateposts and trees and doors, letting others of their kind know a little about the people who live at the houses and farms they pass on their travels. I think cats must leave similar signs; how else to explain the cats who turn up at our door through the year, hungry and flea-ridden and abandoned?

We take them in. We get rid of the fleas and the ticks, feed them, and take them to the vet. We pay for them to get their shots, and, indignity upon indignity, we have them neutered or spayed.

And they stay with us, for a few months, or for a year, or forever.

Most of them arrive in summer. We live in the country, just the right distance out of town for the city dwellers to abandon their cats near us.

We never seem to have more than eight cats, rarely have less than three. The cat population of my house is currently as follows: Hermione and Pod, tabby and black respectively, the mad sisters who live in my attic office and do not mingle; Snowflake, the blue-eyed long-haired white cat, who lived wild in the woods for years before she gave up her wild ways for soft sofas and beds; and, last but largest, Furball, Snowflake's cushionlike calico long-haired daughter, orange and black and white, whom I discovered as a tiny kitten in our garage one day, strangled and almost dead, her head poked through an old badminton net, and who surprised us all by not dying but instead

197

growing up to be the best-natured cat I have ever encountered.

And then there is the black cat. Who has no other name than the Black Cat and who turned up almost a month ago. We did not realize he was going to be living here at first: he looked too well fed to be a stray, too old and jaunty to have been abandoned. He looked like a small panther, and he moved like a patch of night.

One day, in the summer, he was lurking about our ramshackle porch: eight or nine years old, at a guess, male, greenish-yellow of eye, very friendly, quite unperturbable. I assumed he belonged to a neighboring farmer or household.

I went away for a few weeks, to finish writing a book, and when I came home he was still on our porch, living in an old cat bed one of the children had found for him. He was, however, almost unrecognizable. Patches of fur had gone, and there were deep scratches on his gray skin. The tip of one ear was chewed away. There was a gash beneath one eye, a slice gone from one lip. He looked tired and thin.

We took the Black Cat to the vet, where we got him some antibiotics, which we fed him each night, along with soft cat food.

We wondered who he was fighting. Snowflake, our beautiful white near-feral queen? Raccoons? A rat-tailed, fanged possum?

Each night the scratches would be worse—one night his side would be chewed up; the next it would be his underbelly, raked with claw marks and bloody to the touch.

When it got to that point, I took him down to the basement to recover beside the furnace and the piles of boxes. He was surprisingly heavy, the Black Cat, and I picked him up and carried him down there, with a cat basket, and a litter box, and some food and water. I closed the door behind me. I had to wash the blood from my hands when I left the basement.

He stayed down there for four days. At first he seemed too weak to feed himself: a cut beneath one eye had rendered him almost one-eyed, and he limped and lolled weakly, thick yellow pus oozing from the cut in his lip.

I went down there every morning and every night, and I fed him and gave him antibiotics, which I mixed with his canned food, and I dabbed at the worst of the cuts, and spoke to him. He had diarrhea, and, although I changed his litter daily, the basement stank evilly.

The four days that the Black Cat lived in the basement were a bad four days in my house: the baby slipped in the bath and banged her head and might have drowned; I learned that a project I had set my heart on—adapting Hope Mirrlees's novel *Lud-in-the-Mist* for the BBC—was no longer going to happen, and I realized that I did not have the energy to begin again from scratch, pitching it to other networks or to other media; my daughter left for summer camp and immediately began to send home a plethora of heart-tearing letters and cards, five or six each day, imploring us to bring her home; my son had some kind of fight with his best friend, to the point that they were no longer on speaking terms; and, returning home one night, my wife hit a deer that ran out in front of the car. The deer was killed, the car was left undriveable, and my wife sustained a small cut over one eye.

By the fourth day, the cat was prowling the basement, walking haltingly but impatiently between the stacks of books and comics, the boxes of mail and cassettes, of pictures and of gifts and of stuff. He mewed at me to let him out and, reluctantly, I did so.

He went back onto the porch and slept there for the rest of the day.

The next morning there were deep, new gashes in his flanks, and clumps of black cat hair—his—covered the wooden boards of the porch.

Letters arrived that day from my daughter, telling us that camp was going better and she thought she could survive a few days; my son and his friend sorted out their problem, although what the argument was about—trading cards, computer games, *Star Wars*, or A Girl—I would never learn. The BBC executive who had vetoed *Lud-in-the-Mist* was discovered to have been taking bribes (well, "questionable loans") from an independent production company and was sent home on permanent leave: his successor, I was delighted to learn when she faxed me, was the woman who had initially proposed the project to me before leaving the BBC.

I thought about returning the Black Cat to the basement, but decided against it. Instead, I resolved to try and discover what kind of

animal was coming to our house each night and from there to for-
mulate a plan of action—to trap it, perhaps.

For birthdays and at Christmas my family gives me gadgets and giz-
mos, pricy toys which excite my fancy but, ultimately, rarely leave their
boxes. There is a food dehydrator and an electric carving knife, a
bread-making machine, and, last year's present, a pair of see-in-the-
dark binoculars. On Christmas Day I had put the batteries into the
binoculars and had walked about the basement in the dark, too impatient even to wait until nightfall, stalking a flock of imaginary Starlings.
(You were warned not to turn it on in the light: that would have dam-
aged the binoculars and quite possibly your eyes as well.) Afterward I
had put the device back into its box, and it sat there still, in my office,
beside the box of computer cables and forgotten bits and pieces.

Perhaps, I thought, if the creature—dog or cat or raccoon or what
have you—were to see me sitting on the porch, it would not come, so
I took a chair into the box and coatroom, little larger than a closet,
which overlooks the porch, and, when everyone in the house was
asleep, I went out onto the porch and bade the Black Cat good night.

That cat, my wife had said, when he first arrived, *is a person*. And
there was something very person-like in his huge leonine face: his
broad black nose, his greenish-yellow eyes, his fanged but amiable
mouth (still leaking amber pus from the right lower lip).

I stroked his head, and scratched him beneath the chin, and
wished him well. Then I went inside and turned off the light on the
porch.

I sat on my chair, in the darkness inside the house with the see-in-
the-dark binoculars on my lap. I had switched the binoculars on, and
a trickle of greenish light came from the eyepieces.

Time passed, in the darkness.

I experimented with looking at the darkness with the binoculars,
learning to focus, to see the world in shades of green. I found myself
horrified by the number of swarming insects I could see in the night
air: it was as if the night world were some kind of nightmarish soup,
swimming with life. Then I lowered the binoculars from my eyes and
stared out at the rich blacks and blues of the night, empty and peace-
ful and calm.

Time passed. I struggled to keep awake, found myself profoundly missing cigarettes and coffee, my two lost addictions. Either of them would have kept my eyes open. But before I had tumbled too far into the world of sleep and dreams, a yowl from the garden jerked me fully awake. I fumbled the binoculars to my eyes, and was disappointed to see that it was merely Snowflake, the white cat, streaking across the front garden like a patch of greenish-white light. She vanished into the woodland to the left of the house and was gone.

I was about to settle myself back down when it occurred to me to wonder what exactly had startled Snowflake so, and I began scanning the middle distance with the binoculars, looking for a huge raccoon, a dog, or a vicious possum. And there was indeed something coming down the driveway toward the house. I could see it through the binoculars, clear as day.

It was the Devil.

I had never seen the Devil before, and, although I had written about him in the past, if pressed would have confessed that I had no belief in him, other than as an imaginary figure, tragic and Miltonian. The figure coming up the driveway was not Milton's Lucifer. It was the Devil.

My heart began to pound in my chest, to pound so hard that it hurt. I hoped it could not see me, that, in a dark house, behind window glass, I was hidden.

The figure flickered and changed as it walked up the drive. One moment it was dark, bull-like, Minotaurish, the next it was slim and female, and the next it was a cat itself, a scarred, huge gray-green wildcat, its face contorted with hate.

There are steps that lead up to my porch, four white wooden steps in need of a coat of paint (I knew they were white, although they were, like everything else, green through my binoculars). At the bottom of the steps, the Devil stopped and called out something that I could not understand, three, perhaps four words in a whining, howling language that must have been old and forgotten when Babylon was young; and, although I did not understand the words, I felt the hairs rise on the back of my head as it called.

And then I heard, muffled through the glass, but still audible, a low growl, a challenge, and—slowly, unsteadily—a black figure walked down the steps of the house, away from me, toward the Devil. These days the Black Cat no longer moved like a panther, instead he stumbled and rocked, like a sailor only recently returned to land.

The Devil was a woman now. She said something soothing and gentle to the cat, in a tongue that sounded like French, and reached out a hand to him. He sank his teeth into her arm, and her lip curled, and she spat at him.

The woman glanced up at me then, and if I had doubted that she was the Devil before, I was certain of it now: the woman's eyes flashed red fire at me, but you can see no red through the night-vision binoculars, only shades of a green. And the Devil saw me, through the window. It saw me. I am in no doubt about that at all.

The Devil twisted and writhed, and now it was some kind of jackal, a flat-faced, huge-headed, bullnecked creature, halfway between a hyena and a dingo. There were maggots squirming in its mangy fur, and it began to walk up the steps.

The Black Cat leapt upon it, and in seconds they became a rolling, writhing thing, moving faster than my eyes could follow.

All this in silence.

And then a low roar—down the country road at the bottom of our drive, in the distance, lumbered a late-night truck, its blazing headlights burning bright as green suns through the binoculars. I lowered them from my eyes and saw only darkness, and the gentle yellow of headlights, and then the red of rear lights as it vanished off again into the nowhere at all.

When I raised the binoculars once more, there was nothing to be seen. Only the Black Cat on the steps, staring up into the air. I trained the binoculars up and saw something flying away—a vulture, perhaps, or an eagle—and then it flew beyond the trees and was gone.

I went out onto the porch, and picked up the Black Cat, and stroked him, and said kind, soothing things to him. He mewled piteously when I first approached him, but, after a while, he went to sleep on my lap, and I put him into his basket, and went upstairs to my bed, to sleep myself. There was dried blood on my T-shirt and jeans, the following morning.

That was a week ago.

The thing that comes to my house does not come every night. But it comes most nights: we know it by the wounds on the cat, and the pain I can see in those leonine eyes. He has lost the use of his front left paw, and his right eye has closed for good.

I wonder what we did to deserve the Black Cat. I wonder who sent him. And, selfish and scared, I wonder how much more he has to give.

How to Talk to Talk to
Girls at Parties

C OME ON," SAID Vic. "It'll be great."

"No, it won't," I said, although I'd lost this fight hours ago, and I knew it.

"It'll be brilliant," said Vic, for the hundredth time. "Girls! Girls! Girls!" He grinned with white teeth.

We both attended an all-boys' school in south London. While it would be a lie to say that we had no experience with girls—Vic seemed to have had many girlfriends, while I had kissed three of my sister's friends—it would, I think, be perfectly true to say that we both chiefly spoke to, interacted with, and only truly understood, other boys. Well, I did, anyway. It's hard to speak for someone else, and I've not seen Vic for thirty years. I'm not sure that I would know what to say to him now if I did.

We were walking the backstreets that used to twine in a grimy maze behind East Croydon station—a friend had told Vic about a party, and Vic was determined to go whether I liked it or not, and I didn't. But my parents were away that week at a conference, and I was Vic's guest at his house, so I was trailing along beside him.

"It'll be the same as it always is," I said. "After an hour you'll be off somewhere snogging the prettiest girl at the party, and I'll be in the kitchen listening to somebody's mum going on about politics or poetry or something."

"You just have to *talk* to them," he said. "I think it's probably that road at the end here." He gestured cheerfully, swinging the bag with the bottle in it.

"Don't you know?"

"Alison gave me directions and I wrote them on a bit of paper, but I left it on the hall table. S'okay. I can find it."

"How?" Hope welled slowly up inside me.

"We walk down the road," he said, as if speaking to an idiot child. "And we look for the party. Easy."

I looked, but saw no party: just narrow houses with rusting cars or bikes in their concreted front gardens; and the dusty glass fronts of newsagents, which smelled of alien spices and sold everything from birthday cards and secondhand comics to the kind of magazines that were so pornographic that they were sold already sealed in plastic bags. I had been there when Vic had slipped one of those magazines beneath his sweater, but the owner caught him on the pavement outside and made him give it back.

We reached the end of the road and turned into a narrow street of terraced houses. Everything looked very still and empty in the summer's evening. "It's all right for you," I said. "They fancy you. You don't actually *have* to talk to them." It was true: one urchin grin from Vic and he could have his pick of the room.

"Nah. S'not like that. You've just got to talk."

The times I had kissed my sister's friends I had not spoken to them. They had been around while my sister was off doing something elsewhere, and they had drifted into my orbit, and so I had kissed them. I do not remember any talking. I did not know what to say to girls, and I told him so.

"They're just girls," said Vic. "They don't come from another planet."

As we followed the curve of the road around, my hopes that the party would prove unfindable began to fade: a low pulsing noise, music muffled by walls and doors, could be heard from a house up ahead. It was eight in the evening, not that early if you aren't yet sixteen, and we weren't. Not quite.

I had parents who liked to know where I was, but I don't think Vic's parents cared that much. He was the youngest of five boys. That in itself seemed magical to me: I merely had two sisters, both younger than I was, and I felt both unique and lonely. I had wanted a brother as far back as I could remember. When I turned thirteen, I stopped wishing on falling stars or first stars, but back when I did, a brother was what I had wished for.

We went up the garden path, crazy paving leading us past a hedge and a solitary rosebush to a pebble-dashed facade. We rang the doorbell, and the door was opened by a girl. I could not have told you how old she was, which was one of the things about girls I had begun to hate: when you start out as kids you're just boys and girls, going through time at the same speed, and you're all five, or seven, or eleven, together. And then one day there's a lurch and the girls just sort of sprint off into the future ahead of you, and they know all about everything, and they have periods and breasts and makeup and God only knew what else—for I certainly didn't. The diagrams in biology textbooks were no substitute for being, in a very real sense, young adults. And the girls of our age were.

Vic and I weren't young adults, and I was beginning to suspect that even when I started needing to shave every day, instead of once every couple of weeks, I would still be way behind.

The girl said, "Hello?"

Vic said, "We're friends of Alison's." We had met Alison, all freckles and orange hair and a wicked smile, in Hamburg, on a German exchange. The exchange organizers had sent some girls with us, from a local girls' school, to balance the sexes. The girls, our age, more or less, were raucous and funny, and had more or less adult boyfriends with cars and jobs and motorbikes and—in the case of one girl with crooked teeth and a raccoon coat, who spoke to me about it sadly at the end of a party in Hamburg, in, of course, the kitchen—a wife and kids.

"She isn't here," said the girl at the door. "No Alison."

"Not to worry," said Vic, with an easy grin. "I'm Vic. This is Enn." A beat, and then the girl smiled back at him. Vic had a bottle of white wine in a plastic bag, removed from his parents' kitchen cabinet. "Where should I put this, then?"

She stood out of the way, letting us enter. "There's a kitchen in the

209

back," she said. "Put it on the table there, with the other bottles." She had golden, wavy hair, and she was very beautiful. The hall was dim in the twilight, but I could see that she was beautiful.

"What's your name, then?" said Vic.

She told him it was Stella, and he grinned his crooked white grin and told her that that had to be the prettiest name he had ever heard. Smooth bastard. And what was worse was that he said it like he meant it.

Vic headed back to drop off the wine in the kitchen, and I looked into the front room, where the music was coming from. There were people dancing in there. Stella walked in, and she started to dance, swaying to the music all alone, and I watched her.

This was during the early days of punk. On our own record players we would play the Adverts and the Jam, the Stranglers and the Clash and the Sex Pistols. At other people's parties you'd hear ELO or 10cc or even Roxy Music. Maybe some Bowie, if you were lucky. During the German exchange, the only LP that we had all been able to agree on was Neil Young's *Harvest,* and his song "Heart of Gold" had threaded through the trip like a refrain: *I crossed the ocean for a heart of gold. . . .*

The music playing in that front room wasn't anything I recognized. It sounded a bit like a German electronic pop group called Kraftwerk, and a bit like an LP I'd been given for my last birthday, of strange sounds made by the BBC Radiophonic Workshop. The music had a beat, though, and the half-dozen girls in that room were moving gently to it, although I only looked at Stella. She shone.

Vic pushed past me, into the room. He was holding a can of lager. "There's booze back in the kitchen," he told me. He wandered over to Stella and he began to talk to her. I couldn't hear what they were saying over the music, but I knew that there was no room for me in that conversation.

I didn't like beer, not back then. I went off to see if there was something I wanted to drink. On the kitchen table stood a large bottle of Coca-Cola, and I poured myself a plastic tumblerful, and I didn't dare say anything to the pair of girls who were talking in the underlit kitchen. They were animated and utterly lovely. Each of them had very black skin and glossy hair and movie star clothes, and their accents were foreign, and each of them was out of my league.

I wandered, Coke in hand.

The house was deeper than it looked, larger and more complex than the two-up two-down model I had imagined. The rooms were underlit—I doubt there was a bulb of more than 40 watts in the building—and each room I went into was inhabited: in my memory, inhabited only by girls. I did not go upstairs.

A girl was the only occupant of the conservatory. Her hair was so fair it was white, and long, and straight, and she sat at the glass-topped table, her hands clasped together, staring at the garden outside, and the gathering dusk. She seemed wistful.

"Do you mind if I sit here?" I asked, gesturing with my cup. She shook her head, and then followed it up with a shrug, to indicate that it was all the same to her. I sat down.

Vic walked past the conservatory door. He was talking to Stella, but he looked in at me, sitting at the table, wrapped in shyness and awkwardness, and he opened and closed his hand in a parody of a speaking mouth. *Talk*. Right.

"Are you from around here?" I asked the girl.

She shook her head. She wore a low-cut silvery top, and I tried not to stare at the swell of her breasts.

I said, "What's your name? I'm Enn."

"Wain's Wain," she said, or something that sounded like it. "I'm a second."

"That's, uh. That's a different name."

She fixed me with huge, liquid eyes. "It indicates that my progenitor was also Wain, and that I am obliged to report back to her. I may not breed."

"Ah. Well. Bit early for that anyway, isn't it?"

She unclasped her hands, raised them above the table, spread her fingers. "You see?" The little finger on her left hand was crooked, and it bifurcated at the top, splitting into two smaller fingertips. A minor deformity. "When I was finished a decision was needed. Would I be retained, or eliminated? I was fortunate that the decision was with me. Now, I travel, while my more perfect sisters remain at home

211

in stasis. They were firsts. I am a second.

"Soon I must return to Wain, and tell her all I have seen. All my impressions of this place of yours."

"I don't actually live in Croydon," I said. "I don't come from here." I wondered if she was American. I had no idea what she was talking about.

"As you say," she agreed, "neither of us comes from here." She folded her six-fingered left hand beneath her right, as if tucking it out of sight. "I had expected it to be bigger, and cleaner, and more colorful. But still, it is a jewel."

She yawned, covered her mouth with her right hand, only for a moment, before putting it back on the table again. "I grow weary of the journeying, and I wish sometimes that it would end. On a street in Río, at Carnival, I saw them on a bridge, golden and tall and insect-eyed and winged, and elated I almost ran to greet them, before I saw that they were only people in costumes. I said to Hola Colt, 'Why do they try so hard to look like us?' and Hola Colt replied, 'Because they hate themselves, all shades of pink and brown, and so small.' It is what I experience, even me, and I am not grown. It is like a world of children, or of elves." Then she smiled, and said, "It was a good thing they could not any of them see Hola Colt."

"Um," I said, "do you want to dance?"

She shook her head immediately. "It is not permitted," she said. "I can do nothing that might cause damage to property. I am Wain's."

"Would you like something to drink, then?"

"Water," she said.

I went back to the kitchen and poured myself another Coke, and filled a cup with water from the tap. From the kitchen back to the hall, and from there into the conservatory, but now it was quite empty.

I wondered if the girl had gone to the toilet, and if she might change her mind about dancing later. I walked back to the front room and stared in. The place was filling up. There were more girls dancing, and several lads I didn't know, who looked a few years older than me and Vic. The lads and the girls all kept their distance, but

Vic was holding Stella's hand as they danced, and when the song ended he put an arm around her, casually, almost proprietorially, to make sure that nobody else cut in.

I wondered if the girl I had been talking to in the conservatory was now upstairs, as she did not appear to be on the ground floor.

I walked into the living room, which was across the hall from the room where the people were dancing, and I sat down on the sofa. There was a girl sitting there already. She had dark hair, cut short and spiky, and a nervous manner.

Talk, I thought. "Um, this mug of water's going spare," I told her, "if you want it?"

She nodded, and reached out her hand and took the mug extremely carefully, as if she were unused to taking things, as if she could trust neither her vision nor her hands.

"I love being a tourist," she said, and smiled hesitantly. She had a gap between her two front teeth, and she sipped the tap water as if she were an adult sipping a fine wine. "The last tour, we went to sun, and we swam in sunfire pools with the whales. We heard their histories and we shivered in the chill of the outer places, then we swam deepward where the heat churned and comforted us.

"I wanted to go back. This time, I wanted it. There was so much I had not seen. Instead we came to world. Do you like it?"

"Like what?"

She gestured vaguely to the room—the sofa, the armchairs, the curtains, the unused gas fire.

"It's all right, I suppose."

"I told them I did not wish to visit world," she said. "My parent-teacher was unimpressed. 'You will have much to learn,' it told me. I said, 'I could learn more in sun, again. Or in the deeps. Jessa spun webs between galaxies. I want to do that.'

"But there was no reasoning with it, and I came to world. Parent-teacher engulfed me, and I was here, embodied in a decaying lump of meat hanging on a frame of calcium. As I incarnated I felt things deep inside me, fluttering and pumping and squishing. It was my first experience with pushing air through the mouth, vibrating the vocal cords on the way, and I used it to tell parent-teacher that I

213

wished that I would die, which it acknowledged was the inevitable exit strategy from world."

There were black worry beads wrapped around her wrist, and she fiddled with them as she spoke. "But knowledge is there, in the meat," she said, "and I am resolved to learn from it."

We were sitting close at the center of the sofa now. I decided I should put an arm around her, but casually. I would extend my arm along the back of the sofa and eventually sort of creep it down, almost imperceptibly, until it was touching her. She said, "The thing with the liquid in the eyes, when the world blurs. Nobody told me, and I still do not understand. I have touched the folds of the Whisper and pulsed and flown with the tachyon swans, and I still do not understand."

She wasn't the prettiest girl there, but she seemed nice enough, and she was a girl, anyway. I let my arm slide down a little, tentatively, so that it made contact with her back, and she did not tell me to take it away.

Vic called to me then, from the doorway. He was standing with his arm around Stella, protectively, waving at me. I tried to let him know, by shaking my head, that I was onto something, but he called my name and, reluctantly, I got up from the sofa and walked over to the door. "What?"

"Er. Look. The party," said Vic apologetically. "It's not the one I thought it was. I've been talking to Stella and I figured it out. Well, she sort of explained it to me. We're at a different party."

"Christ. Are we in trouble? Do we have to go?"

Stella shook her head. He leaned down and kissed her, gently, on the lips. "You're just happy to have me here, aren't you darlin'?"

"You know I am," she told him.

He looked from her back to me, and he smiled his white smile: roguish, lovable, a little bit Artful Dodger, a little bit wide-boy Prince Charming. "Don't worry. They're all tourists here anyway. It's a foreign exchange thing, innit? Like when we all went to Germany."

"It is?"

"Enn. You got to *talk* to them. And that means you got to listen to them, too. You understand?"

"I *did*. I already talked to a couple of them."

"You getting anywhere?"

"I was till you called me over."

"Sorry about that. Look, I just wanted to fill you in. Right?"

And he patted my arm and he walked away with Stella. Then, together, the two of them went up the stairs.

Understand me, all the girls at that party, in the twilight, were lovely; they all had perfect faces but, more important than that, they had whatever strangeness of proportion, of oddness or humanity it is that makes a beauty something more than a shop window dummy. Stella was the most lovely of any of them, but she, of course, was Vic's, and they were going upstairs together, and that was just how things would always be.

There were several people now sitting on the sofa, talking to the gap-toothed girl. Someone told a joke, and they all laughed. I would have had to push my way in there to sit next to her again, and it didn't look like she was expecting me back or cared that I had gone, so I wandered out into the hall. I glanced in at the dancers, and found myself wondering where the music was coming from. I couldn't see a record player or speakers.

From the hall I walked back to the kitchen.

Kitchens are good at parties. You never need an excuse to be there, and, on the good side, at this party I couldn't see any signs of someone's mum. I inspected the various bottles and cans on the kitchen table, then I poured a half an inch of Pernod into the bottom of my plastic cup, which I filled to the top with Coke. I dropped in a couple of ice cubes and took a sip, relishing the sweet-shop tang of the drink.

"What's that you're drinking?" A girl's voice.

"It's Pernod," I told her. "It tastes like aniseed balls, only it's alcoholic." I didn't say that I only tried it because I'd heard someone in the crowd ask for a Pernod on a live Velvet Underground LP.

"Can I have one?" I poured another Pernod, topped it off with Coke, passed it to her. Her hair was a coppery auburn, and it tumbled around her head in ringlets. It's not a hairstyle you see much now, but you saw it a lot back then.

"What's your name?" I asked.

"Triolet," she said.

"Pretty name," I told her, although I wasn't sure that it was. She was pretty, though.

"It's a verse form," she said proudly. "Like me."

"You're a poem?"

She smiled, and looked down and away, perhaps bashfully. Her profile was almost flat—a perfect Grecian nose that came down from her forehead in a straight line. We did *Antigone* in the school theater the previous year. I was the messenger who brings Creon the news of Antigone's death. We wore half-masks that made us look like that. I thought of that play, looking at her face, in the kitchen, and I thought of Barry Smith's drawings of women in the *Conan* comics: five years later I would have thought of the Pre-Raphaelites, of Jane Morris and Lizzie Siddall. But I was only fifteen then.

"You're a poem?" I repeated.

She chewed her lower lip. "If you want. I am a poem, or I am a pattern, or a race of people whose world was swallowed by the sea."

"Isn't it hard to be three things at the same time?"

"What's your name?"

"Enn."

"So you are Enn," she said. "And you are a male. And you are a biped. Is it hard to be three things at the same time?"

"But they aren't different things. I mean, they aren't contradictory." It was a word I had read many times but never said aloud before that night, and I put the stresses in the wrong places. *Con*tradic*tory*.

She wore a thin dress made of a white, silky fabric. Her eyes were a pale green, a color that would now make me think of tinted contact lenses; but this was thirty years ago; things were different then. I remember wondering about Vic and Stella, upstairs. By now, I was sure that they were in one of the bedrooms, and I envied Vic so much it almost hurt.

Still, I was talking to this girl, even if we were talking nonsense, even if her name wasn't really Triolet (my generation had not been given hippie names: all the Rainbows and the Sunshines and the

Moons, they were only six, seven, eight years old back then). She said, "We knew that it would soon be over, and so we put it all into a poem, to tell the universe who we were, and why we were here, and what we said and did and thought and dreamed and yearned for. We wrapped our dreams in words and patterned the words so that they would live forever, unforgettable. Then we sent the poem as a pattern of flux, to wait in the heart of a star, beaming out its message in pulses and bursts and fuzzes across the electromagnetic spectrum, until the time when, on worlds a thousand sun systems distant, the pattern would be decoded and read, and it would become a poem once again."

"And then what happened?"

She looked at me with her green eyes, and it was as if she stared out at me from her own Antigone half-mask; but as if her pale green eyes were just a different, deeper, part of the mask. "You cannot hear a poem without it changing you," she told me. "They heard it, and it colonized them. It inherited them and it inhabited them, its rhythms becoming part of the way that they thought; its images permanently transmuting their metaphors; its verses, its outlook, its aspirations becoming their lives. Within a generation their children would be born already knowing the poem, and, sooner rather than later, as these things go, there were no more children born. There was no need for them, not any longer. There was only a poem, which took flesh and walked and spread itself across the vastness of the known."

I edged closer to her, so I could feel my leg pressing against hers. She seemed to welcome it: she put her hand on my arm, affectionately, and I felt a smile spreading across my face.

"There are places that we are welcomed," said Triolet, "and places where we are regarded as a noxious weed, or as a disease, something immediately to be quarantined and eliminated. But where does contagion end and art begin?"

"I don't know," I said, still smiling. I could hear the unfamiliar music as it pulsed and scattered and boomed in the front room.

She leaned into me then and—I suppose it was a kiss. . . . I suppose. She pressed her lips to my lips, anyway, and then, satisfied, she pulled back, as if she had now marked me as her own.

217

"Would you like to hear it?" she asked, and I nodded, unsure what she was offering me, but certain that I needed anything she was willing to give.

She began to whisper something in my ear. It's the strangest thing about poetry—you can tell it's poetry, even if you don't speak the language. You can hear Homer's Greek without understanding a word, and you still know it's poetry. I've heard Polish poetry, and Inuit poetry, and I knew what it was without knowing. Her whisper was like that. I didn't know the language, but her words washed through me, perfect, and in my mind's eye I saw towers of glass and diamond; and people with eyes of the palest green; and, unstoppable, beneath every syllable, I could feel the relentless advance of the ocean.

Perhaps I kissed her properly. I don't remember. I know I wanted to.

And then Vic was shaking me violently. "Come on!" he was shouting. "Quickly. Come on!"

In my head I began to come back from a thousand miles away.

"Idiot. Come on. Just get a move on," he said, and he swore at me. There was fury in his voice.

For the first time that evening I recognized one of the songs being played in the front room. A sad saxophone wail followed by a cascade of liquid chords, a man's voice singing cut-up lyrics about the sons of the silent age. I wanted to stay and hear the song.

She said, "I am not finished. There is yet more of me."

"Sorry, love," said Vic, but he wasn't smiling any longer. "There'll be another time," and he grabbed me by the elbow and he twisted and pulled, forcing me from the room. I did not resist. I knew from experience that Vic could beat the stuffing out of me if he got it into his head to do so. He wouldn't do it unless he was upset or angry, but he was angry now.

Out into the front hall. As Vic pulled open the door, I looked back one last time, over my shoulder, hoping to see Triolet in the doorway to the kitchen, but she was not there. I saw Stella, though, at the top of the stairs. She was staring down at Vic, and I saw her face.

This all happened thirty years ago. I have forgotten much, and I will forget more, and in the end I will forget everything; yet, if I have any certainty of life beyond death, it is all wrapped up not in psalms or hymns, but in this one thing alone: I cannot believe that I will ever forget that moment, or forget the expression on Stella's face as she watched Vic hurrying away from her. Even in death I shall remember that.

Her clothes were in disarray, and there was makeup smudged across her face, and her eyes—

You wouldn't want to make a universe angry. I bet an angry universe would look at you with eyes like that.

We ran then, me and Vic, away from the party and the tourists and the twilight, ran as if a lightning storm was on our heels, a mad helter-skelter dash down the confusion of streets, threading through the maze, and we did not look back, and we did not stop until we could not breathe; and then we stopped and panted, unable to run any longer. We were in pain. I held on to a wall, and Vic threw up, hard and long, into the gutter.

He wiped his mouth.

"She wasn't a—" He stopped.

He shook his head.

Then he said, "You know . . . I think there's a thing. When you've gone as far as you dare. And if you go any further, you wouldn't be *you* anymore? You'd be the person who'd done *that*? The places you just can't go. . . . I think that happened to me tonight."

I thought I knew what he was saying. "Screw her, you mean?" I said.

He rammed a knuckle hard against my temple, and twisted it violently. I wondered if I was going to have to fight him—and lose—but after a moment he lowered his hand and moved away from me, making a low, gulping noise.

I looked at him curiously, and I realized that he was crying: his face was scarlet; snot and tears ran down his cheeks. Vic was sobbing in the street, as unself-consciously and heartbreakingly as a little boy. He walked away from me then, shoulders heaving, and he hurried down the road so he was in front of me and I could no longer see his face. I wondered what had occurred in that upstairs room to make

219

him behave like that, to scare him so, and I could not even begin to guess.

The streetlights came on, one by one; Vic stumbled on ahead, while I trudged down the street behind him in the dusk, my feet treading out the measure of a poem that, try as I might, I could not properly remember and would never be able to repeat.

SUNBIRD

THEY WERE A rich and a rowdy bunch at the Epicurean Club in those days. They certainly knew how to party. There were five of them:

There was Augustus TwoFeathers McCoy, big enough for three men, who ate enough for four men and who drank enough for five. His great-grandfather had founded the Epicurean Club with the proceeds of a tontine, which he had taken great pains, in the traditional manner, to ensure that he had collected in full.

There was Professor Mandalay, small and twitchy and gray as a ghost (and perhaps he was a ghost; stranger things have happened), who drank nothing but water and who ate doll portions from plates the size of saucers. Still, you do not need the gusto for the gastronomy, and Mandalay always got to the heart of every dish placed in front of him.

There was Virginia Boote, the food and restaurant critic, who had once been a great beauty but was now a grand and magnificent ruin, and who delighted in her ruination.

There was Jackie Newhouse, the descendant (on the left-handed route) of the great lover, gourmand, violinist, and duelist Giacomo Casanova. Jackie Newhouse had, like his notorious ancestor, both broken his share of hearts and eaten his share of great dishes.

And there was Zebediah T. Crawcrustle, who was the only one of the Epicureans who was flat-out broke: he shambled in unshaven from the street when they had their meetings, with half a bottle of rotgut in a brown paper bag, hatless and coatless and, too often, partly shirtless, but he ate with more of an appetite than any of them.

Augustus TwoFeathers McCoy was talking—

"We have eaten everything that can be eaten," said Augustus TwoFeathers McCoy, and there was regret and glancing sorrow in his voice. "We have eaten vulture, mole, and fruit bat."

Mandalay consulted his notebook. "Vulture tasted like rotten pheasant. Mole tasted like carrion slug. Fruit bat tasted remarkably like sweet guinea pig."

"We have eaten kakapo, aye-aye, and giant panda—"

"Oh, that broiled panda steak," sighed Virginia Boote, her mouth watering at the memory.

"We have eaten several long-extinct species," said Augustus TwoFeathers McCoy. "We have eaten flash-frozen mammoth and Patagonian giant sloth."

"If we had but gotten to the mammoth a little faster," sighed Jackie Newhouse. "I could tell why the hairy elephants went so fast, though, once people got a taste of them. I am a man of elegant pleasures, but after only one bite, I found myself thinking only of Kansas City barbecue sauce and what the ribs on those things would be like, if they were fresh."

"Nothing wrong with being on ice for a millennium or two," said Zebediah T. Crawcrustle. He grinned. His teeth may have been crooked, but they were sharp and strong. "Even so, for real taste you had to go for honest-to-goodness mastodon every time. Mammoth was always what people settled for, when they couldn't get mastodon."

"We've eaten squid, and giant squid, and humongous squid," said Augustus TwoFeathers McCoy. "We've eaten lemmings and Tasmanian tigers. We've eaten bowerbird and ortolan and peacock. We've eaten the dolphin fish (which is not the mammal dolphin) and the giant sea turtle and the Sumatran rhino. We've eaten everything there is to eat."

"Nonsense. There are many hundreds of things we have not yet tasted," said Professor Mandalay. "Thousands, perhaps. Think of all the species of beetle there are, still untasted."

"Oh Mandy," sighed Virginia Boote. "When you've tasted one beetle, you've tasted them all. And we all tasted several hundred species. At least the dung beetles had a real kick to them."

"No," said Jackie Newhouse, "that was the dung-beetle balls. The beetles themselves were singularly unexceptional. Still, I take your point. We have scaled the heights of gastronomy, we have plunged down into the depths of gustation. We have become cosmonauts exploring undreamed of worlds of delectation and gourmanderie."

"True, true, true," said Augustus TwoFeathers McCoy. "There has been a meeting of the Epicureans every month for over a hundred and fifty years, in my father's time, and my grandfather's time, and my great-grandfather's time, and now I fear that I must hang it up for there is nothing left that we, or our predecessors in the club, have not eaten."

"I wish I had been here in the twenties," said Virginia Boote, "when they legally had Man on the menu."

"Only after it had been electrocuted," said Zebediah T. Crawcrustle. "Half-fried already it was, all char and crackling. It left none of us with a taste for long pig, save one who was already that way inclined, and he went out pretty soon after that anyway."

"Oh, Crusty, *why* must you pretend that you were there?" asked Virginia Boote, with a yawn. "Anyone can see you aren't that old. You can't be more than sixty, even allowing for the ravages of time and the gutter."

"Oh, they ravage pretty good," said Zebediah T. Crawcrustle. "But not as good as you'd imagine. Anyway there's a host of things we've not eaten yet."

"Name one," said Mandalay, his pencil poised precisely above his notebook.

"Well, there's Suntown Sunbird," said Zebediah T. Crawcrustle. And he grinned his crookedy grin at them, with his teeth ragged but sharp.

"I've never heard of it," said Jackie Newhouse. "You're making it up."

"I've heard of it," said Professor Mandalay, "but in another context. And besides, it is imaginary."

"Unicorns are imaginary," said Virginia Boote, "but, gosh, that unicorn flank tartare was tasty. A little bit horsey, a little bit goatish, and all the better for the capers and raw quail eggs."

"There's something about the Sunbird in one of the minutes of the Epicurean Club from bygone years," said Augustus TwoFeathers McCoy. "But what it was, I can no longer remember."

"Did they say how it tasted?" asked Virginia.

"I do not believe that they did," said Augustus, with a frown. "I would need to inspect the bound proceedings, of course."

"Nah," said Zebediah T. Crawcrustle. "That's only in the charred volumes. You'll never find out about it from there."

Augustus TwoFeathers McCoy scratched his head. He really did have two feathers, which went through the knot of black hair shot with silver at the back of his head, and the feathers had once been golden although by now they were looking kind of ordinary and yellow and ragged. He had been given them when he was a boy.

"Beetles," said Professor Mandalay. "I once calculated that, if a man such as myself were to eat six different species of beetle each day, it would take him more than twenty years to eat every beetle that has been identified. And over that twenty years enough new species of beetle might have been discovered to keep him eating for another five years. And in those five years enough beetles might have been discovered to keep him eating for another two and a half years, and so on, and so on. It is a paradox of inexhaustibility. I call it Mandalay's Beetle. You would have to enjoy eating beetles, though," he added, "or it would be a very bad thing indeed."

"Nothing wrong with eating beetles if they're the right kind of beetle," said Zebediah T. Crawcrustle. "Right now, I've got a hankering on me for lightning bugs. There's a kick from the glow of a lightning bug that might be just what I need."

"While the lightning bug or firefly (*Photinus pyralis*) is more of a beetle than it is a glowworm," said Mandalay, "it is by no stretch of the imagination edible."

"They may not be edible," said Crawcrustle, "but they'll get you into shape for the stuff that is. I think I'll roast me some. Fireflies and habañero peppers. Yum."

Virginia Boote was an eminently practical woman. She said, "Suppose we did want to eat Suntown Sunbird. Where should we start looking for it?"

Zebediah T. Crawcrustle scratched the bristling seventh-day beard that was sprouting on his chin (it never grew any longer than that; seventh-day beards never do). "If it was me," he told them, "I'd head down to Suntown of a noon in midsummer, and I'd find somewhere comfortable to sit—Mustapha Stroheim's coffeehouse, for example—and I'd wait for the Sunbird to come by. Then I'd catch him in the traditional manner, and cook him in the traditional manner as well."

"And what would the traditional manner of catching him be?" asked Jackie Newhouse.

"Why, the same way your famous ancestor poached quails and wood grouse," said Crawcrustle.

"There's nothing in Casanova's memoirs about poaching quail," said Jackie Newhouse.

"Your ancestor was a busy man," said Crawcrustle. "He couldn't be expected to write everything down. But he poached a good quail nonetheless."

"Dried corn and dried blueberries, soaked in whiskey," said Augustus TwoFeathers McCoy. "That's how my folk always did it."

"And that was how Casanova did it," said Crawcrustle, "although he used barley grains mixed with raisins, and he soaked the raisins in brandy. He taught me himself."

Jackie Newhouse ignored this statement. It was easy to ignore much that Zebediah T. Crawcrustle said. Instead, Jackie Newhouse asked, "And where is Mustapha Stroheim's coffeehouse in Suntown?"

"Why, where it always is, third lane after the old market in the Suntown district, just before you reach the old drainage ditch that was once an irrigation canal, and if you find yourself outside One-eye Khayam's carpet shop you have gone too far," began Crawcrustle. "But I see by the expressions of irritation upon your faces that you were expecting a less succinct, less accurate description. Very well. It is in Suntown, and Suntown is in Cairo, in Egypt, where it always is, or almost always."

"And who will pay for an expedition to Suntown?" asked Augustus TwoFeathers McCoy. "And who will be on this expedition? I ask the question although I already know the answer, and I do not like it."

"Why, you will pay for it, Augustus, and we will all come," said Zebediah T. Crawcrustle. "You can deduct it from our Epicurean membership dues. And I shall bring my chef's apron and my cooking utensils."

Augustus knew that Crawcrustle had not paid his Epicurean Club membership in much too long a time, but the Epicurean Club would cover him; Crawcrustle had been a member of the Epicureans in Augustus's father's day. He simply said, "And when shall we leave?"

Crawcrustle fixed him with a mad old eye and shook his head in disappointment. "Why, Augustus," he said. "We're going to Suntown, to catch the Sunbird. When else should we leave?"

"Sunday!" sang Virginia Boote. "Darlings, we'll leave on a Sunday!"

"There's hope for you yet, young lady," said Zebediah T. Crawcrustle. "We shall leave Sunday indeed. Three Sundays from now. And we shall travel to Egypt. We shall spend several days hunting and trapping the elusive Sunbird of Suntown, and, finally, we shall deal with it in the traditional way."

Professor Mandalay blinked a small gray blink. "But," he said, "I am teaching a class on Monday. On Mondays I teach mythology, on Tuesdays I teach tap dancing, and on Wednesdays, woodwork."

"Get a teaching assistant to take your course, Mandalay, O Mandalay. On Monday you'll be hunting the Sunbird," said Zebediah T. Crawcrustle. "And how many other professors can say that?"

They went, one by one, to see Crawcrustle, in order to discuss the journey ahead of them, and to announce their misgivings.

Zebediah T. Crawcrustle was a man of no fixed abode. Still, there were places he could be found, if you were of a mind to find him. In the early mornings he slept in the bus terminal, where the benches were comfortable and the transport police were inclined to let him lie; in the heat of the afternoons he hung in the park by the statues of long-forgotten generals, with the dipsos and the winos and the

228

hopheads, sharing their company and the contents of their bottles, and offering his opinion, which was, as that of an Epicurean, always considered and always respected, if not always welcomed.

Augustus TwoFeathers McCoy sought out Crawcrustle in the park; he had with him his daughter, Hollyberry NoFeathers McCoy. She was small, but she was sharp as a shark's tooth.

"You know," said Augustus, "there is something very familiar about this."

"About what?" asked Zebediah.

"All of this. The expedition to Egypt. The Sunbird. It seemed to me like I heard about it before."

Crawcrustle merely nodded. He was crunching something from a brown paper bag.

Augustus said, "I went to the bound annals of the Epicurean Club, and I looked it up. And there was what I took to be a reference to the Sunbird in the index for forty years ago, but I was unable to learn anything more."

"And why was that?" asked Zebediah T. Crawcrustle, swallowing noisily.

Augustus TwoFeathers McCoy sighed. "I found the relevant page in the annals," he said, "but it was burned away, and afterward there was some great confusion in the administration of the Epicurean Club."

"You're eating lightning bugs from a paper bag," said Hollyberry NoFeathers McCoy. "I seen you doing it."

"I am indeed, little lady," said Zebediah T. Crawcrustle.

"Do you remember the days of great confusion, Crawcrustle?" asked Augustus.

"I do indeed," said Crawcrustle. "And I remember you. You were only the age that young Hollyberry is now. But there is always confusion, Augustus, and then there is no confusion. It is like the rising and the setting of the sun."

Jackie Newhouse and Professor Mandalay found Crawcrustle that evening, behind the railroad tracks. He was roasting something in a tin can over a small charcoal fire.

"What are you roasting, Crawcrustle?" asked Jackie Newhouse.

"More charcoal," said Crawcrustle. "Cleans the blood, purifies the spirit."

There was basswood and hickory, cut up into little chunks at the bottom of the can, all black and smoking.

"And will you actually eat this charcoal, Crawcrustle?" asked Professor Mandalay.

In response, Crawcrustle licked his fingers and picked out a lump of charcoal from the can. It hissed and fizzed in his grip.

"A fine trick," said Professor Mandalay. "That's how fire-eaters do it, I believe."

Crawcrustle popped the charcoal into his mouth and crunched it between his ragged old teeth. "It is indeed," he said. "It is indeed."

Jackie Newhouse cleared his throat. "The truth of the matter is," he said, "Professor Mandalay and I have deep misgivings about the journey that lies ahead."

Zebediah merely crunched his charcoal. "Not hot enough," he said. He took a stick from the fire and nibbled off the orange-hot tip of it. "That's good," he said.

"It's all an illusion," said Jackie Newhouse.

"Nothing of the sort," said Zebediah T. Crawcrustle primly. "It's prickly elm."

"I have extreme misgivings about all this," said Jackie Newhouse. "My ancestors and I have a finely tuned sense of personal preservation, one that has often left us shivering on roofs and hiding in rivers—one step away from the law, or from gentlemen with guns and legitimate grievances—and that sense of self-preservation is telling me not to go to Suntown with you."

"I am an academic," said Professor Mandalay, "and thus have no finely developed senses that would be comprehensible to anyone who has not ever needed to grade papers without actually reading the blessed things. Still, I find the whole thing remarkably suspicious. If this Sunbird is so tasty, why have I not heard of it?"

"You have, Mandy old fruit. You have," said Zebediah T. Crawcrustle.

"And I am, in addition, an expert on geographical features from Tulsa, Oklahoma, to Timbuktu," continued Professor Mandalay. "Yet

I have never seen a mention in any book of a place called Suntown in Cairo."

"Seen it mentioned? Why, you've taught it," said Crawcrustle, and he doused a lump of smoking charcoal with hot pepper sauce before popping it in his mouth and chomping it down.

"I don't believe you're really eating that," said Jackie Newhouse. "But even being around the trick of it is making me uncomfortable. I think it is time that I was elsewhere."

And he left. Perhaps Professor Mandalay left with him: that man was so gray and so ghostie it was always a toss-up whether he was there or not.

Virginia Boote tripped over Zebediah T. Crawcrustle while he rested in her doorway, in the small hours of the morning. She was returning from a restaurant she had needed to review. She got out of a taxi, tripped over Crawcrustle, and went sprawling. She landed nearby. "Whee!" she said. "That was some trip, wasn't it?"

"Indeed it was, Virginia," said Zebediah T. Crawcrustle. "You would not happen to have such a thing as a box of matches on you, would you?"

"I have a book of matches on me somewhere," she said, and she began to rummage in her purse, which was very large and very brown. "Here you are."

Zebediah T. Crawcrustle was carrying a bottle of purple methylated spirits, which he proceeded to pour into a plastic cup.

"Meths?" said Virginia Boote. "Somehow you never struck me as a meths drinker, Zebby."

"Nor am I," said Crawcrustle. "Foul stuff. It rots the guts and spoils the taste buds. But I could not find any lighter fluid at this time of night."

He lit a match, then dipped it near the surface of the cup of spirits, which began to burn with a flickery light. He ate the match. Then he gargled with the flaming liquid, and blew a sheet of flame into the street, incinerating a sheet of newspaper as it blew by.

"Crusty," said Virginia Boote, "that's a good way to get yourself killed."

Zebediah T. Crawcrustle grinned through black teeth. "I don't actually drink it," he told her. "I just gargle and breathe it out."

"You're playing with fire," she warned him.

"That's how I know I'm alive," said Zebediah T. Crawcrustle.

Virginia said, "Oh, Zeb. I *am* excited. I am so excited. What do you think the Sunbird tastes like?"

"Richer than quail and moister than turkey, fatter than ostrich and lusher than duck," said Zebediah T. Crawcrustle. "Once eaten it's never forgotten."

"We're going to Egypt," she said. "I've never been to Egypt." Then she said, "Do you have anywhere to stay the night?"

He coughed, a small cough that rattled around in his old chest. "I'm getting too old to sleep in doorways and gutters," he said. "Still, I have my pride."

"Well," she said, looking at the man, "you could sleep on my sofa."

"It is not that I am not grateful for the offer," he said, "but there is a bench in the bus station that has my name on it."

And he pushed himself away from the wall and tottered majestically down the street.

There really *was* a bench in the bus station that had his name on it. He had donated the bench to the bus station back when he was flush, and his name was attached to the back of it, engraved upon a small brass plaque. Zebediah T. Crawcrustle was not always poor. Sometimes he was rich, but he had difficulty in holding on to his wealth, and whenever he had become wealthy he discovered that the world frowned on rich men eating in hobo jungles at the back of the railroad, or consorting with the winos in the park, so he would fritter his wealth away as best he could. There were always little bits of it here and there that he had forgotten about, and sometimes he would forget that he did not like being rich, and then he would set out again and seek his fortune, and find it.

He had needed a shave for a week, and the hairs of his seven-day beard were starting to come through snow white.

They left for Egypt on a Sunday, the Epicureans. There were five of them there, and Hollyberry NoFeathers McCoy waved good-bye to them at the airport. It was a very small airport, which still permitted waves good-bye.

232

"Good-bye, Father!" called Hollyberry NoFeathers McCoy.

Augustus TwoFeathers McCoy waved back at her as they walked along the asphalt to the little prop plane, which would begin the first leg of their journey.

"It seems to me," said Augustus TwoFeathers McCoy, "that I remember, albeit dimly, a day like this long, long ago. I was a small boy, in that memory, waving good-bye. I believe it was the last time I saw my father, and I am struck once more with a sudden presentiment of doom." He waved one last time at the small child at the other end of the field, and she waved back at him.

"You waved just as enthusiastically back then," agreed Zebediah T. Crawcrustle, "but I think she waves with slightly more aplomb."

It was true. She did.

They took a small plane and then a larger plane, then a smaller plane, a blimp, a gondola, a train, a hot-air balloon, and a rented Jeep.

They rattled through Cairo in the Jeep. They passed the old market, and they turned off on the third lane they came to (if they had continued on they would have come to a drainage ditch that was once an irrigation canal). Mustapha Stroheim himself was sitting outside in the street, perched on an elderly wicker chair. All of the tables and chairs were on the side of the street, and it was not a particularly wide street.

"Welcome, my friends, to my *kahwa*," said Mustapha Stroheim. "*Kahwa* is Egyptian for café or for coffeehouse. Would you like tea? Or a game of dominoes?"

"We would like to be shown to our rooms," said Jackie Newhouse.

"Not me," said Zebediah T. Crawcrustle. "I'll sleep in the street. It's warm enough, and that doorstep over there looks mighty comfortable."

"I'll have coffee, please," said Augustus TwoFeathers McCoy.

"Of course."

"Do you have water?" asked Professor Mandalay.

"Who said that?" said Mustapha Stroheim. "Oh, it was you, little gray man. My mistake. When I first saw you I thought you were someone's shadow."

"I will have *shay sokkar bosta*," said Virginia Boote, which is a glass of hot tea with the sugar on the side. "And I will play backgammon with anyone who wishes to take me on. There's not a soul in Cairo I cannot beat at backgammon, if I can remember the rules."

Augustus TwoFeathers McCoy was shown to his room. Professor Mandalay was shown to his room. Jackie Newhouse was shown to his room. This was not a lengthy procedure; they were all in the same room, after all. There was another room in the back where Virginia would sleep, and a third room for Mustapha Stroheim and his family.

"What's that you're writing?" asked Jackie Newhouse.

"It's the procedures, annals, and minutes of the Epicurean Club," said Professor Mandalay. He was writing in a large leather-bound book with a small black pen. "I have chronicled our journey here, and all the things that we have eaten on the way. I shall keep writing as we eat the Sunbird, to record for posterity all the tastes and textures, all the smells and the juices."

"Did Crawcrustle say how he was going to cook the Sunbird?" asked Jackie Newhouse.

"He did," said Augustus TwoFeathers McCoy. "He says that he will drain a beer can, so it is only a third full. And then he will add herbs and spices to the beer can. He will stand the bird up on the can, with the can in its inner cavity, and place it up on the barbecue to roast. He says it is the traditional way."

Jackie Newhouse sniffed. "It sounds suspiciously modern to me."

"Crawcrustle says it is the traditional method of cooking the Sunbird," repeated Augustus.

"Indeed I did," said Crawcrustle, coming up the stairs. It was a small building. The stairs weren't that far away, and the walls were not thick ones. "The oldest beer in the world is Egyptian beer, and they've been cooking the Sunbird with it for over five thousand years now."

"But the beer can is a relatively modern invention," said Professor Mandalay, as Zebediah T. Crawcrustle came through the door. Crawcrustle was holding a cup of Turkish coffee, black as tar, which steamed like a kettle and bubbled like a tar pit.

"That coffee looks pretty hot," said Augustus TwoFeathers McCoy.

Crawcrustle knocked back the cup, draining half the contents. "Nah," he said. "Not really. And the beer can isn't really that new an invention. We used to make them out of an amalgam of copper and tin in the old days, sometimes with a little silver in there, sometimes not. It depended on the smith, and what he had to hand. You needed something that would stand up to the heat. I see that you are all looking at me doubtfully. Gentlemen, consider: of course the ancient Egyptians made beer cans; where else would they have kept their beer?"

From outside the window, at the tables in the street, came a wailing, in many voices. Virginia Boote had persuaded the locals to start playing backgammon for money, and she was cleaning them out. That woman was a backgammon shark.

Out back of Mustapha Stroheim's coffeehouse there was a courtyard containing a broken-down old barbecue, made of clay bricks and a half-melted metal grating, and an old wooden table. Crawcrustle spent the next day rebuilding the barbecue and cleaning it, oiling down the metal grille.

"That doesn't look like it's been used in forty years," said Virginia Boote. Nobody would play backgammon with her any longer, and her purse bulged with grubby piasters.

"Something like that," said Crawcrustle. "Maybe a little more. Here, Ginnie, make yourself useful. I've written a list of things I need from the market. It's mostly herbs and spices and wood chips. You can take one of the children of Mustapha Stroheim to translate for you."

"My pleasure, Crusty."

The other three members of the Epicurean Club were occupying themselves in their own way. Jackie Newhouse was making friends with many of the people of the area, who were attracted by his elegant suits and his skill at playing the violin. Augustus TwoFeathers McCoy went for long walks. Professor Mandalay spent time translating the hieroglyphics he had noticed were incised upon the clay bricks in the barbecue. He said that a foolish man might believe that they proved the barbecue in Mustapha Stroheim's backyard was once sacred to the Sun. "But I, who am an intelligent man," he said, "I see immediately that what has happened is that bricks that were once, long ago, part of a temple, have, over the millennia, been reused. I doubt that these people know the value of what they have here."

"Oh, they know all right," said Zebediah T. Crawcrustle. "And these bricks weren't part of any temple. They've been right here for five thousand years, since we built the barbecue. Before that we made do with stones."

Virginia Boote returned with a filled shopping basket. "Here," she said. "Red sandalwood and patchouli, vanilla beans, lavender twigs and sage and cinnamon leaves, whole nutmegs, garlic bulbs, cloves, and rosemary: everything you wanted and more."

Zebediah T. Crawcrustle grinned with delight. "The Sunbird will be so happy," he told her.

He spent the afternoon preparing a barbecue sauce. He said it was only respectful, and besides, the Sunbird's flesh was often slightly on the dry side.

The Epicureans spent that evening sitting at the wicker tables in the street out front, while Mustapha Stroheim and his family brought them tea and coffee and hot mint drinks. Zebediah T. Crawcrustle had told the Epicureans that they would be having the Sunbird of Suntown for Sunday lunch, and that they might wish to avoid food the night before, to ensure that they had an appetite.

"I have a presentiment of doom upon me," said Augustus Two-Feathers McCoy that night, in a bed that was far too small for him, before he slept. "And I fear it shall come to us with barbecue sauce."

They were all so hungry the following morning. Zebediah T. Crawcrustle had a comedic apron on, with the words kiss the cook written upon it in violently green letters. He had already sprinkled the brandy-soaked raisins and grain beneath the stunted avocado tree behind the house, and he was arranging the scented woods, the herbs, and the spices on the bed of charcoal. Mustapha Stroheim and his family had gone to visit relatives on the other side of Cairo.

"Does anybody have a match?" Crawcrustle asked.

Jackie Newhouse pulled out a Zippo lighter, and passed it to Crawcrustle, who lit the dried cinnamon leaves and dried laurel leaves beneath the charcoal. The smoke drifted up into the noon air.

"The cinnamon and sandalwood smoke will bring the Sunbird," said Crawcrustle.

"Bring it from where?" asked Augustus TwoFeathers McCoy.

"From the Sun," said Crawcrustle. "That's where he sleeps."

Professor Mandalay coughed discreetly. He said, "The Earth is, at its closest, ninety-one million miles from the Sun. The fastest dive by a bird ever recorded is that of the peregrine falcon, at two hundred and seventy-three miles per hour. Flying at that speed, from the Sun, it would take a bird a little over thirty-eight years to reach us—if it could fly through the dark and cold and vacuum of space, of course."

"Of course," agreed Zebediah T. Crawcrustle. He shaded his eyes and squinted and looked upward. "Here it comes," he said.

It looked almost as if the bird was flying out of the sun; but that could not have been the case. You could not look directly at the noonday sun, after all.

First it was a silhouette, black against the sun and against the blue sky, then the sunlight caught its feathers, and the watchers on the ground caught their breath. You have never seen anything like sunlight on the Sunbird's feathers; seeing something like that would take your breath away.

The Sunbird flapped its wide wings once, then it began to glide in ever-decreasing circles in the air above Mustapha Stroheim's coffeehouse.

The bird landed in the avocado tree. Its feathers were golden, and purple, and silver. It was smaller than a turkey, larger than a rooster, and had the long legs and high head of a heron, though its head was more like the head of an eagle.

"It is very beautiful," said Virginia Boote. "Look at the two tall feathers on its head. Aren't they lovely?"

"It is indeed quite lovely," said Professor Mandalay.

"There is something familiar about that bird's headfeathers," said Augustus TwoFeathers McCoy.

"We pluck the headfeathers before we roast the bird," said

Zebediah T. Crawcrustle. "It's the way it's always done."

The Sunbird perched on a branch of the avocado tree, in a patch of sun. It seemed almost as if it were glowing, gently, in the sunlight, as if its feathers were made of sunlight, iridescent with purples and greens and golds. It preened itself, extending one wing in the sunlight. It nibbled and stroked at the wing with its beak until all the feathers were in their correct position, and oiled. Then it extended the other wing, and repeated the process. Finally, the bird emitted a contented chirrup, and flew the short distance from the branch to the ground.

It strutted across the dried mud, peering from side to side short-sightedly.

"Look!" said Jackie Newhouse. "It's found the grain."

"It seemed almost that it was looking for it," said Augustus TwoFeathers McCoy. "That it was expecting the grain to be there."

"That's where I always leave it," said Zebediah T. Crawcrustle.

"It's so lovely," said Virginia Boote. "But now I see it closer, I can see that it's much older than I thought. Its eyes are cloudy and its legs are shaking. But it's still lovely."

"The Bennu bird is the loveliest of birds," said Zebediah T. Crawcrustle.

Virginia Boote spoke good restaurant Egyptian, but beyond that she was all at sea. "What's a Bennu bird?" she asked. "Is that Egyptian for Sunbird?"

"The Bennu bird," said Professor Mandalay, "roosts in the Persea tree. It has two feathers on its head. It is sometimes represented as being like a heron, and sometimes like an eagle. There is more, but it is too unlikely to bear repeating."

"It's eaten the grain and the raisins!" exclaimed Jackie Newhouse. "Now it's stumbling drunkenly from side to side—such majesty, even in its drunkenness!"

Zebediah T. Crawcrustle walked over to the Sunbird, which, with a great effort of will, was staggering back and forth on the mud beneath the avocado tree, not tripping over its long legs. He stood directly in front of the bird, and then, very slowly, he bowed to it. He bent like an extremely old man, slowly and creakily, but still he bowed. And the Sunbird bowed back to him, then it toppled to the mud. Zebediah T. Crawcrustle picked it up reverently, and placed it in his arms, carrying it as one would carry a child, and he took it back to the plot of land behind Mustapha Stroheim's coffeehouse, and the others followed him.

First he plucked the two majestic headfeathers, and set them aside.

And then, without plucking the bird, he gutted it, and placed the guts on the smoking twigs. He put the half-filled beer can inside the body cavity, and placed the bird upon the barbecue.

"Sunbird cooks fast," warned Crawcrustle. "Get your plates ready."

The beers of the ancient Egyptians were flavored with cardamom and coriander, for the Egyptians had no hops; their beers were rich and flavorsome and thirst quenching. You could build pyramids after drinking that beer, and sometimes people did. On the barbecue the beer steamed the inside of the Sunbird, keeping it moist. As the heat of the charcoal reached them, the feathers of the bird burned off, igniting with a flash like a magnesium flare, so bright that the Epicureans were forced to avert their eyes.

The smell of roast fowl filled the air, richer than peacock, lusher than duck. The mouths of the assembled Epicureans began to water. It seemed like it had been cooking for no time at all, but Zebediah lifted the Sunbird from the charcoal bed and put it on the table. Then, with a carving knife, he sliced it up and placed the steaming meat on the plates. He poured a little barbecue sauce over each piece of meat. He placed the carcass directly onto the flames.

Each member of the Epicurean Club sat in the back of Mustapha Stroheim's coffeehouse, sat around an elderly wooden table, and they ate with their fingers.

"Zebby, this is amazing!" said Virginia Boote, talking as she ate. "It melts in your mouth. It tastes like heaven."

"It tastes like the sun," said Augustus TwoFeathers McCoy, putting his food away as only a big man can. He had a leg in one hand, and some breast in the other. "It is the finest thing I have ever eaten, and I do not regret eating it, but I do believe that I shall miss my daughter."

"It is perfect," said Jackie Newhouse. "It tastes like love and fine music. It tastes like truth."

Professor Mandalay was scribbling in the bound annals of the Epicurean Club. He was recording his reaction to the meat of the bird, and recording the reactions of the other Epicureans, and trying not to drip on the page while he wrote, for with the hand that was not writing he was holding a wing, and, fastidiously, he was nibbling the meat off it.

"It is strange," said Jackie Newhouse, "for as I eat it, it gets hotter and hotter in my mouth and in my stomach."

"Yup. It'll do that. It's best to prepare for it ahead of time," said Zebediah T. Crawcrustle. "Eat coals and flames and lightning bugs to get used to it. Otherwise it can be a trifle hard on the system."

Zebediah T. Crawcrustle was eating the head of the bird, crunching its bones and beak in his mouth. As he ate, the bones sparked small lightnings against his teeth. He just grinned and chewed the more.

The bones of the Sunbird's carcass burned orange on the barbecue, and then they began to burn white. There was a thick heat haze in the courtyard at the back of Mustapha Stroheim's coffeehouse, and in it everything shimmered, as if the people around the table were seeing the world through water or a dream.

"It is so good!" said Virginia Boote as she ate. "It is the best thing I have ever eaten. It tastes like my youth. It tastes like forever." She licked her fingers, then picked up the last slice of meat from her plate. "The Sunbird of Suntown," she said. "Does it have another name?"

"It is the Phoenix of Heliopolis," said Zebediah T. Crawcrustle. "It is the bird that dies in ashes and flame, and is born again, generation after generation. It is the Bennu bird, which flew across the waters when all was dark. When its time is come it is burned on the fire of rare woods and spices and herbs, and in the ashes it is reborn, time after time, world without end."

"Fire!" exclaimed Professor Mandalay. "It feels as if my insides are burning up!" He sipped his water, but seemed no happier.

"My fingers," said Virginia Boote. "Look at my fingers." She held them up. They were glowing inside, as if lit with inner flames.

Now the air was so hot you could have baked an egg in it.

There was a spark and a sputter. The two yellow feathers in Augustus TwoFeathers McCoy's hair went up like sparklers. "Crawcrustle," said Jackie Newhouse, aflame, "answer me truly. How long have you been eating the Phoenix?"

"A little over ten thousand years," said Zebediah. "Give or take a few thousand. It's not hard, once you master the trick of it; it's just mastering the trick of it that's hard. But this is the best Phoenix I've ever prepared. Or do I mean, 'This is the best I've ever cooked this Phoenix'?"

"The years!" said Virginia Boote. "They are burning off you!"

"They do that," admitted Zebediah. "You've got to get used to the heat, though, before you eat it. Otherwise you can just burn away."

"Why did I not remember this?" said Augustus TwoFeathers McCoy, through the bright flames that surrounded him. "Why did I not remember that this was how my father went, and his father before him, that each of them went to Heliopolis to eat the Phoenix? And why do I only remember it now?"

"Because the years are burning off you," said Professor Mandalay. He had closed the leather book as soon as the page he had been writing on caught fire. The edges of the book were charred, but the rest of the book would be fine. "When the years burn, the memories of those years come back." He looked more solid now, through the wavering burning air, and he was smiling. None of them had ever seen Professor Mandalay smile before.

"Shall we burn away to nothing?" asked Virginia, now incandescent. "Or shall we burn back to childhood and burn back to ghosts and angels and then come forward again? It does not matter. Oh Crusty, this is all such *fun!*"

"Perhaps," said Jackie Newhouse, through the fire, "there might have been a little more vinegar in the sauce. I feel a meat like this could have dealt with something more robust." And then he was gone, leaving only an afterimage.

"Chacun à son goût," said Zebediah T. Crawcrustle, which is French for "each to his own taste," and he licked his fingers and he shook his

head. "Best it's ever been," he said, with enormous satisfaction.

"Good-bye, Crusty," said Virginia. She put her flame-white hand out, and held his dark hand tightly for one moment, or perhaps for two.

And then there was nothing in the courtyard back of Mustapha Stroheim's *kahwa* (or coffeehouse) in Heliopolis (which was once the city of the Sun, and is now a suburb of Cairo) but white ash, which blew up in the momentary breeze, and settled like powdered sugar or like snow; and nobody there but a young man with dark, dark hair and even, ivory-colored teeth, wearing an apron that said KISS THE COOK.

A tiny golden-purple bird stirred in the thick bed of ashes on top of the clay bricks, as if it were waking for the first time. It made a high-pitched *peep!* and it looked directly into the sun, as an infant looks at a parent. It stretched its wings as if to dry them, and, eventually, when it was quite ready, it flew upward, toward the sun, and nobody watched it leave but the young man in the courtyard.

There were two long golden feathers at the young man's feet, beneath the ash that had once been a wooden table, and he gathered them up, and brushed the white ash from them and placed them, reverently, inside his jacket. Then he removed his apron, and he went upon his way.

Hollyberry TwoFeathers McCoy is a grown woman, with children of her own. There are silver hairs on her head, in there with the black, beneath the golden feathers in the bun at the back. You can see that once the feathers must have looked pretty special, but that would have been a long time ago. She is the president of the Epicurean Club—a rich and rowdy bunch—having inherited the position, many long years ago, from her father.

I hear that the Epicureans are beginning to grumble once again. They are saying that they have eaten everything.

(For HMG—a belated birthday present)

242

THE WITCH'S
HEADSTONE

THERE WAS A witch buried at the edge of the graveyard; it was common knowledge. Bod had been told to keep away from that corner of the world by Mrs. Owens as far back as he could remember.

"Why?" he asked.

"'Tain't healthy for a living body," said Mrs. Owens. "There's damp down that end of things. It's practically a marsh. You'll catch your death."

Mr. Owens himself was more evasive and less imaginative. "It's not a good place" was all he said.

The graveyard proper ended at the bottom of the hill, beneath the old apple tree, with a fence of rust-brown iron railings, each topped with a small, rusting spearhead, but there was a wasteland beyond that, a mass of nettles and weeds, of brambles and autumnal rubbish, and Bod, who was a good boy, on the whole, and obedient, did not push between the railings, but he went down there and looked through. He knew he wasn't being told the whole story, and it irritated him.

Bod went back up the hill, to the abandoned church in the middle of the graveyard, and he waited until it got dark. As twilight edged from gray to purple there was a noise in the spire, like a fluttering of heavy velvet, and Silas left his resting place in the belfry and clambered headfirst down the spire.

"What's in the far corner of the graveyard," asked Bod. "Past Harrison Westwood, Baker of this Parish, and his wives, Marion and Joan?"

"Why do you ask?" said his guardian, brushing the dust from his black suit with ivory fingers.

Bod shrugged. "Just wondered."

"It's unconsecrated ground," said Silas. "Do you know what that means?"

"Not really," said Bod.

Silas walked across the path without disturbing a fallen leaf, and sat down on the stone bench, beside Bod. "There are those," he said in his silken voice, "who believe that all land is sacred. That it is sacred before we come to it, and sacred after. But here, in your land, they bless the churches and the ground they set aside to bury people in, to make it holy. But they leave land unconsecrated beside the sacred ground, potter's fields to bury the criminals and the suicides or those who were not of the faith."

"So the people buried in the ground on the other side of the fence are bad people?"

Silas raised one perfect eyebrow. "Mm? Oh, not at all. Let's see, it's been a while since I've been down that way. But I don't remember anyone particularly evil. Remember, in days gone by you could be hanged for stealing a shilling. And there are always people who find their lives have become so unsupportable they believe the best thing they could do would be to hasten their transition to another plane of existence."

"They kill themselves, you mean?" said Bod. He was about eight years old, wide-eyed and inquisitive, and he was not stupid.

"Indeed."

"Does it work? Are they happier dead?"

Silas grinned so wide and sudden that he showed his fangs. "Sometimes. Mostly, no. It's like the people who believe they'll be happy if they go and live somewhere else, but who learn it doesn't work that way. Wherever you go, you take yourself with you. If you see what I mean."

"Sort of," said Bod.

Silas reached down and ruffled the boy's hair.

Bod said, "What about the witch?"

"Yes. Exactly," said Silas. "Suicides, criminals, and witches. Those who died unshriven." He stood up, a midnight shadow in the twilight. "All this talking," he said, "and I have not even had my breakfast. While you will be late for lessons." In the twilight of the graveyard there was a silent implosion, a flutter of velvet darkness, and Silas was gone.

The moon had begun to rise by the time Bod reached Mr. Pennyworth's mausoleum, and Thomes Pennyworth (*here he lyes in the certainty of the moft glorious refurrection*) was already waiting, and was not in the best of moods.

"You are late," he said.

"Sorry, Mr. Pennyworth."

Pennyworth tutted. The previous week Mr. Pennyworth had been teaching Bod about Elements and Humors, and Bod had kept forgetting which was which. He was expecting a test, but instead Mr. Pennyworth said, "I think it is time to spend a few days on practical matters. Time is passing, after all."

"Is it?" asked Bod.

"I am afraid so, young Master Owens. Now, how is your Fading?"

Bod had hoped he would not be asked that question.

"It's all right," he said. "I mean. You know."

"No, Master Owens. I do not know. Why do you not demonstrate for me?"

Bod's heart sank. He took a deep breath, and did his best, squinching up his eyes and trying to fade away.

Mr. Pennyworth was not impressed.

"Pah. That's not the kind of thing. Not the kind of thing at all. Slipping and fading, boy, the way of the dead. Slip through shadows. Fade from awareness. Try again."

Bod tried harder.

"You're as plain as the nose on your face," said Mr. Pennyworth. "And your nose is remarkably obvious. As is the rest of your face, young man. As are you. For the sake of all that is holy, empty your mind. Now. You are an empty alleyway. You are a vacant doorway. You are nothing. Eyes will not see you. Minds will not hold you. Where you are is nothing and nobody."

Bod tried again. He closed his eyes and imagined himself fading into the stained stonework of the mausoleum wall, becoming a shadow on the night and nothing more. He sneezed.

"Dreadful," said Mr. Pennyworth with a sigh. "Quite dreadful. I believe I shall have a word with your guardian about this." He shook his head. "So. The humors. List them."

"Um. Sanguine. Choleric. Phlegmatic. And the other one. Um, Melancholic, I think."

And so it went, until it was time for Grammar and Composition with Miss Letitia Borrows, Spinster of this Parish (*Who Did No Harm to No Man all the Dais of Her Life. Reader, Can You Say Lykewise?*). Bod liked Miss Borrows, and the coziness of her little crypt, and that she could all too easily be led off the subject.

"They say there's a witch in the uncons—unconsecrated ground," he said.

"Yes, dear. But you don't want to go over there."

"Why not?"

Miss Borrows smiled the guileless smile of the dead. "They aren't our sort of people," she said.

"But it *is* the graveyard, isn't it? I mean, I'm allowed to go there if I want to?"

"That," said Miss Borrows, "would not be advisable."

Bod was obedient but curious, and so, when lessons were done for the night, he walked past Harrison Westwood, Baker, and family's memorial, a broken-headed angel, but did not climb down the hill to the potter's field. Instead he walked up the side of the hill to where a picnic some thirty years before had left its mark in the shape of a large apple tree.

There were some lessons that Bod had mastered. He had eaten a bellyful of unripe apples, sour and white-pipped, from the tree some years before, and had regretted it for days, his guts cramping and painful while Mrs. Owens lectured him on what not to eat. Now he waited until the apples were ripe before eating them, and never ate more than two or three a night. He had finished the last of the apples the week before, but he liked the apple tree as a place to think.

He edged up the trunk, to his favorite place in the crook of two branches, and looked down at the potter's field below him, a brambly patch of weeds and unmown grass in the moonlight. He wondered whether the witch would be old and iron-toothed and travel in a house on chicken legs, or whether she would be thin and sharp-nosed and carry a broomstick.

And then he was hungry. He wished he had not devoured all the apples on the tree. That he had left just one . . .

He glanced up, and thought he saw something. He looked once, looked twice to be certain. An apple, red and ripe.

Bod prided himself on his tree-climbing skills. He swung himself up, branch by branch, and imagined he was Silas swarming smoothly up a sheer brick wall. The apple, the red of it almost black in the moonlight, hung just out of reach. Bod moved slowly forward along the branch, until he was just below the apple. Then he stretched up, and the tips of his fingers touched the perfect apple.

He was never to taste it.

A snap, loud as a hunter's gun, as the branch gave way beneath him.

A flash of pain woke him, sharp as ice, the color of slow thunder, down in the weeds that summer's night.

The ground beneath him seemed relatively soft, and oddly warm. He pushed a hand down and felt something like warm fur beneath him. He had landed on the grass pile, where the graveyard's gardener threw the cuttings from the mower, and it had broken his fall. Still, there was a pain in his chest, and his leg hurt as if he had landed on it first and twisted it.

Bod moaned.

"Hush-a-you-hush-a-boy," said a voice from behind him. "Where did you come from? Dropping like a thunderstone. What way is that to carry on?"

"I was in the apple tree," said Bod.

"Ah. Let me see your leg. Broken like the tree's limb, I'll be

249

bound." Cool fingers prodded his left leg. "Not broken. Twisted, yes, sprained perhaps. You have the Devil's own luck, boy, falling into the compost. 'Tain't the end of the world."

"Oh, good," said Bod. "Hurts, though."

He turned his head, looked up and behind him. She was older than him but not a grown-up, and she looked neither friendly nor unfriendly. Wary, mostly. She had a face that was intelligent and not even a little bit beautiful.

"I'm Bod," he said.

"The live boy?" she asked.

Bod nodded.

"I thought you must be," she said. "We've heard of you, even over here, in the potter's field. What do they call you?"

"Owens," he said. "Nobody Owens. Bod, for short."

"How-de-do, young Master Bod."

Bod looked her up and down. She wore a plain white shift. Her hair was mousy and long, and there was something of the goblin in her face—a sideways hint of a smile that seemed to linger, no matter what the rest of her face was doing.

"Were you a suicide?" he asked. "Did you steal a shilling?"

"Never stole nuffink," she said, "not even a handkerchief. Anyway," she said pertly, "the suicides is all over there, on the other side of that hawthorn, and the gallows birds are in the blackberry patch, both of them. One was a coiner, t'other a highwayman, or so he says, although if you ask me I doubt he was more than a common footpad and nightwalker."

"Ah," said Bod. Then, suspicion forming, tentatively, he said, "They say a witch is buried here."

She nodded. "Drownded and burnded and buried here without as much as a stone to mark the spot."

"You were drowned *and* burned?"

She settled down on the hill of grass cuttings beside him, and held his throbbing leg with her chilly hands. "They come to my little cottage at dawn, before I'm proper awake, and drags me out onto the green. 'You're a witch!' they shouts, fat and fresh-scrubbed all pink in the morning, like so many pigwiggins scrubbed clean for market day.

250

One by one they gets up beneath the sky and tells of milk gone sour and horses gone lame, and finally Mistress Jemima gets up, the fattest, pinkest, best scrubbed of them all, and tells how as Solomon Porritt now cuts her dead and instead hangs around the washhouse like a wasp about a honeypot, and it's all my magic, says she, that made him so and the poor young man must be bespelled. So they strap me to the cucking stool and forces it under the water of the duck pond, saying if I'm a witch I'll neither drown nor care, but if I am not a witch I'll feel it. And Mistress Jemima's father gives them each a silver groat to hold the stool down under the foul green water for a long time, to see if I'd choke on it."

"And did you?"

"Oh yes. Got a lungful of water. It done for me."

"Oh," said Bod. "Then you weren't a witch after all."

The girl fixed him with her beady ghost eyes and smiled a lopsided smile. She still looked like a goblin, but now she looked like a pretty goblin, and Bod didn't think she would have needed magic to attract Solomon Porritt, not with a smile like that. "What nonsense. Of course I was a witch. They learned that when they untied me from the cucking stool and stretched me on the green, nine parts dead and all covered with duckweed and stinking pond muck. I rolled my eyes back in my head, and I cursed each and every one of them there on the village green that morning, that none of them would ever rest easily in a grave. I was surprised at how easily it came, the cursing. Like dancing it was, when your feet pick up the steps of a new measure your ears have never heard and your head don't know, and they dance it till dawn." She stood, and twirled, and kicked, and her bare feet flashed in the moonlight. "That was how I cursed them, with my last gurgling pond-watery breath. And then I expired. They burned my body on the green until I was nothing but blackened charcoal, and they popped me in a hole in the potter's field without so much as a headstone to mark my name," and it was only then that she paused, and seemed, for a moment, wistful.

"Are any of them buried in the graveyard, then?" asked Bod.

"Not a one," said the girl, with a twinkle. "The Saturday after they drownded and toasted me, a carpet was delivered to Master

Porringer, all the way from London Town, and it was a fine carpet. But it turned out there was more in that carpet than strong wool and good weaving, for it carried the plague in its pattern, and by Monday five of them were coughing blood, and their skins were gone as black as mine when they hauled me from the fire. A week later and it had taken most of the village, and they threw the bodies all promiscuous in a plague pit they dug outside of the town, that they filled in after."

"Was everyone in the village killed?"

She shrugged. "Everyone who watched me get drownded and burned. How's your leg now?"

"Better," he said. "Thanks."

Bod stood up slowly, and limped down from the grass pile. He leaned against the iron railings. "So were you always a witch?" he asked. "I mean, before you cursed them all?"

"As if it would take witchcraft," she said with a sniff, "to get Solomon Porritt mooning 'round my cottage."

Which, Bod thought, but did not say, was not actually an answer to the question, not at all.

"What's your name?" he asked.

"Got no headstone," she said, turning down the corners of her mouth. "Might be anybody. Mightn't I?"

"But you must have a name."

"Liza Hempstock, if you please," she said tartly. Then she said, "It's not that much to ask, is it? Something to mark my grave. I'm just down there, see? With nothing but nettles to show where I rest." And she looked so sad, just for a moment, that Bod wanted to hug her. And then it came to him, and as he squeezed between the railings of the fence. He would find Liza Hempstock a headstone, with her name upon it. He would make her smile.

He turned to wave good-bye as he began to clamber up the hill, but she was already gone.

There were broken lumps of other people's stones and statues in the graveyard, but, Bod knew, that would have been entirely the wrong sort of thing to bring to the gray-eyed witch in the potter's field. It was going to take more than that. He decided not to tell anyone what he was planning, on the not entirely unreasonable basis that they would have told him not to do it.

Over the next few days his mind filled with plans, each more complicated and extravagant than the last. Mr. Pennyworth despaired.

"I do believe," he announced, scratching his dusty mustache, "that you are getting, if anything, worse. You are not Fading. You are *obvious*, boy. You are difficult to miss. If you came to me in company with a purple lion, a green elephant, and a scarlet unicorn astride which was the King of England in his royal robes, I do believe that it is you and you alone that people would stare at, dismissing the others as minor irrelevancies."

Bod simply stared at him, and said nothing. He was wondering whether there were special shops in the places where the living people gathered that sold only headstones, and if so how he could go about finding one, and Fading was the least of his problems.

He took advantage of Miss Borrow's willingness to be diverted from the subjects of grammar and composition to the subject of anything else at all to ask her about money—how exactly it worked, how one used it to get things one wanted. Bod had a number of coins he had found over the years (he had learned that the best place to find money was to go, afterward, to wherever courting couples had used the grass of the graveyard as a place to cuddle and snuggle and kiss and roll about. He would often find metal coins on the ground, in the place where they had been), and he thought perhaps he could finally get some use from them.

"How much would a headstone be?" he asked Miss Borrows.

"In my time," she told him, "they were fifteen guineas. I do not know what they would be today. More, I imagine. Much, much more."

Bod had fifty-three pence. It would, he was quite certain, not be enough.

It had been four years, almost half a lifetime, since Bod had visited the Indigo Man's tomb. But he still remembered the way. He climbed to the top of the hill, until he was above the whole town, above even the top of the apple tree, above even the steeple of the ruined church, up where the Frobisher vault stood like a rotten tooth. He slipped down into it, and down and down and still farther down, down to the tiny stone steps cut into the center of the hill, and those he descended until he reached the stone chamber at the base of the hill. It was dark in that tomb, dark as a deep mine, but Bod saw as the dead see and the room gave up its secrets to him.

The Sleer was coiled around the wall of the barrow. It was as he remembered it, all smoky tendrils and hate and greed. This time, however, he was not afraid of it.

FEAR ME, whispered the Sleer. FOR I GUARD THINGS PRECIOUS AND NEVER-LOST.

"I don't fear you," said Bod. "Remember? And I need to take something away from here."

NOTHING EVER LEAVES, came the reply from the coiled thing in the darkness. THE KNIFE, THE BROOCH, THE GOBLET. I GUARD THEM IN THE DARKNESS. I WAIT.

In the center of the room was a slab of rock, and on it they lay: a stone knife, a brooch, and a goblet.

"Pardon me for asking," said Bod, "but was this your grave?"

MASTER SETS US HERE ON THE PLAIN TO GUARD, BURIES OUR SKULLS BENEATH THIS STONE, LEAVES US HERE KNOWING WHAT WE HAVE TO DO. WE GUARDS THE TREASURES UNTIL MASTER COMES BACK.

"I expect that he's forgotten all about you," pointed out Bod. "I'm sure he's been dead himself for ages."

WE ARE THE SLEER. WE GUARD.

Bod wondered just how long ago you had to go back before the deepest tomb inside the hill was on a plain, and he knew it must have been an extremely long time ago. He could feel the Sleer winding its waves of fear around him, like the tendrils of some carnivorous plant. He was beginning to feel cold, and slow, as if he had been bitten in the heart by some arctic viper and it was starting to pump its icy venom through his body.

He took a step forward, so he was standing against the stone slab, and he reached down and closed his fingers around the coldness of the brooch.

HISH! whispered the Sleer. WE GUARDS THAT FOR THE MASTER.

"He won't mind," said Bod. He took a step backward, walking toward the stone steps, avoiding the desiccated remains of people and animals on the floor.

The Sleer writhed angrily, twining around the tiny chamber like ghost smoke. Then it slowed. IT COMES BACK, said the Sleer in its tangled triple voice. ALWAYS COMES BACK.

Bod went up the stone steps inside the hill as fast as he could. At one point he imagined that there was something coming after him, but when he broke out of the top, into the Frobisher vault, and he could breathe the cool dawn air, nothing moved or followed.

Bod sat in the open air on the top of the hill and held the brooch. He thought it was all black, at first, but then the sun rose, and he could see that the stone in the center of the black metal was a swirling red. It was the size of a robin's egg, and Bod stared into the stone wondering if there were things moving in its heart, his eyes and soul deep in the crimson world. If Bod had been smaller he would have wanted to put it into his mouth.

The stone was held in place by a black metal clasp, by something that looked like claws, with something else crawling around it. The something else looked almost snakelike, but it had too many heads. Bod wondered if that was what the Sleer looked like, in the daylight.

He wandered down the hill, taking all the shortcuts he knew, through the ivy tangle that covered the Bartleby family vault (and inside, the sound of the Bartlebies grumbling and readying for sleep) and on and over and through the railings and into the potter's field.

He called, "Liza! Liza!" and looked around.

"Good morrow, young lummox," said Liza's voice. Bod could not see her, but there was an extra shadow beneath the hawthorn tree, and, as he approached it, the shadow resolved itself into something pearlescent and translucent in the early-morning light. Something girl-like. Something gray eyed. "I should be decently sleeping," she said. "What kind of carrying-on is this?"

"Your headstone," he said. "I wanted to know what you want on it."

"My name," she said. "It must have my name on it, with a big E, for Elizabeth, like the old queen that died when I was born, and a big haitch, for Hempstock. More than that I care not, for I did never master my letters."

"What about dates?" asked Bod.

"Willyum the Conker ten sixty-six," she sang, in the whisper of the dawn wind in the hawthorn bush. "A big E if you please. And a big haitch."

"Did you have a job?" asked Bod. "I mean, when you weren't being a witch?"

"I done laundry," said the dead girl, and then the morning sunlight flooded the wasteland, and Bod was alone.

It was nine in the morning, when all the world is sleeping. Bod was determined to stay awake. He was, after all, on a mission. He was eight years old, and the world beyond the graveyard held no terrors for him.

Clothes. He would need clothes. His usual dress, of a gray winding sheet, was, he knew, quite wrong. It was good in the graveyard, the same color as stone and as shadows. But if he was going to dare the world beyond the graveyard walls, he would need to blend in there.

There were some clothes in the crypt beneath the ruined church, but Bod did not want to go down to the crypt, not even in daylight. While Bod was prepared to justify himself to Master and Mistress Owens, he was not about to explain himself to Silas; the very thought of those dark eyes angry, or worse still, disappointed, filled him with shame.

There was a gardener's hut at the far end of the graveyard, a small green building that smelled like motor oil and in which the old mower sat and rusted, unused, along with an assortment of ancient garden tools. The hut had been abandoned when the last gardener had retired, before Bod was born, and the task of keeping the graveyard had been shared between the council (who sent in a man to cut the grass, once a month from April to September) and local volunteers.

A huge padlock on the door protected the contents of the hut, but Bod had long ago discovered the loose wooden board in the back. Sometimes he would go to the gardener's hut, and sit, and think, when he wanted to be by himself.

As long as he had been going to the hut there had been a brown workingman's jacket hanging on the back of the door, forgotten or abandoned years before, along with a green-stained pair of gardening jeans. The jeans were much too big for him, but he rolled up the cuffs until his feet showed, then he made a belt out of brown garden twine, and tied it around his waist. There were boots in one corner, and he tried putting them on, but they were so big and encrusted with mud and concrete that he could barely shuffle them, and if he took a step, the boots remained on the floor of the shed. He pushed the jacket out through the space in the loose board, squeezed himself out, then put it on. If he rolled up the sleeves, he decided, it worked quite well. It had big pockets, and he thrust his hands into them, and felt quite the dandy.

Bod walked down to the main gate of the graveyard, and looked out through the bars. A bus rattled past in the street; there were cars there and noise and shops. Behind him, a cool green shade, overgrown with trees and ivy: home.

His heart pounding, Bod walked out into the world.

Abanazer Bolger had seen some odd types in his time; if you owned a shop like Abanazer's, you'd see them too. The shop, in the warren of streets in the Old Town—a little bit antique shop, a little bit junk shop, a little bit pawnbroker's (and not even Abanazer himself was entirely certain which bit was which)—brought odd types and strange people, some of them wanting to buy, some of them needing to sell. Abanazer Bolger traded over the counter, buying and selling, and he did a better trade behind the counter and in the back room, accepting objects that may not have been acquired entirely honestly, and then quietly shifting them on. His business was an iceberg. Only the dusty little shop was visible on the surface. The rest of it was underneath, and that was just how Abanazer Bolger wanted it.

Abanazer Bolger had thick spectacles and a permanent expression of mild distaste, as if he had just realized that the milk in his tea had been on the turn and he could not get the sour taste of it out of his mouth. The expression served him well when people tried to sell him things. "Honestly," he would tell them, sour faced, "it's not really

257

worth anything at all. I'll give you what I can, though, as it has senti-mental value." You were lucky to get anything like what you thought you wanted from Abanazer Bolger.

A business like Abanazer Bolger's brought in strange people, but the boy who came in that morning was one of the strangest Abanazer could remember in a lifetime of cheating strange people out of their valuables. He looked to be about seven years old, and dressed in his grandfather's clothes. He smelled like a shed. His feet were bare. His hair was long and shaggy, and he looked extremely grave. His hands were deep in the pockets of a dusty brown jacket, but even with the hands out of sight, Abanazer could see that something was clutched extremely tightly—protectively—in the boy's right hand.

"Excuse me," said the boy.

"Aye, aye, Sonny Jim," said Abanazer Bolger warily. *Kids,* he thought. *They've nicked something, or they're trying to sell their toys.* Whichever it was, he usually said no. Buy stolen property from a kid, and next thing you knew you'd have an enraged adult accusing you of having given little Johnnie or Matilda a tenner for their wedding ring. More trouble than they was worth, kids.

"I need something for a friend of mine," said the boy. "And I thought maybe you could buy something I've got."

"I don't buy stuff from kids," said Abanazer Bolger flatly.

Bod took his hand out of his pocket and put the brooch down on the grimy counter top. Bolger glanced at it, then he looked at it. He removed his spectacles. He took an eyepiece from the counter top and he screwed it into his eye. He turned on a little light on the counter and examined the brooch through the eyeglass. "Snakestone?" he said, to himself, not to the boy. Then he took the eyepiece out, replaced his glasses, and fixed the boy with a sour and suspicious look.

"Where did you get this?" Abanazer Bolger asked.

Bod said, "Do you want to buy it?"

"You stole it. You've nicked this from a museum or somewhere, didn't you?"

"No," said Bod flatly. "Are you going to buy it, or shall I go and find somebody who will?"

Abanazer Bolger's sour mood changed then. Suddenly he was all affability. He smiled broadly. "I'm sorry," he said. "It's just you don't see many pieces like this. Not in a shop like this. Not outside of a museum. But I would certainly like it. Tell you what. Why don't we sit down over tea and biscuits—I've got a packet of chocolate chip cookies in the back room—and decide how much something like this is worth? Eh?"

Bod was relieved that the man was finally being friendly. "I need enough to buy a stone," he said. "A headstone for a friend of mine. Well, she's not really my friend. Just someone I know. I think she helped make my leg better, you see."

Abanazer Bolger, paying little attention to the boy's prattle, led him behind the counter, and opened the door to the storeroom, a windowless little space every inch of which was crammed high with teetering cardboard boxes, each filled with junk. There was a safe in there, in the corner, a big old one. There was a box filled with violins, an accumulation of stuffed dead animals, chairs without seats, books and prints.

There was a small desk beside the door, and Abanazer Bolger pulled up the only chair, and sat down, letting Bod stand. Abanazer rummaged in a drawer, in which Bod could see a half-empty bottle of whiskey, and pulled out an almost-finished packet of chocolate chip cookies, and he offered one to the boy; he turned on the desk light, looked at the brooch again, the swirls of red and orange in the stone, and he examined the black metal band that encircled it, suppressing a little shiver at the expression on the heads of the snake things. "This is old," he said. "It's—" *priceless*, he thought, "—probably not really worth much, but you never know." Bod's face fell. Abanazer Bolger tried to look reassuring. "I just need to be sure that it's not stolen, though, before I can give you a penny. Did you take it from your mum's dresser? Nick it from a museum? You can tell me. I'll not get you into trouble. I just need to know."

Bod shook his head. He munched on his cookie.

"Then where did you get it?"

Bod said nothing.

Abanazer Bolger did not want to put down the brooch, but he

pushed it across the desk to the boy. "If you can't tell me," he said, "you'd better take it back. There has to be trust on both sides, after all. Nice doing business with you. Sorry it couldn't go any further."

Bod looked worried. Then he said, "I found it in an old grave. But I can't say where." And then he stopped, because naked greed and excitement had replaced the friendliness on Abanazer Bolger's face.

"And there's more like this there?"

Bod said, "If you don't want to buy it, I'll find someone else. Thank you for the biscuit."

Bolger said, "You're in a hurry, eh? Mum and Dad waiting for you, I expect?"

The boy shook his head, then wished he had nodded.

"Nobody waiting. Good." Abanazer Bolger closed his hands around the brooch. "Now, you tell me exactly where you found this. Eh?"

"I don't remember," said Bod.

"Too late for that," said Abanazer Bolger. "Suppose you have a serious think for a bit about where it came from. Then, when you've thought, we'll have a little chat, and you'll tell me."

He got up, and walked out of the room, closing the door behind him. He locked it, with a large metal key.

He opened his hand, and looked at the brooch and smiled, hungrily.

There was a *ding* from the bell above the shop door, to let him know someone had entered, and he looked up guiltily, but there was nobody there. The door was slightly ajar though, so Bolger pushed it shut, and then for good measure, he turned around the sign in the window, so it said CLOSED. He pushed the bolt shut. Didn't want any busybodies turning up today.

The autumn day had turned from sunny to gray, and a light patter of rain ran down the grubby shop window.

Abanazer Bolger picked up the telephone from the counter and pushed at the buttons with fingers that barely shook.

"Paydirt, Tom," he said. "Get over here, soon as you can."

Bod realized that he was trapped when he heard the lock turn in the door. He pulled on the door, but it held fast. He felt stupid for having been lured inside, foolish for not trusting his first impulses to get as far away from the sour-faced man as possible. He had broken all the rules of the graveyard, and everything had gone wrong. What would Silas say? Or the Owens? He could feel himself beginning to panic, and he suppressed it, pushing the worry back down inside him. It would all be good. He knew that. Of course, he needed to get out. . . .

He examined the room he was trapped in. It was little more than a storeroom with a desk in it. The only entrance was the door.

He opened the desk drawer, finding nothing but small pots of paint (used for brightening up antiques) and a paintbrush. He wondered if he would be able to throw paint in the man's face and blind him for long enough to escape. He opened the top of a pot of paint and dipped in his finger.

"What're you doin'?" asked a voice close to his ear.

"Nothing," said Bod, screwing the top on the paintpot and dropping it into one of the jacket's enormous pockets.

Liza Hempstock looked at him, unimpressed. "Why are you in here?" she asked. "And who's the old bag of lard out there?"

"It's his shop. I was trying to sell him something."

"Why?"

"None of your beeswax."

She sniffed. "Well," she said, "you should get on back to the graveyard."

"I can't. He's locked me in."

"Course you can. Just slip through the wall—"

He shook his head. "I can't. I can only do it at home because they gave me the freedom of the graveyard when I was a baby." He looked up at her, under the electric light. It was hard to see her properly, but Bod had spent his life talking to dead people. "Anyway, what are you doing here? What are you doing out from the graveyard? It's daytime. And you're not like Silas. You're meant to stay in the graveyard."

She said, "There's rules for those in graveyards, but not for those as was buried in unhallowed ground. Nobody tells *me* what to do or where to go." She glared at the door. "I don't like that man," she said. "I'm going to see what he's doing."

A flicker, and Bod was alone in the room once more. He heard a rumble of distant thunder.

In the cluttered darkness of Bolger's Antiquities, Abanazer Bolger looked up suspiciously, certain that someone was watching him, then realized he was being foolish. "The boy's locked in the room," he told himself. "The front door's locked." He was polishing the metal clasp surrounding the snakestone, as gently and as carefully as an archaeologist on a dig, taking off the black and revealing the glittering silver beneath it.

He was beginning to regret calling Tom Hustings over, although Hustings was big and good for scaring people. He was also beginning to regret that he was going to have to sell the brooch when he was done. It was special. The more it glittered, under the tiny light on his counter, the more he wanted it to be his, and only his.

There was more where this came from, though. The boy would tell him. The boy would lead him to it.

The boy . . .

And then an idea struck him. He put down the brooch reluctantly, and opened a drawer behind the counter, taking out a metal biscuit tin filled with envelopes and cards and slips of paper.

He reached in, and took out a card only slightly larger than a business card. It was black edged. There was no name or address printed on it, though. Only one word, handwritten in the center in an ink that had faded to brown: *Jack*.

On the back of the card, in pencil, Abanazer Bolger had written instructions to himself, in his tiny, precise handwriting, as a reminder, although he would not have been likely to forget the use of the card, how to use it to summon the man Jack. No, not summon. *Invite*. You did not summon people like him.

A knocking on the outer door of the shop.

Bolger tossed the card down onto the counter, and walked over to the door, peering out into the wet afternoon.

"Hurry up," called Tom Hustings. "It's miserable out here. Dismal. I'm getting soaked."

Bolger unlocked the door and Tom Hustings pushed his way in, his raincoat and hair dripping. "What's so important that you can't

262

talk about it over the phone, then?"

"Our fortune," said Abanazer Bolger, with his sour face. "That's what."

Hustings took off his raincoat and hung it on the back of the shop door. "What is it? Something good fell off the back of a lorry?"

"Treasure," said Abanazer Bolger. "Two kinds." He took his friend over to the counter, showed him the brooch, under the little light.

"It's old, isn't it?"

"From pagan times," said Abanazer. "Before. From Druid times. Before the Romans came. It's called a snakestone. Seen 'em in museums. I've never seen metalwork like that, or one so fine. Must have belonged to a king. The lad who found it says it come from a grave— think of a barrow filled with stuff like this."

"Might be worth doing it legit," said Hustings thoughtfully. "Declare it as treasure trove. They have to pay us market value for it, and we could make them name it for us. The Hustings-Bolger Bequest."

"Bolger-Hustings," said Abanazer automatically. Then he said, "There's a few people I know of, people with real money, would pay more than market value, if they could hold it as you are—" for Tom Hustings was fingering the brooch gently, like a man stroking a kitten—"and there'd be no questions asked." He reached out his hand and, reluctantly, Tom Hustings passed him the brooch.

"You said two kinds of treasure," said Hustings. "What's t'other?"

Abanazer Bolger picked up the black-edged card, held it out for his friend's inspection. "Do you know what this is?"

His friend shook his head.

Abanazer put the card down on the counter. "There's a party is looking for another party."

"So?"

"The way I heard it," said Abanazer Bolger, "the other party is a boy."

"There's boys everywhere," said Tom Hustings. "Running all around. Getting into trouble. I can't abide them. So, there's a party looking for a particular boy?"

"This lad looks to be the right sort of age. He's dressed—well, you'll see how he's dressed. And he found this. It could be him."

"And if it is him?"

Abanazer Bolger picked up the card again, by the edge, and waved it back and forth slowly, as if running the edge along an imaginary flame. "Here comes a candle to light you to bed . . ." he began.

". . . and here comes a chopper to chop off your head," concluded Tom Hustings thoughtfully. "But look you. If you call the man Jack, you lose the boy. And if you lose the boy, you lose the treasure."

And the two men went back and forth on it, weighing the merits and disadvantages of reporting the boy or of collecting the treasure, which had grown in their minds to a huge underground cavern filled with precious things, and as they debated Abanazer pulled a bottle of sloe gin from beneath the counter and poured them both a generous tot, "to assist the cerebrations."

Liza was soon bored with their discussions, which went around and around like a whirligig, getting nowhere, and so she went back into the storeroom, to find Bod standing in the middle of the room with his eyes tightly closed and his fists clenched and his face all screwed up as if he had a toothache, almost purple from holding his breath.

"What you a-doin' of now?" she asked, unimpressed.

He opened his eyes and relaxed. "Trying to Fade," he said.

Liza sniffed. "Try again," she said.

He did, holding his breath even longer this time.

"Stop that," she told him, "or you'll pop."

Bod took a deep breath and then sighed. "It doesn't work," he said. "Maybe I could hit him with a rock and just run for it." There wasn't a rock, so he picked up a colored-glass paperweight, hefted it in his hand, wondering if he could throw it hard enough to stop Abanazer Bolger in his tracks.

"There's two of them out there now," said Liza. "And if the one don't get you, t'other one will. They say they want to get you to show them where you got the brooch, and then dig up the grave and take the treasure." She did not tell him about the other discussions they were having, nor about the black-edged card. She shook her head.

264

"Why did you do something as stupid as this anyway? You know the rules about leaving the graveyard. Just asking for trouble, it was."

Bod felt very insignificant, and very foolish. "I wanted to get you a headstone," he admitted in a small voice. "And I thought it would cost more money. So I was going to sell him the brooch, to buy you your headstone."

She didn't say anything.

"Are you angry?"

She shook her head. "It's the first nice thing anyone's done for me in five hundred years," she said with a hint of a goblin smile. "Why would I be angry?" Then she said, "What do you do, when you try to Fade?"

"What Mr. Pennyworth told me. *I am an empty doorway, I am a vacant alley, I am nothing. Eyes will not see me, glances slip over me.*' But it never works."

"It's because you're alive," said Liza with a sniff. "There's stuff as works for us, the dead, who have to fight to be noticed at the best of times, that won't never work for you people."

She hugged herself tightly, moving her body back and forth, as if she was debating something. Then she said, "It's because of me you got into this. . . . Come here, Nobody Owens."

He took a step toward her, in that tiny room, and she put her cold hand on his forehead. It felt like a wet silk scarf against his skin.

"Now," she said. "Perhaps I can do a good turn for you."

And with that, she began to mutter to herself, mumbling words that Bod could not make out. Then she said, clear and loud,

"Be hole, be dust, be dream, be wind,
Be night, be dark, be wish, be mind,
Now slip, now slide, now move unseen,
Above, beneath, betwixt, between."

Something huge touched him, brushed him from head to feet, and he shivered. His hair prickled, and his skin was all gooseflesh. Something had changed. "What did you do?" he asked.

"Just gived you a helping hand," she said. "I may be dead, but I'm

265

a dead witch, remember. And we don't forget."

"But—"

"Hush up," she said. "They're coming back."

The key rattled in the storeroom lock. "Now then, chummy," said a voice Bod had not heard clearly before, "I'm sure we're all going to be great friends," and with that Tom Hustings pushed open the door. Then he stood in the doorway looking around, looking puzzled. He was a big, big man, with foxy-red hair and a bottle-red nose. "Here. Abanazer? I thought you said he was in here."

"I did," said Bolger from behind him.

"Well, I can't see hide nor hair of him."

Bolger's face appeared behind the ruddy man's and he peered into the room. "Hiding," he said, staring straight at where Bod was standing. "No use hiding," he announced loudly. "I can see you there. Come on out."

The two men walked into the little room, and Bod stood stock-still between them and thought of Mr. Pennyworth's lessons. He did not react, he did not move. He let the men's glances slide over him without seeing him.

"You're going to wish you'd come out when I called," said Bolger, and he shut the door. "Right," he said to Tom Hustings. "You block the door, so he can't get past." And with that he walked around the room, peering behind things, and bending awkwardly, to look beneath the desk. He walked straight past Bod and opened the cupboard. "Now I see you!" he shouted. "Come out!"

Liza giggled.

"What was that?" asked Tom Hustings, spinning around.

"I didn't hear nothing," said Abanazer Bolger.

Liza giggled again. Then she put her lips together and blew, making a noise that began as a whistling and then sounded like a distant wind. The electric lights in the little room flickered and buzzed. Then they went out.

"Bloody fuses," said Abanazer Bolger. "Come on. This is a waste of time."

The key clicked in the lock, and Liza and Bod were left alone in the room.

"He's got away," said Abanazer Bolger. Bod could hear him now, through the door. "Room like that. There wasn't anywhere he could have been hiding. We'd've seen him if he was."

"The man Jack won't like that."

"Who's going to tell him?"

A pause.

"Here. Tom Hustings. Where's the brooch gone?"

"Mm? That? Here. I was keeping it safe."

"Keeping it safe? In your pocket? Funny place to be keeping it safe, if you ask me. More like you were planning to make off with it— like you was planning to keep my brooch for your own."

"Your brooch, Abanazer? *Your* brooch? Our brooch, you mean."

"Ours, indeed. I don't remember you being here when I got it from that boy."

"That boy that you couldn't even keep safe for the man Jack, you mean? Can you imagine what he'll do, when he finds *you* had the boy he was looking for, and *you* let him go?"

"Probably not the same boy. Lots of boys in the world—what're the odds it was the one he was looking for? Out the back door as soon as my back was turned, I'll bet." And then Abanazer Bolger said, in a high, wheedling voice, "Don't you worry about the man Jack, Tom Hustings. I'm sure that it was a different boy. My old mind playing tricks. And we're almost out of sloe gin—how would you fancy a good Scotch? I've whiskey in the back room. You just wait here a moment."

The storeroom door was unlocked, and Abanazer entered, holding a walking stick and a flashlight, looking even more sour of face than before.

"If you're still in here," he said in a sour mutter, "don't even think of making a run for it. I've called the police on you, that's what I've done." A rummage in a drawer produced the half-filled bottle of whiskey, and then a tiny black bottle. Abanazer poured several drops from the little bottle into the larger, then he pocketed the tiny bottle. "My brooch, and mine alone," he mouthed, and followed it with a barked, "Just coming, Tom!"

He glared around the dark room, staring past Bod, then he left the storeroom, carrying the whiskey in front of him. He locked the door behind him.

"Here you go," came Abanazer Bolger's voice through the door. "Give us your glass then, Tom. Nice drop of Scotch, put hairs on your chest. Say when."

Silence. "Cheap muck. Aren't you drinking?"

"That sloe gin's gone to my innards. Give it a minute for my stomach to settle. . . ." Then, "Here—Tom! What have you done with my brooch?"

"*Your* brooch is it now? Whoa—I feel a bit queasy . . . you put something in my drink, you little grub!"

"What if I did? I could read on your face what you was planning, Tom Hustings. Thief."

And then there was shouting, and several crashes, and loud bangs, as if heavy items of furniture were being overturned . . .

. . . then silence.

Liza said, "Quickly now. Let's get you out of here."

"But the door's locked." He looked at her. "Is there something you can do to get us out?"

"Me? I don't have any magics will get you out of a locked room, boy."

Bod crouched, and peered out through the keyhole. It was blocked; the key sat in the keyhole. Bod thought, then he smiled momentarily, and it lit his face like the flash of a lightbulb. He pulled a crumpled sheet of newspaper from a packing case, flattened it out as best he could, then pushed it underneath the door, leaving only a corner on his side of the doorway.

"What are you playing at?" asked Liza impatiently.

"I need something like a pencil. Only thinner . . ." he said. "Here we go." And he took a thin paintbrush from the top of the desk, and pushed the brushless end into the lock, jiggled it, and pushed some more.

There was a muffled *clunk* as the key was pushed out, as it dropped from the lock onto the newspaper. Bod pulled the paper back under the door, now with the key sitting on it.

Liza laughed, delighted. "That's wit, young man," she said. "That's wisdom."

Bod put the key in the lock, turned it, and pushed open the storeroom door.

There were two men on the floor in the middle of the crowded antique shop. Furniture had indeed fallen; the place was a chaos of wrecked clocks and chairs, and in the midst of it the bulk of Tom Hustings lay, fallen on the smaller figure of Abanazer Bolger. Neither of them was moving.

"Are they dead?" asked Bod.

"No such luck," said Liza.

On the floor beside the men was a brooch of glittering silver; a crimson-orange-banded stone, held in place with claws and with snake heads, and the expression on the snake heads was one of triumph and avarice and satisfaction.

Bod dropped the brooch into his pocket, where it sat beside the heavy glass paperweight, the paintbrush, and the little pot of paint.

"Take this too," said Liza.

Bod looked at the black-edged card with the word *Jack* handwritten on one side. It disturbed him. There was something familiar about it, something that stirred old memories, something dangerous. "I don't want it."

"You can't leave it here with them," said Liza. "They were going to use it to hurt you."

"I don't want it," said Bod. "It's bad. Burn it."

"No!" Liza gasped. "Don't do that. You mustn't do that."

"Then I'll give it to Silas," said Bod. And he put the little card into an envelope, so he had to touch it as little as possible, and put the envelope into the inside pocket of his old gardening jacket beside his heart.

Two hundred miles away, the man Jack woke from his sleep, and sniffed the air. He walked downstairs.

"What is it?" asked his grandmother, stirring the contents of a big iron pot on the stove. "What's got into you now?"

"I don't know," he said. "Something's happening. Something . . ."

interesting." And then he licked his lips. "Smells tasty," he said. "Very tasty."

Lightning illuminated the cobbled street.

Bod hurried through the rain through the Old Town, always heading up the hill toward the graveyard. The gray day had become an early night while he was inside the storeroom, and it came as no surprise to him when a familiar shadow swirled beneath the streetlamps. Bod hesitated, and a flutter of night-black velvet resolved itself into man-shape.

Silas stood in front of him, arms folded. He strode forward impatiently.

"Well?" he said.

Bod said, "I'm sorry, Silas."

"I'm disappointed in you, Bod," Silas said, and he shook his head. "I've been looking for you since I woke. You have the smell of trouble all around you. And you know you're not allowed to go out here, into the living world."

"I know. I'm sorry." There was rain on the boy's face, running down like tears.

"First of all, we need to get you back to safety." Silas reached down and enfolded the living child inside his cloak, and Bod felt the ground fall away beneath him.

"Silas," he said.

Silas did not answer.

"I *was* a bit scared," he said. "But I knew you'd come and get me if it got too bad. And Liza was there. She helped a lot."

"Liza?" Silas's voice was sharp.

"The witch. From the potter's field."

"And you say she helped you?"

"Yes. She especially helped me with my Fading. I think I can do it now."

Silas grunted. "You can tell me all about it when we're home." And Bod was quiet until they landed beside the church. They went inside, into the empty hall, as the rain redoubled, splashing up from the puddles that covered the ground.

Bod produced the envelope containing the black-edged card. "Um," he said. "I thought you should have this. Well, Liza did, really."

Silas looked at it. Then he opened it, removed the card, stared at it, turned it over, and read Abanazer Bolger's penciled note to himself, in tiny handwriting, explaining the precise manner of use of the card.

"Tell me everything," he said.

Bod told him everything he could remember about the day. And at the end, Silas shook his head slowly, thoughtfully.

"Am I in trouble?" asked Bod.

"Nobody Owens," said Silas. "You are indeed in trouble. However, I believe I shall leave it to your foster parents to administer whatever discipline and reproach they believe to be needed. In the meantime, I need to deal with this."

The black-edged card vanished inside the velvet cloak, and then, in the manner of his kind, Silas was gone.

Bod pulled the jacket up over his head, and clambered up the slippery paths to the top of the hill, to the Frobisher vault, and then he went down, and down, and still farther down.

He dropped the brooch beside the goblet and the knife.

"Here you go," he said. "All polished up. Looking pretty."

IT COMES BACK, whispered the Sleer, with satisfaction in its smoke-tendril voice. IT ALWAYS COMES BACK.

The night had been long, but it was almost dawn.

Bod was walking, sleepily and a little gingerly, past the small tomb of the wonderfully named Miss Liberty Roach (*What she spent is lost, what she gave away remains with her always. Reader, be charitable*), past the final resting place of Harrison Westwood, Baker of this Parish, and his wives, Marion and Joan, to the potter's field. Mr. and Mrs. Owens had died several hundred years before it had been decided that beating children was wrong, and Mr. Owens had, regretfully, that night, done what he saw as his duty, and Bod's bottom stung like anything. Still, the look of worry on Mrs. Owens's face had hurt Bod worse than any beating could have done.

He reached the iron railings that bounded the potter's field, and slipped between them.

"Hullo?" he called. There was no answer. Not even an extra shadow in the hawthorn bush. "I hope I didn't get you into trouble too," he said.

Nothing.

He had replaced the jeans in the gardener's hut—he was more comfortable in just his gray winding sheet—but he had kept the jacket. He liked having the pockets.

When he had gone to the shed to return the jeans, he had taken a small hand scythe from the wall where it hung, and with it he had attacked the nettle patch in the potter's field, sending the nettles flying, slashing and gutting them till there was nothing but stinging stubble on the ground.

From his pocket he took the large glass paperweight, its insides a multitude of bright colors, along with the paintpot, and the paintbrush.

He dipped the brush into the paint and carefully painted, in brown paint, on the surface of the paperweight, the letters

E H

and beneath them he wrote

We don't forget

It was almost daylight. Bedtime, soon, and it would not be wise for him to be late to bed for some time to come.

He put the paperweight down on the ground that had once been a nettle patch, placed it in the place that he estimated her head would have been, and, pausing only to look at his handiwork for a moment, he went through the railings and made his way, rather less gingerly, back up the hill.

"Not bad," said a pert voice from the potter's field behind him. "Not bad at all."

But when he turned to look, there was nobody there.

INSTRUCTIONS

Touch the wooden gate in the wall you never saw
      before,
Say "please" before you open the latch,
go through,
walk down the path.
A red metal imp hangs from the
      green-painted front door,
as a knocker,
do not touch it; it will bite your fingers.
Walk through the house. Take nothing. Eat nothing.
However,
if any creature tells you that it hungers,
feed it.
If it tells you that it is dirty,
clean it.
If it cries to you that it hurts,
if you can,
ease its pain.

From the back garden you will be able to see the wild
      wood.
The deep well you walk past leads down to Winter's
      realm;

there is another land at the bottom of it.
If you turn around here,
you can walk back, safely;
you will lose no face. I will think no less of you.

Once through the garden you will be in the wood.
The trees are old. Eyes peer from the undergrowth.
Beneath a twisted oak sits an old woman.
        She may ask for something;
give it to her. She
will point the way to the castle. Inside it
are three princesses.
Do not trust the youngest. Walk on.
In the clearing beyond the castle the
        twelve months sit about a fire,
warming their feet, exchanging tales.
They may do favors for you, if you are polite.
You may pick strawberries in December's frost.

Trust the wolves, but do not tell them
        where you are going.
The river can be crossed by the ferry.
        The ferryman will take you.
(The answer to his question is this:
If he hands the oar to his passenger, he
        will be free to leave the boat.
Only tell him this from a safe distance.)

If an eagle gives you a feather, keep it safe.
Remember: that giants sleep too soundly; that
witches are often betrayed by their appetites;
dragons have one soft spot, somewhere, always;
hearts can be well hidden,
and you betray them with your tongue.
Do not be jealous of your sister:
know that diamonds and roses

are as uncomfortable when they tumble
        from one's lips as toads and frogs:
colder, too, and sharper, and they cut.

Remember your name.
Do not lose hope—what you seek will be found.
Trust ghosts. Trust those that you have
        helped to help you in their turn.
Trust dreams.
Trust your heart, and trust your story.

When you come back, return the way you came.
Favors will be returned, debts be repaid.
Do not forget your manners.
Do not look back.
Ride the wise eagle (you shall not fall)
Ride the silver fish (you will not drown)
Ride the gray wolf (hold tightly to his fur).

There is a worm at the heart of the tower;
        that is why it will not stand.

When you reach the little house, the
        place your journey started,
you will recognize it, although it will seem
        much smaller than you remember.
Walk up the path, and through the garden
        gate you never saw before but once.
And then go home. Or make a home.

Or rest.

THE HISTORY OF
BLOOMSBURY PUBLISHING

Bloomsbury Publishing was founded in 1986 to publish books of excellence and originality. Its authors include Margaret Atwood, John Berger, William Boyd, David Guterson, Khaled Hosseini, John Irving, Anne Michaels, Michael Ondaatje, J.K. Rowling, Donna Tartt and Barbara Trapido. Its logo is Diana, the Roman Goddess of Hunting.

In 1994 Bloomsbury floated on the London Stock Exchange and added both a paperback and a children's list. Bloomsbury is based in Soho Square in London and expanded to New York in 1998 and Berlin in 2003. In 2000 Bloomsbury acquired A&C Black and now publishes *Who's Who*, *Whitaker's Almanack*, *Wisden Cricketers' Almanack* and the *Writers' & Artists' Yearbook*. Many books, bestsellers and literary awards later, Bloomsbury is one of the world's leading independent publishing houses.

To read extracts from the introductions to other Bloomsbury Phantastics and to find out more on the books in this series visit www.bloomsbury.com/thebloomsburyphantastics

For more information on all Bloomsbury authors and for all the latest news please visit www.bloomsbury.com